DRIVING A HARD BARGAIN

"We aren't embarking on a lovematch, we're marrying solely because of duty," Louisa pointed out to Lord Christopher Highclare.

"It's still a marriage," the lord pointed out.

"In name, maybe," Louisa said.

Highclare's eyes were very blue as they held hers. "You're going to be my wife in every way."

The color heightened on Louisa's cheeks. She felt very warm now, her hands clasping and unclasping in her lap. "F-forgive me, but I imagined . . ."

"That it was to be a purely platonic arrangement?" he said implacably. "You imagined incorrectly."

She met his eyes. "I accept that you'll be my husband in every meaning of the word."

Lord Highclare raised a wry eyebrow. "Intimate strangers," he murmured. . . .

Dear Reader:

As you know, Signet is proud to keep bringing you the best in romance and now we're happy to announce that we are now presenting you with even more of what you love!

The Regency has long been one of the most popular settings for romances and it's easy to see why. It was an age of elegance and opulence, of wickedness and wit. It was also a time of tumultuous change, the beginning of the modern age and the end of illusion, when money began to mean as much as birth, but still an age when manners often meant more than morality.

Now Signet has commissioned some of its finest authors to write some bigger romances—longer, lusher, more exquisitely sensuous than ever before—wonderful love stories that encompass even more of the flavor of this glittering and flamboyant age. We are calling them "Super Regencies" because they have been liberated from category conventions and have the room to take the Regency novel even further—to the limits of the Regency itself.

Because we want to bring you only the very best, we are publishing these books only on an occasional basis, only when we feel that we can bring you something special. The first of the Super Regencies, *Love in Disguise* by Edith Layton, was published in August to rave reviews and has won two awards. It was followed by two other outstanding titles, *The Guarded Heart* by Barbara Hazard, published in October and *Indigo Moon* by Patricia Rice, published in February. Watch for future Signet Super Regencies in upcoming months in your favorite bookstore.

Sincerely,

Hilary Ross
Associate Executive Editor

SANDRA HEATH
A MATTER OF DUTY

A SIGNET BOOK

NEW AMERICAN LIBRARY

NAL BOOKS ARE AVAILABLE AT QUANTITY DISCOUNTS WHEN USED TO
PROMOTE PRODUCTS OR SERVICES. FOR INFORMATION PLEASE WRITE TO
PREMIUM MARKETING DIVISION, NEW AMERICAN LIBRARY,
1633 BROADWAY, NEW YORK, NEW YORK 10019.

SIGNET TRADEMARK REG. U.S.PAT. OFF. AND FOREIGN COUNTRIES
REGISTERED TRADEMARK—MARCA REGISTRADA
HECHO EN CHICAGO, U.S.A.

SIGNET, SIGNET CLASSIC,MENTOR, ONYX, PLUME,
MERIDIAN and NAL BOOKS are published by NAL PENGUIN,
INC., 1633 Broadway, New York, New York 10019

First Printing, March, 1988

1 2 3 4 5 6 7 8 9

PRINTED IN THE UNITED STATES OF AMERICA

1

The August night was hot and still, and at Lawrence Park by the Thames Sir Ashley Lawrence's eight-year-old daughter, Emma, tossed in her immense four-poster bed, her sleep disturbed by the approaching thunderstorm.

Outside, there wasn't any moonlight. The lights of Brentford town shone across the meadows, and the silhouette of London rose faintly on the horizon. On the opposite bank of the river, the gables of the royal residences at Kew could be seen among the shadowy trees.

Lawrence Park was a fine Palladian house, with grounds sweeping down to the river steps. Its parterre boasted tall fountains, and on the newly laid croquet lawn, a very recent innovation, the ghostly shapes of white peacocks strutted in the moonless darkness. There were few lights in the house, for Sir Ashley, his beautiful new bride, and Captain Geoffrey Lawrence, Sir Ashley's son and heir by his first marriage, were attending a reception at Devonshire House and weren't expected home until the early hours.

Suddenly there was a bright flash of lightning, followed closely by a loud clap of thunder, and Emma awoke with a frightened start, her brown ringlets tumbling down from beneath her frilled night bonnet as she sat up. She was afraid of the dark, and even more afraid of thunder. Where was the lighted candle that had been there when she'd gone to sleep? And where was her governess?

Her lips began to tremble. "Cherry?" she ventured timorously. "Cherry, where are you?"

The door opened almost straightaway, and a slender young woman came in with the lighted candle. She was about twenty-two years old and wore a high-waisted white muslin gown. Her long dark-red hair was piled up in a knot on top of her graceful head, and her complexion was pale and clear in the flickering light. She had large gray eyes, and her generous mouth curved in a way that suggested a warm nature and a willingness to smile. There was an indefinable air of quality about her, for she was that most unfortunate of creatures, a lady fallen on hard times. But for the gambling ways of her much-loved wastrel of a brother, she'd have been assured of a Season in London, with the prospect, if not of marrying into the aristocracy, certainly of into the landed gentry. Miss Louisa Cherington, once of Cherington Court in the county of Wiltshire, was now reduced to being a governess and had no hope at all of ever being mistress of a house like Lawrence Park.

She quickly set the candlestick down on the table and went to sit on the edge of the bed, taking the child's trembling hands. "It's all right, Emma, I'm here now," she said soothingly.

The candle flame still flickered and the shadows moved monstrously against the walls. Emma watched them fearfully. "I'm frightened, Cherry," she said, tears shining in her brown eyes.

Louisa hugged her quickly. "It's only another storm, sweeting; it won't hurt you. We've had lots of them this summer, and nothing's befallen you yet, has it?" She spoke lightly and a little teasingly, hoping to make the child smile at her fears.

"But it's going to happen, Cherry! Stepmama said it would. I was naughty yesterday, and she said that the next thunderstorm would punish me for my wickedness."

"What nonsense," murmured Louisa, her voice still light. Her gray eyes were angry that the new Lady

Lawrence could say something so deliberately cruel and frightening to a child, especially one as lonely and timid as Emma. Sir Ashley's second wife was a cold, spiteful woman who'd only married him in order to advance herself socially, for he was no longer the man he'd once been. His age and health were beginning to tell; indeed, he was sometimes confined to his bed, but he was exceeding wealthy, and that was all that mattered to his beloved Anne.

Emma clung to Louisa. "Wh-where were you? I woke up and the candle had gone, and—"

"The candle went out, sweetheart, and I just slipped out to light it from the one that's always left burning in the passage. I was only gone for a moment."

Emma was a little reassured. "Is Papa back yet?"

"No, he and Lady Lawrence will be at Devonshire House for some time yet."

"Isn't Geoffrey back either?"

"No, sweeting, I'm afraid he'll be there for a long while yet as well. It's a very grand reception, you know—the Prince Regent will be there."

"Oh." Emma drew back forlornly. She loved her handsome elder brother, even though he didn't have a lot of time for her. He was an officer in a crack hussar regiment and was home on leave from Spain; he seemed somehow to always manage to be free at this time of year for the newly fashionable regatta at Cowes on the Isle of Wight, where he liked more than anything to race his fast cutter, the *Cyclops*. This year, however, his plans had been frustrated because his other great passion, gambling, had finally caught up with him. The moment he'd set foot in England the duns had pounced, demanding full settlement of his mountainous debts, and for once Sir Ashley had refused to come across with the necessary sum. Nothing Geoffrey said would change his father's mind on the matter, and so the *Cyclops*, a costly vessel that would fetch a good price, awaited a purchaser. She rocked at her moorings by the river steps, a constant reminder to Geoffrey that his father was being very unreasonable indeed; at least, that was how Geoffrey saw it. As a consequence, the atmosphere at Lawrence Park was chill, for Captain Geoffrey Lawrence wasn't one to appreciate being thwarted.

Louisa had only been the governess for a year, but in that time she'd seen a sad change come over the household. From being a lonely but cheerful widower who doted on his small daughter, Sir Ashley had become a tired, short-tempered old man, beset by an arrogant, self-centered son and badgered by a new wife into doing everything she wanted, whether he approved or not. It was his grave misfortune to be cursed with such a bride; it was even more his misfortune to be cursed with a son who matched her in every unpleasant way. Anne, Lady Lawrence, had already been bored with her marriage when her handsome stepson had come home for the first time, and in retrospect Louisa saw that it had been inevitable that she'd been immediately attracted to the young man, who had all the swagger and virility her elderly husband lacked. But it was one thing to be attracted, quite another to actually indulge in an improper liaison, and to their eternal discredit it had been upon the latter course that they'd immediately embarked.

Louisa had regarded it as none of her concern—her duty was toward Emma—but through no fault of her own she'd been dragged into the tangled web, because Geoffrey Lawrence's roving eye didn't stop at his beautiful stepmother, it wandered toward his sister's pretty governess as well. He'd made little secret of finding Louisa Cherington desirable, a fact that aroused Anne's considerable jealousy and vindictiveness, and it wasn't long before Louisa realized that her position at Lawrence Park had become very precarious indeed.

Anne's method of ridding herself of a rival was very simple indeed: remove the need for a governess, and Louisa would be dismissed. And so Sir Ashley had in recent weeks found himself under constant pressure to send Emma away to a certain highly recommended

seminary for young ladies in Kensington, a move Anne
justified by pointing out the deterioration in the child's
conduct. The apparent deterioration was there for all to
see, for, unknown to trusting Sir Ashley, his wife was
working upon the little girl, goading her into misconduct that could be laid fairly and squarely at the feet
of her seemingly incompetent governess. He was
resisting so far, because he adored his daughter, but
how much longer he would withstand such concentrated
pressure was a matter of conjecture. Louisa could see
the time fast approaching when she'd be without a
position, forced by a spiteful woman's jealousy and an
unprincipled young man's selfish arrogance, to find
another situation in order to keep a roof over her
head.

Another loud crash of thunder reverberated across
the night sky, and Emma gave a frightened cry, flinging
her arms tightly around Louisa's neck. "D-do you think
Geoffrey will keep his promise?"

"What promise?"

"To come home early from Devonshire House."

Louisa's heart sank, for there could only be one
reason for him doing that: he intended to see if he could
make progress with her while his stepmother was otherwise engaged.

Emma looked at her. "Will he come home early,
Cherry?"

"I-I don't know, sweeting. Come, now, it's gone
midnight and you really should go back to sleep. Don't
forget you have extra lessons to do in the morning."

Emma scowled. "Because of *her*," she said, referring
to her stepmother. "She'd do anything to make me
unhappy. She only said I had to do extra lessons because
she wanted to stop me going for a ride with Geoffrey.
She's going with him herself now, did you know?"

Louisa did know. "Never mind, Emma, there'll be
other days to go riding."

"She'll find reasons to stop me, I know she will. I
hate her."

"You mustn't talk like that, Emma. Now, then, please try to sleep."

"I won't be able to, Cherry," said the little girl, shrinking against her as another roll of thunder grumbled through the night.

"But I'll be here now, the room will be lit, and I promise to sit with you."

"Will you ring for a glass of milk? If I could drink that and listen to a story, I think I'll be able to sleep." Emma looked hopefully at her.

"Emma . . ."

"Please, Cherry."

"Oh, all right, you minx, but I'll have to go down for the milk, you know the servants never answer the bell when your parents are out and they know it's just me ringing. Will you be all right on your own for a few minutes?"

Emma's face fell a little. "Couldn't I come with you like I used to?"

"I don't think you'd better. Lady Lawrence has said you're not to go to the kitchens, and she'd be bound to find out if you'd disobeyed." Yes, the servants had very quickly discovered they could curry favor with the mistress of the house if they told tales on the child or the governess.

Emma's expression was sullen. "I hate her," she said again. "You won't be long, will you?" she added nervously as Louisa went to the mantelpiece to take down another candle to light.

"Of course I won't." Louisa shielded the new flame with her hand, waiting until it had gained strength before going to the door. She glanced back at the bed, where Emma had curled up tightly beneath the bed-clothes and was now only a trembling mound. Smiling, she went out, closing the door softly behind her.

She moved swiftly along the spacious passage, where past members of the Lawrence family gazed down from the gilt-framed canvases lining the elegant walls. The solitary night candle on the console table near the top of the stairs fluttered in the draft of her passing, the light shimmering in the beautiful mirror above.

The grand staircase swept down between Corinthian columns to the unlit entrance hall below. Her shadow leapt and danced against the soaring columns as she began to descend, and the moving light flashed on the magnificent chandeliers suspended from the domed roof far above. Another growl of thunder echoed across the sky outside, and she paused immediately, listening for Emma, but there wasn't a sound from the little girl.

Louisa waited for a moment more. From this point on the staircase it was possible to see between the columns and chandeliers to the main doors, above which a very fine fanlight allowed a view over the park. A flash of lightning illuminated everything, and she saw the fountains in the parterre and the ghostly white peacocks moving on the croquet lawn. Beyond she caught a fragmentary glimpse of the *Cyclops* at her moorings by the river steps, but then all was darkness again. There was still no sound from Emma, and so Louisa continued on her way down to the entrance hall. The main doors were once again obscured from her view by the columns and chandeliers.

A sudden draft almost extinguished the candle, and cool air swept fleetingly over her. She halted in alarm, protecting the guttering flame with her hand. Such a draft could only have been caused by someone opening the main doors. She hadn't heard anything, but she knew nevertheless that someone had come in. Who was it? Why hadn't they knocked? She felt suddenly very cold, and her heart began to beat more swiftly as she sensed that she was no longer alone.

Slow footsteps sounded on the black-and-white-tiled floor below, and her alarm heightened, touching her skin with ice in spite of the heat of the summer night.

2

The candle trembled in her hand, but then a tall figure in hussar's uniform came into the faint arc of moving light. It was Geoffrey Lawrence.

He smiled up at her, placing a gleaming, spurred cavalry boot on the lowermost tread of the staircase. His dark-blue dolman was braided with silver, and his tight white breeches might have been molded to his figure. A pelisse trimmed with black fur was fixed casually over his left shoulder, and a red-and-white-striped sash accentuated his slender waist. His dark-brown hair was thick and luxuriant, and he wore it with side whiskers and a mustache, as did all fashionable young hussar officers. He was twenty-seven years old, and only too aware of how attractive he was; but there wasn't anything remotely attractive about the knowing way he allowed his gaze to rake over her, taking in the outline of her figure through the flimsy muslin of her gown. She felt as if she were naked.

He smiled again. "Good evening, Miss Cherington," he said softly.

"Captain Lawrence?"

"I trust I didn't startle you."

"I didn't realize anyone had returned." She looked past him, half-expecting to see Sir Ashley and Lady Lawrence as well.

He interpreted the glance correctly. "I'm alone, my father and stepmother are still basking in the royal presence at Devonshire House. I grew bored with the company." Bored indeed, his dear stepmama was becoming tiresome and he thirsted for pastures new, pastures like the delightful governess. Seduction was very much on his mind, more so than ever now he'd seen again the soft curves beneath the so-revealing muslin she wore so innocently. He hoped she was as vulnerable as she seemed, for his kind preyed upon such vulnerability. His smile didn't falter, he was all that was agreeable and charming. "You seem a little uneasy, Miss Cherington, I promise you're quite safe."

She hadn't liked him from the moment he'd returned to the house, and she certainly distrusted his facile and rather superficial charm. "I-I didn't for one moment think otherwise, sir," she replied a little coolly.

"Tell me, Miss Cherington, are you much given to wandering around the house at night?"

"I'm going to get a glass of milk for Emma."

"There are servants to do that."

"They don't answer bells rung by governesses, sir."

"No, I don't suppose they do," he murmured, and she could see by his eyes that he was well aware of how the servants behaved because of the situation his return had brought about. He studied her. "Why is Emma still awake?"

"She's afraid of the storm." Another rumble of thunder chose that moment to roll overhead, rolling away into the distance for some time before becoming silent again.

"Afraid? And so you rush to comfort her with glasses of milk—and stories, no doubt. No wonder she worships the ground you tread, trilling constantly about her beloved Cherry." His glance moved over her again. "Mind you, I suppose I cannot blame her, for to be sure you're a truly delightful person, Miss Cherington, and had I known before that you were residing beneath the parental roof, I vow I'd have returned sooner."

She wished he wouldn't speak to her like this, and she remained cool and unresponsive. "You wouldn't have returned earlier, sir, you'd still have come for Cowes."

"Ah, cruel heart, determined to dash my romantic

aspirations.'' His eyes were warm and dark, inviting so much. "But nothing will dash the fact that I find you a most enchanting diversion, my sweet Miss Cherington.''

She drew warily back. "Sir, you shouldn't—"

"Say such wickedly improper things? Probably not, but then I'm a wickedly improper fellow.''

She said nothing to this, and her silence was eloquent.

He raised an eyebrow. "You have surprising spirit, for a governess. You intrigue me, for you're obviously from a good family and yet you're reduced to seeking a position. What happened? Did your father lose all on the turn of a card?''

She flushed. She hadn't said anything to anyone about her family background, for to do so would be like being disloyal to her brother Tom, who may have been at fault but was still loved very much. "My parents are both dead, sir, and neither of them was at fault.''

He noted the emotion he'd accidentally tapped. Maybe he could throw her off guard by pressing the point. "Was it your brother, then? Or maybe a cousin? Who was it, Miss Cherington? I know it was the turn of a card, it always is. Devil take it, I should know the truth of that.''

"I don't wish to discuss it, Captain Lawrence.''

"You may not, Miss Cherington, but I'm afraid I do. Come now, satisfy my vulgar curiosity. Who was the selfish bounder who squandered it all and robbed you of your chance to make an advantageous match?''

The color still stained her cheeks. "Please, sir, I really don't wish to discuss it.''

"Humor me, Miss Cherington," he said softly, giving her not an inch. "Name the black sheep.''

She knew he had no intention of dropping the subject. Perhaps it would be wiser to say. "It was my brother, and please don't call him a black sheep.''

"Your brother, eh? And is this disreputable sibling still with us? Or has he passed into the hereafter as well?''

"He's still alive, sir, and he most certainly isn't disreputable." She was stiff and on the defensive.

"Why, I do believe you're still fond of the wretch. My dear Miss Cherington, the knave doesn't deserve your affection, he deserves to be castigated for his sins, because instead of protecting you, he's failed in his duty in every way."

"That isn't so!"

"No? Does he visit you? He doesn't, does he? I've made it my business to inquire about you, and I've ascertained that you haven't received a single visitor in the year you've been here."

Her eyes flashed at that. "Sir, you had no right to pry into my affairs." Her anger made her forget for a moment that she was only the governess, whereas he was the son of the house.

"On the contrary, Miss Cherington, I had every right. You are, after all, employed in this house."

She colored, looking quickly away. Another echo of thunder rolled in the distance.

He watched her. Dear God, how tempting she was, so virginal and fresh, just waiting to be aroused. And that spirit, oh, how satisfying it would be to master it, to master everything about her . . .

She made to go on down the staircase. "Please, sir, I must get the glass of milk."

He remained firmly in her way. "We haven't finished yet, Miss Cherington. I believe we were discussing your brother. Why doesn't he visit you? Is he ashamed of having reduced you to this?"

Her tongue passed nervously over her lips. How was she going to escape from him? She glanced back up the staircase.

"My sister's asleep, I'm sure of it," he said. "You haven't answered my question, Miss Cherington. Why does your brother ignore you?"

"He doesn't ignore me, sir; we write regularly and meet in Brentford whenever we can. We hope to meet in two days' time, if Lady Lawrence will allow me to.''

"Which is hardly likely, under the circumstances."

"The circumstances aren't my fault, sir," she replied stiffly.

"Oh, but they are, Miss Cherington. You shouldn't be so desirable, should you?"

Her cheeks were aflame, and her heart was beating more swiftly again. Please let someone come. But all was silent, except for the distant rattle of thunder.

"Don't look so frightened, Miss Cherington. I'm a gentleman and would no more dream of thrusting unwelcome attentions upon you than I would of flying."

"You're forcing your attentions upon me now, sir, by not allowing me to pass."

"But I only wish to talk to you, Miss Cherington," he said reasonably, spreading his hands innocently, but nevertheless remaining squarely in her way. "We haven't finished discussing your brother."

"I don't intend to discuss him, sir, not with you or with anyone else."

"Why not? Have you something to hide?"

"No!"

"Then tell me about him. Does he reside in luxury in London while you exist here in a miserable room on the top floor?"

"He's sharing a friend's apartment in New Bond Street."

"Ah, so the cad's living at someone else's expense. No doubt he's still frittering things away at the green baize."

"Don't judge others . . ." She bit the words back.

"By myself? Why not, for it's my experience that others *are* like myself, willfully going their own sweet way no matter what the consequences."

"My brother isn't like that, he didn't willfully lose everything; it just happened, and there's no one more saddened by his dereliction of his family duty than he is." Her eyes were angry as she met his. "Did you willfully bring about the situation that now requires you to sell the *Cyclops* or risk imprisonment for debt?''

He seemed to find this amusing. ''Of course I did, Miss Cherington. I continued to play even when I knew my hand couldn't possibly win, just as your worthless brother continued and thus lost you everything. He thought only of his own pleasure, and family duty couldn't have been further from his mind.''

Who was Captain Geoffrey Lawrence to pronounce upon family duty? He didn't even begin to understand what it meant. She was suddenly determined to end the conversation, making once again to pass him. ''Please let me go, sir, Emma will be—''

''Emma's asleep,'' he replied, moving to bar her way. ''Come now, it isn't often that we're at liberty to talk like this.'' Without warning, he put out his hand to touch her cheek.

With a gasp, she recoiled. The candle fluttered and smoked, and some hot wax splashed onto her wrist. She was a little frightened now. ''Captain Lawrence, we aren't at liberty at *all* to speak like this,'' she cried.

''This is 1811, Miss Cherington, not the Middle Ages.''

''That makes no difference, sir, for there are barriers between us. Now, will you please allow me to pass?''

''Only after you've paid a small forfeit,'' he replied. It was time to remove the kid gloves.

Her heart almost stopped. ''F-forfeit?'' she asked very warily.

''Just a little one,'' he said softly, reaching out to touch her cheek again.

With a quick intake of breath, she pulled sharply away, but he reached out swiftly to put his other hand to her waist, pulling her roughly toward him. The light in his eyes frightened her, as did the force he used, and momentarily her strength seemed to desert her. She was so shocked that she simply couldn't move; he had her completely at his mercy.

As another roll of thunder growled through the night,

he was oblivious to everything but the soft, pliant warmth of her body through the thin stuff of her gown. Desire rose sharply within him, arousing him to the point of madness. He had to possess her, he had to be the first to know the secret delights of her body. He succumbed to passion, forcing his lips down upon hers. He kissed her hungrily and without finesse, intent only upon slaking the desire that consumed him.

At last she began to struggle, trying to thrust him away, but he was too strong for her and nothing she did deterred him from his purpose. The candle slipped from her hand and the flame was immediately extinguished, engulfing them both in darkness. Still she struggled, trying to beat him with her fists, but then a new sound penetrated her fear—the patter of childish footsteps and muffled sobs as Emma left her room and came tearfully to look for her.

"Cherry? Cherry, where are you? I'm frightened!"

With a savage curse, Geoffrey started back from her, just as another flickering light appeared at the head of the staircase. Emma stood there in her white nightgown, a candle in her hand as she peered down toward them, calling Louisa's name.

Louisa needed no second bidding; she turned to dash up to the child, kneeling to gather her into her arms. "It's all right, sweeting, I'm here." Her heart was thundering, her senses still in turmoil.

Emma saw Geoffrey. Her fear evaporated and she hurried down to him. "Geoffrey! You came back just like you promised!"

He was in no mood to be pleasant. "You should be in bed, Emma," he said shortly, his eyes furious still as he looked past her toward Louisa.

Emma's steps faltered. "Are you angry with me?"

"Yes, I am. Get back to bed, or I'll tell Stepmama that you've been disobedient behind her back."

The child's eyes were wide with hurt.

"Didn't you hear me? I said you were to get back to your bed!"

With a choked sob, Emma turned to run back up the staircase, the candle streaming and smoking. She dashed past Louisa, who lingered a moment, looking contemptuously down at him. "I find you abhorrent and totally despicable," she said in a low, shaking voice.

He gave her a mocking, derisive bow, turned on his heel, and strode back toward the main doors. God damn Emma for interrupting. A few minutes more and he'd have succeeded. Now he'd have to wait, for he wasn't deterred by the way it had gone; on the contrary, he was more fired than before to possess what was being denied him.

He emerged beneath the portico, where the approaching storm had brought a light breeze that whispered between the columns. Searching in his pockets, he took out a Spanish cigar and some lucifers, and a moment later the sweet smoke was curling up to be snatched at by the night breeze. He gazed down through the park toward the river, where a flash of lightning fleetingly picked out the mast and rigging of the *Cyclops*. Louisa faded from his mind as his thoughts turned to his financial difficulties. A plague on the old man for choosing to make a stand! Geoffrey drew on the cigar. Cowes had an added enticement this year, for Lord Rowe's champion yacht, the *Mercury*, had foundered on rocks off the island earlier in the year after taking foolish risks against Lord Highclare's brilliant challenger, the *Spindrift*. Rowe's vessel had gone down like a stone, taking five of her crew of ten with her, and Rowe's bitter thirst for revenge was no secret—he'd voiced it many a time. Geoffrey gave a thin smile, pondering what might have been, for in the *Mercury*'s absence he'd intended to challenge Highclare's *Spindrift* himself and thus maybe snatch the crown. That had to go by the board now, for the *Cyclops* had to be sold.

He raised the cigar to his lips again, but then paused. What a fool he was! Why hadn't he thought of it before? The answer was obvious: Rowe must be persuaded to buy the *Cyclops*, one of the few cutters in England capable of tackling the *Spindrift*. Rowe was still in London, at his house in Berkeley Square, and could be approached the day after tomorrow, when an appointment at the War Office with Lord Palmerston would be taking Captain Geoffrey Lawrence to the capital.

He dropped the cigar and crushed it with his heel. And in the meantime, there was the delicious Miss Cherington to provide a diversion. She'd be his before he went to London, he promised himself she would.

Turning, he went back inside. Behind him the first heavy drops of rain began to fall and another roll of thunder echoed across the night.

3

There were thunderstorms all over the south of England that night, and Cowes didn't escape their attention. The Isle of Wight lay about two hours' sailing time due south from the mainland, across the stretch of water known as the Solent. Before the battle of Trafalgar had made the high seas safe for British merchantmen, the Solent had been a collecting place for convoys awaiting a Royal Navy escort, but now these waters were peaceful and each August society had begun to descend upon Cowes, on the island's northern shore, for a regatta and private yacht racing.

The town nestled around the mouth of the Medina, the river that flowed from south to north of the island, almost dividing it in two. On the mainland opposite, across the Solent, was the wide mouth of Southampton Water, the seven-mile-long inlet that had since Roman times made the port of Southampton one of the safest and most important in England. The Solent and the waters around the island were ideal for yacht racing, and this year, for the first time, the regatta had the royal seal of approval, in the presence of Prince William, Duke of Gloucester, and his sister, Princess Sophia; as a consequence there were more stylish persons to be seen on the island than ever before.

Cowes' new fashionability had seen great changes to the town, with many fine villas appearing on the rising hills on either side of the Medina, and several new Gothic castles standing grandly against the skyline. But there were great houses on the island that had been there before the regatta, and foremost among them was Highclare, some two miles west of Cowes, facing across the Solent toward Southampton Water and the New Forest. It was an elegant property, set in a noble park, and had been the seat for nearly two centuries of the Earls of Redway, aristocrats of proud lineage. The present earl, the sixth, was a reclusive old gentleman who'd shunned society since the deaths in a carriage accident some five years before of his beloved wife, son, and daughter-in-law. He very rarely left Highclare now, although he occasionally had houseguests, and the family was represented in society by his handsome grandson, Christopher, Lord Highclare, known as Kit to his many friends.

Kit was most definitely not a recluse; indeed, he was much sought after because of his wit, charm, and considerable eligibility. He was a leading light in yachting circles, and was master of the celebrated racing cutter, the *Spindrift*, which vessel had emerged victorious when Lord Rowe's reckless sailing had led to the sinking of the *Mercury*. There were many gentlemen who aspired to the *Spindrift*'s new crown, and foremost among them was Lord Grantham, who'd issued a challenge to a race around the island. Now Cowes talked of little else but this forthcoming event, on the outcome of which there was much wagering.

But on this rain-washed, thundery night, yacht racing was far from everyone's mind as society crushed into the Fountain Inn to attend a concert in the presence of the Duke of Gloucester and Princess Sophia. Very few cared to stay away, for to be seen with royalty was *de rigueur*, and so the town's narrow twisting streets were quiet, with lantern light reflecting dismally on the wet cobbles. The Medina was windswept, and the elegant yachts rocked at their moorings on the choppy water. Growls of thunder rolled over the lowering skies, and the darkness was punctuated now and then by stabs of brilliant lightning.

There were some yachts tied up at the harbor

wharves, their sleek, costly shapes a sharp contrast to the sturdy ketches and wherries that were to be found at Cowes all the year round. On the quayside the Mermaid Inn was bright with lights, and the sound of male laughter issued from its doorway as a lone fisherman staggered out into the night, his sea boots ringing unsteadily on the cobbles as he began to make his way home. The nearby shipyards were dark and silent, but a lantern swayed on the corner of a warehouse, lit especially to illuminate the deck of one of the racing yachts moored nearby. The fisherman hardly noticed the yacht as he wended his uneven way past, but had society witnessed the vessel's hasty preparations to sail on the night tide, it would have been very surprised indeed, for the yacht was the *Spindrift* and it was quite unthinkable that she should leave while the regatta was at its height.

Kit was on the deck with his small crew. His fair hair was ruffled by the blustering wind, and his voluminous cloak flapped around his tall, athletic figure. He knew the hazards of sailing in weather like this, but felt he had to respond to the urgent note he'd received from a close friend in distress in London. Storm or no storm, the *Spindrift* would cross the Solent tonight and be in Southampton as quickly as possible.

Kit only hoped his mistress would be able to slip away from the concert at the Fountain Inn to see him before he left. He'd sent a message, but maybe it wouldn't reach her in time; maybe, too, she'd choose to ignore it, for he was supposed to be with her right now and there was nothing she disliked more than being let down. As he worked to make the *Spindrift* ready, he pondered what society would say if it knew about the liaison, because the lady was none other than Lady Rowe, wife of the man who already had so much cause to loathe the future Earl of Redway.

Rowe wasn't a man to cross; he was a ruthless duelist who'd dispatched a number of opponents to the hereafter, and so Kit knew his affair with Thea was unwise in the extreme. But there was no place for wisdom where love was concerned, and Kit was very much in love. He hadn't entered lightly into the affair—it went against his principles to put horns on another man, even such a man as the unpleasant Rowe—but because he loved Thea so very much, he'd thrown all caution to the winds. She was the love of his life, the woman he wanted as his wife, and his commitment to her was total; he only wished he could be certain she felt the same way.

Tonight he knew he'd somehow reached a crossroad. His honor forbade him from continuing with the affair if she wouldn't leave Rowe and come finally to him, and so she had to decide which man meant more to her: the husband who treated her with cold possessiveness, or the lover she professed to adore. Kit's heart was heavy as he worked, for Thea had no idea that he'd finally reached this stage; what her reaction would be to having such a decision forced upon her without warning was in the lap of the gods.

At that very moment, Thea was sitting impatiently in the crush in the Fountain Inn. Her fan tapped irritably against her white-gloved palm, and the plumes springing from the golden circlet around her head quivered with barely suppressed anger. She was an exceedingly beautiful woman, with warm honey-blond hair cut into fashionably short curls, and violet eyes that were both haughty and challenging. Her figure was full and slender-waisted, and her skin alabaster clear. The spangles adorning her damson silk gown flashed in the overheated air, and her face was as stormy as the night outside. Where *was* Kit? He'd promised to be here by now after spending the day out at Highclare with his grandfather. It wasn't often that she and Rowe were so providently apart so that she could spend so much time with her secret lover, and Kit chose now to absent himself without reason!

The orchestra continued playing, and her fan tapped ever more impatiently. She glared at the musicians, among whom a certain Mr. Griesley was distinguishing himself on the hautbois, or at least was endeavoring to do so above the disgraceful chatter of the audience.

A plague on Mr. Griesley, she thought uncharitably, and the devil take his wretched hautbois! Kit had never let her down before, and it was an experience she resented very much indeed.

A footman approached her discreetly. "My lady?"

"Yes? What is it?"

"I'm charged to give you this." He handed her a note and then quickly withdrew.

To the strains of the hautbois and the loud drone of conversation, she read the brief communication: "My darling, forgive me for not being with you, but I must see you as quickly as possible on board the *S*. Don't delay, I beg you. K."

Slowly she folded the note and slipped it into her sequinned velvet reticule. Why on earth was Kit on the *Spindrift* at this hour? What could possibly be more important than his promise to be with her? For a moment she considered ignoring the note, as a token of her severe displeasure, but then she thought again. Kit was an exciting lover, and she enjoyed the danger of a liaison with the man her husband hated most in all the world. Perhaps she'd be wiser to answer the note. She glanced toward the Duke of Gloucester and Princess Sophia, seated in golden chairs directly in front of the unfortunate Mr. Griesley. Their permission would have to be sought if she was to leave the concert halfway through. What would be the best excuse? She thought for a moment. A headache, yes, that would be ideal, for the princess was a martyr to them herself.

Thea rose discreetly to her feet, slipping around the edge of the tightly packed audience to curtsy before the royal brother and sister. Sophia Mathilda was a plain but charming spinster of thirty-eight, with a diamond tiara in her prematurely graying hair, and a heavily embroidered green velvet gown encasing her plump person. The duke was a few years younger, with a large, stout body and spindly legs, and he liked to dress very grandly, with much gold braiding and as many orders and decorations as he could muster. He was pompous and boring, and always expected to be treated with full ceremony, but even though he was staring fixedly at the orchestra, it was nevertheless he who noticed Thea first.

"Lady Rowe?" he murmured, his popping eyes moving slowly over her.

"Your highness, I crave your pardon, but I'm exceedingly indisposed with a headache and beg your understanding and indulgence to—"

Princess Sophia's attention was dragged away from Mr. Griesley's excellence. "Certainly, Lady Rowe," she said quickly, waving her away. "I trust you will soon be recovered."

"Your highness is very kind," replied Thea, bowing her lovely head gratefully and then withdrawing as quickly as possible.

She hurried from the packed room, her damson silk skirt whispering richly and the plumes of her head streaming softly.

Behind her, Mr. Griesley gave his all with the hautbois.

4

As Thea's landau drove onto the quay, a flash of lightning illuminated everything, and then there was darkness again, broken by a loud roll of thunder directly overhead. The rain seemed to intensify, tamping on every surface and running in rivulets along the gutters. From the Mermaid Inn there still came the sound of laughter and singing, and the lantern swung on the warehouse close to the *Spindrift*.

Kit heard the landau approaching, and he immediately came ashore. He took out his fob watch. The tide was almost ready, there were only minutes to go before he'd have to set sail for the mainland.

The landau drew to a standstill, the team stamping and tossing their heads as the downpour soaked them. Kit flung open the door and looked in at Thea. His top hat threw his face in shadow, but she saw his quick smile.

"I'm glad you came," he said softly, his voice almost drowned by the noise of the storm.

The wind was chill, making her shiver a little as it touched her bare arms. She drew her shawl more closely. "Why are you here, Kit? What's happened?"

"I have to go to the mainland tonight."

Her eyes widened. "In *this* weather?"

"Yes."

"But it's madness! What possible reason can you have that's important enough?"

"I can't tell you here. Come aboard."

She was loath to agree, for she still felt angry with

him for failing to join her at the concert, but she slipped
her hand into his and alighted from the landau. The rain
was cold and the wind snatched at her flimsy damson
skirt.

He led her quickly across the quay and over the gangplank onto the deck of the cutter, ushering her toward
the stern, where a narrow hatch led belowdeck to the
vessel's single, exceedingly small cabin. As Kit closed
the hatch behind them, the noise of the storm was
immediately stifled.

The cabin was spartan, containing a narrow, curtained bunk, a small table and chair, and a sea trunk.
During the day it was lit by a fine window in the stern,
but now, in the darkness, light was provided by two
gimbel-mounted candlesticks on the wall. The flames
had shivered as the hatch was opened and the night air
swept in, but they swiftly settled again.

Kit untied his wet cloak, hanging it on a hook, then he
removed his top hat and gloves, tossing both onto the
table before turning to face Thea. He was wearing a
plain, excellently cut brown coat and very tight buckskin breeches that outlined his fine form to perfection,
leaving very little of his anatomy to the imagination. His
top boots were the work of Hoby of St. James's Street,
and his cravat was tied in the very latest fashion. He was
above average height, with broad shoulders and slender
hips, and always managed to look effortlessly elegant
and graceful. There were centuries of breeding and
quality in his lean, sunburnt face and clear blue eyes,
and a hint of devil-may-care in his finely chiseled lips.
His tousled fair hair was usually just a little wavy, but
tonight, because of the downpour, it was wet and tightly
curled. There was something of the prince and the
Viking about him, and it was an exciting mixture that
never failed to stimulate her. Looking at him now, she
wanted nothing more than to submit to him, but she was
still angry, and anger always made her contrary.

She faced him haughtily. "Why did you ask me to
come here, Kit? If there's something so vastly important

waiting for you on the mainland that you must up and go even on a night like this, I marvel that you bothered to send word to me at all.''

He smiled a little. ''You know full well that I'd never leave without good reason, and you also know that I wouldn't go without seeing you first.''

''Without sending for me like a lackey, you mean,'' she said petulantly.

''Some lackey,'' he murmured, allowing his glance to move appreciatively over her.

She flushed a little, pleased in spite of herself. ''You presume, sir.''

''So I do.''

She felt her pulse quicken. ''Why are you leaving Cowes so quickly?'' she asked.

''I've received an urgent note from Tom Cherington. He needs me in London.''

''*Needs* you? What can that good-for-nothing wastrel possibly need you for?''

''I know your opinion of him, Thea, but he happens to have recently become a very good friend of mine. He also happens to have got himself embroiled in a duel at dawn the day after tomorrow, with your husband.''

She stared at him then. ''He *what*? A duel with *Rowe*? Is he mad?''

''Mad? No. Unfortunate? Yes, most probably, for he was unwise enough to detect Rowe cheating at cards. Anyway, the upshot of it all is that Tom has asked me to be his second. I regard it as my duty to go, and I must be there well before time if I'm to stand any chance of dissuading him.'' He met her eyes. ''It has to be Tom who retracts, for we know full well that Rowe never will.''

She looked away. ''Any man fool enough to cross Rowe deserves all he gets.''

A light passed through his eyes. ''Thank you.''

''I didn't mean—''

''It doesn't matter if you did or didn't, the fact remains that if anyone deserves to have to face your husband, it's my good self. However, I'm not the one in question, poor Tom Cherington is, and I intend to offer him whatever support I can. He hasn't any family—they're all dead—and so he needs me.''

''I need you too,'' she said quickly, wanting to persuade him to stay. She didn't care a fig for Tom Cherington, who disliked her as much as she disliked him.

''Thea, in this particular instance he needs me much more.''

She tossed her lovely head again, her anger still simmering. ''Am I to hope you'll deign to return within a few days? Maybe you've forgotten the race with Lord Grantham?''

''I'd hardly forget that.''

''And while you're away I suppose I'm expected to amuse myself with my embroidery?''

He smiled, allowing his glance to move lazily over her. Thea, Lady Rowe, was fashioned for pastimes much more stimulating than embroidery. He found her totally fascinating, totally adorable, and he needed to have her as his wife, nothing less would do anymore. And that was what he needed to broach before the *Spindrift* set sail.

The warmth of his glance affected her, as it always did, and suddenly she found herself setting her anger aside to go to him. She slipped her slender arms around his waist, pressing close as she reached up to kiss him on the lips. She lingered over the kiss, moving her body sensuously against his and savoring the beguiling warmth that began to steal deliciously through her, as always happened with this man.

For a long, long moment he responded, folding her in his arms and almost crushing her, but then he drew back, cupping her face in his hands and looking deep into her eyes. ''My darling,'' he said softly, ''much as I'd like to take you right here and now, I fear I must resist the temptation, for I really do have to leave in a minute or so.'' He hesitated. ''Thea, you don't have to stay here, you could come with me.''

She stared at him, caught completely off guard. ''Are you moonstruck? Go with you and have the world—and Rowe—know the truth about us?''

''Yes. Thea, I want you to be my wife.''

She was at a loss for words, for she'd just been enjoying the illicit excitement of an affair with someone whose lovemaking turned her whole being to fire. She'd always known that he loved her, but although she was infatuated with him, she didn't feel any deep and lasting love for him, and leaving Rowe on his account had never figured in her plans. Deserting her husband for Kit, of all men, would mean certain ruin, for Rowe would move heaven and earth to destroy her reputation. Her character would be tainted forever, because Rowe wouldn't rest in his vendetta against her. She shrank from such notoriety and didn't intend to risk it, not even for a lover like this and not even for the prospect of becoming the Countess of Redway.

She lowered her eyes. ''Kit, can't things remain as they are?''

One of the crew was at the hatch. ''Begging your pardon, my lord, but the tide's up.''

''Very well.'' Kit continued to look at her. ''No, Thea, things can't remain as they are.''

''But there's no need to change . . .''

''I'm afraid there is. It's no longer enough that you're my mistress; my love demands more, and so does my honor.'' His eyes were incredibly blue and piercing as she looked unwillingly into them again. ''Thea, you could leave him if you really wanted to.''

She didn't reply.

Slowly he released her. ''I don't think there's anything more to be said; your decision is only too clear.''

She stared at him then. ''What are you saying?''

''That it's over.''

"You can't possibly mean that! Kit, it's nonsense, there's no need to end anything!"

"There's every need. I may not like Rowe, but I like even less the way I've been making a cuckold of him. There's little honor in bedding another man's wife, and I've been guilty of doing just that because I love you so very much." His eyes were cool. "Now it seems that that love has been a little one-sided all along, for if you felt the way I do, you wouldn't hesitate."

She still couldn't believe the sudden turn things had taken. "Kit, you're being very unreasonable."

"Maybe I am, but I've realized that I can't go on as before, it's just not enough. I'm in love with you, Thea, I'm not just indulging in an affair to amuse my idle hours."

"I-I love you too . . ." she began, thinking to somehow regain control of the situation. She put a hesitant, trembling hand out, summoning tears into her magnificent eyes. "Oh, Kit . . ."

"If you love me, leave him and come with me now."

"I can't."

"You mean, you won't."

She raised her chin defiantly then. "All right, I won't. I see no reason to suddenly change things."

"And I see every reason." He went to take down his wet cloak, swinging it around his shoulders. Outside, another roll of thunder rumbled over the sky, and on deck the crew were waiting for him. He snatched up his hat and gloves, putting both on and then looking at her. "I think it's time to return you to your carriage."

"Kit, when will you return?"

"Of what possible interest can that be to you? Our affair is at an end, and when next we meet, it will be as acquaintances, and nothing more."

She stared at him as he went to the hatch and opened it. Cool, damp air blustered into the cabin, and thunder echoed through the darkness, rolling slowly away beyond the noise of the rain. He turned, holding a hand out to assist her onto the deck.

Slowly she took it. Anger swept willfully over her. How dared he treat her like this! How dared he cast her off simply because she wouldn't come at his whim!

She said nothing as he helped her from the *Spindrift* and across the rainswept quay to the waiting carriage. She'd intended to give him a haughty look before driving off, but he'd already slammed the door and instructed the postilion to drive on. She sat numbly back against the rich upholstery, gazing out at the lantern swinging on the corner of the warehouse.

He remained on the quay, watching until the landau had turned the corner and passed out of sight.

A crewman was waiting anxiously. "We should be leaving, my lord."

Kit turned and strode back on board, his wet cloak flapping around him as the wind picked up still more.

A few minutes later, the *Spindrift* slipped out of the shelter of Cowes harbor into the stormblown waters of the Solent. Behind, the lights of Cowes were invisible in the gloom, and the cutter's sails strained as the full force of the weather caught them.

The rain lashed Kit's face as he stared through the storm toward the mainland. What sort of madness was this? He was risking his own life for the somewhat dubious honor of watching Tom Cherington almost certainly forfeiting his.

5

The storm had gone by the next morning, and England awoke to brilliant August sunshine. At Lawrence Park, the grounds seemed to have been refreshed by the overnight rain, and the flower beds in the parterre were particularly bright and colorful. The fountains splashed like diamonds and on the croquet lawn the white peacocks moved like delicate living fans, their shrill calls carrying clearly over the park and nearby meadows. On the horizon the outline of London shimmered in a heat haze, while closer the spires and rooftops of Brentford seemed very still and clear. At the top of the river steps, surrounded by flowering shrubs, stood a small summerhouse; in the past it had been used by elegant parties taking wine and wafers while watching the river.

As Louisa rose from her bed, she looked from her top floor window and decided that on such a beautiful morning, poor Emma's extra lessons should at least take place in pleasant surroundings, and what could be more pleasant than the summerhouse?

She and Emma breakfasted alone in the schoolroom, as they always did because the new Lady Lawrence disapproved of children at the breakfast table—or at any other table, come to that. Afterward they dressed to go outside. Emma put on a neat white lawn dress with a wide blue sash, and frilly pantalettes that protruded beneath its dainty hem. She had red morocco shoes, and wore her brown hair in ringlets beneath a little straw bonnet tied on with blue ribbons. Louisa wore one of her three day dresses, the peach seersucker with small

puffed sleeves and a very high waistline gathered in by a
ribbon of matching silk. Her dark-red hair was worn up
beneath a wide-brimmed gypsy hat, and there was a
light white shawl resting over her arms. After they'd
selected the various textbooks they'd need for the
lessons, they proceeded down through the house to the
entrance hall, with Louisa exhorting Emma to walk, not
canter like a small pony on the stairs.

Sir Ashley and Lady Lawrence were emerging from
the breakfast room. He was a gray-haired, kindly faced
gentleman, thin and frail-looking. He had on a long
green paisley dressing gown, and there was a tasseled
cap on his head. His hand rested fondly over his young
wife's as she walked at his side. He doted on her, and
had yet to see her in her true colors.

Anne, Lady Lawrence, had a doll-like face and raven
hair, and her lips were sweetly shaped. She looked
angelic in her fine pale-pink jaconet gown by Madame
Coty, London's foremost couturiere, but there was a
steely glint in her green eyes as she perceived Emma and
the hated governess coming down toward the entrance
hall. Her humor was already poor this morning, for
she'd guessed why Geoffrey had left the reception at
Devonshire House the night before, and over the breakfast table she'd been endeavoring, without success, to
persuade Ashley that his brat of a daughter really would
benefit from a sojourn at Miss Ryden's School for the
Daughters of Gentlefolk in Kensington.

Emma was delighted to see her father, whom she
adored, and she ran impulsively toward him. "Good
morning, Papa," she cried, flinging her arms about him
and hugging him in a most undisciplined way.

He didn't seem to mind, smiling and patting her head
fondly. "Good morning, m'dear."

Emma then looked at her stepmother, and her face
became a little surly, although she executed an
accomplished enough curtsy. "Good morning, Stepmama."

Anne's eyes flickered coldly and she gave a brief

inclination of her head. "Good morning, Emma. Would it be too much to ask that you conduct yourself with a little decorum? This is a house, not a barnyard."

Emma's lips were pressed together sulkily, and she said nothing.

Anne's glance moved on to Louisa. "Am I to understand from your clothes that you intend to go outside, Miss Cherington?"

"Yes, Lady Lawrence."

"I understood that mornings were to be set aside solely for lessons. I also seem to remember ordering that she had to do extra lessons today."

"You did, my lady, and she will do them; it's just that I thought it would be pleasant for her to do her work in the summerhouse on such a lovely morning."

"Lessons are for learning, Miss Cherington, not enjoyment."

Emma's face fell and she looked imploringly at her father. "Oh, *please* let me go outside, Papa. I promise to learn everything. I'll learn a whole poem and recite it for you afterward, and two new French verbs," she added.

Sir Ashley patted his wife's hand. "There, m'dear, is that not a valiant offer?"

"No, sir, it is not," she replied icily. "Emma's lessons must take place in the sober surroundings of the schoolroom if she's to achieve the necessary standards. Her boisterous behavior this morning must surely have gone some way toward convincing you that what I've been saying is only too correct."

A new voice interrupted them from the staircase. It was Geoffrey, his dark-blue uniform as splendidly attractive as ever as he descended. He'd been listening to every word, and it didn't suit him that Emma should stay inside this morning; it certainly didn't suit him that she should be sent away from the house, not yet anyway, for he had to conquer the governess first. He came toward them, his glance resting rather angrily on Anne. "Come now," he said to her, "aren't you being a little severe? What harm is there in the lessons taking place in the summerhouse?''

She was equally angry, for she knew why he was interfering. ''This isn't any concern of yours, Geoffrey.''

''On the contrary, it's very much my concern, for if you do not relent, then I shall be forced to sulk and refuse to go riding with you today.'' He smiled and spoke in a bantering tone, but he meant every word. He wanted the lessons to take place in the summerhouse, for then there would be an opportunity of getting the governess on her own.

Anne colored. He was impossible to please these days, finding fault with everything she said or did. His interest in her was waning, whereas hers in him was as strong and vital as ever. She was losing her hold on him, and the reason stood watching in the shapely form of Miss Louisa Cherington. Anne knew that if she was to stand any chance of keeping his interest, she had to be with him whenever possible, and that meant giving in now or forfeiting the chance of riding alone with him later on. Managing a stiff smile, she nodded. ''Oh, very well, let the lessons take place outside if it's so important, but I've no doubt that in the end I'll be proved right about all this, for Emma will become unmanageable, and it will all be due to the influence of a governess too weak to impose the necessary discipline.'' There was a serpentine chill in her green eyes as they swung to Louisa. ''Miss Cherington, I believe you wish to be permitted to meet your brother in Brentford in a day or so's time.''

Louisa's glance fled toward Geoffrey. He must have said something. ''Yes, my lady.''

''I'm afraid I cannot see my way clear to granting such permission, for Emma's education, such as it is, must come before your personal pleasures.'' With a cool nod of her head, Anne walked on. Her jaconet skirt hissed as she mounted the staircase, and soon the columns and chandeliers obscured her from their view.

Sir Ashley looked and felt most uncomfortable. He loathed awkwardness, and there seemed to have been so much of it recently. Maybe Anne was right and it was all due to Emma's misconduct. He'd have to give the matter of sending her away his full consideration. His hands clasped behind his back, he followed his wife.

Geoffrey glanced at Emma. "I trust you're suitably grateful for my interference on your behalf."

She looked stormily at him. "You were horrid to me last night."

"Then I've made amends," he replied shortly, his glance moving on to Louisa. "Good morning, Miss Cherington, I trust you slept well in spite of everything."

"Very well," she replied coolly, her dislike shining only too clearly in her gray eyes.

He waved Emma away. "Run along to the summer-house with your French verbs. I want to speak privately with Miss Cherington."

"Oh, but, Geoffrey—"

"Do as you're told!"

Emma's eyes filled with tears and without another word she hurried away, leaving the main door open as she dashed out of the house.

Louisa looked angrily at him. "That was inexcusable," she breathed. "Why must you hurt her? It isn't her fault!"

"No, it's *my* fault, and I'm not angry with her, I'm angry with myself. I behaved monstrously toward you last night, and I'm thoroughly ashamed of the fact."

She stared at him, caught completely unawares. "I-I beg your pardon?"

He smiled a little, having intended to catch her off guard. "Can you forgive me, Miss Cherington?"

"For what? Your gross miscalculation?"

"Miscalculation?"

"Yes. You thought that your charm was irresistible and that I'd succumb. You were very wrong."

Behind his smile he was angry, but he'd decided on a

new approach this morning, and that meant concealing the truth. "I'm afraid to say that you're right, Miss Cherington, but it wasn't what it seemed. If I hoped my charm *was* irresistible, it was because I'm so very drawn to you. I want to redeem myself in your eyes, because if it's possible to start again—"

"There's nothing to start, sir," she replied quickly, not trusting such a complete turnabout.

"But there is. I hold you in very high regard, Miss Cherington, too high to be happy with my conduct last night. You must at least allow me the chance to redeem myself. Please say that you will."

"Sir, I am only the governess, and you—"

"And I'm the son of the house. I know. I am also a man very much attracted to you, and as such I'm your equal, not your better." A door opened and closed on the floor above, and he looked up sharply. "We can't talk here, please say you'll meet me somewhere tonight."

She drew back. "Certainly not."

"Please, I beg of you. I promise on my honor to behave like a gentleman. My parents have a card party tonight, but I'll be able to slip away at ten. We could meet at the summerhouse. Please agree, for I need the opportunity to speak properly to you."

"I said no, sir, and I meant it. You revealed yourself for what you really are last night, and I'd be a fool indeed to expose myself to more of the same. Well, I'm not a fool, sir, so please don't treat me like one."

He dissembled again. "I know you're not a fool, Miss Cherington, and I also know that you set great store by fair play. Last night you were very quick to point out that I was wrong to condemn your brother out of hand, but now you're condemning me out of hand, and what could be more unfair than that? You mustn't deny me the chance to prove that I'm truly repentant. I've tried already this morning to right a little of the wrong."

"I don't understand."

"I mentioned the matter of your wish to meet your

brother in Brentford. Maybe I wasn't successful, but I did try. I feel truly appalled about what I did last night, Miss Cherington, you must believe me."

"Please, sir . . ."

"Meet me, for I must speak properly to you," he pressed, his brown eyes bright with earnest imploring.

She hesitated. She *had* insisted on defending Tom's good name, and now she was being equally insistent that Captain Geoffrey Lawrence didn't have a good name to defend. But what if last night had been a momentary transgression? What if he was genuinely repentant? She was torn, and in her quandary forgot all his other sins, such as embarking upon the distasteful affair with his father's new bride.

"Do me the honor of hearing me out," he said softly, knowing that she was wavering.

"I . . ."

"Please."

"Very well," she said reluctantly.

He smiled.

6

As Louisa was making her ill-judged assignation with treacherous, predatory Geoffrey, Kit was posting with all haste toward London to see her brother. The passage across the Solent had been worse than he'd expected, and the *Spindrift* had been delayed outside Southampton Water for some time so that it was well after dawn when at last she'd entered the port. He'd intended to rest awhile at an inn before continuing with his journey, but the delay meant that there wasn't time for that, so he'd immediately hired a post chaise, only to find his progress hampered by flash floods after the night's torrential rain.

It was almost dark and the streetlamps were being lit as the chaise at last reached the capital, traveling through Mayfair and turning into New Bond Street. Glancing wearily out of the window, he saw Brindley's famous bookshop on the left, one of several such emporiums in this most fashionable and stylish of all London's shopping streets. It was a throughfare created for gentlemen, renowned for its hotels, bachelor apartments, tailors, bootmakers, and other such masculine establishments; after dark, it was also renowned as the haunt of prostitutes and other persons of a lower order. During the journey, he'd thought of little else but the breaking up of his relationship with Thea, but now she was far from his thoughts, for it was Tom Cherington who was his prime concern.

The friend whose apartment Tom shared resided above the premises of Messrs. Lucas & Mackintosh, tea merchants, on the western side of the street, almost on the crossroad with Bruton Street and Conduit Street. As the chaise halted at the curb outside, Kit prepared to alight. He felt decidedly jaded after traveling for so long, and wished that he'd driven first to his house in Grosvenor Square to change, but seeing Tom must come before anything else. Besides, Tom was hardly likely to be in the mood to notice any lack of sartorial excellence.

Tapping his top hat on his head, he climbed down from the chaise, paying the postboy and tipping him a little extra to go to Grosvenor Square and leave word that his private carriage was to come to the rooms in New Bond Street an hour before dawn. Pray God it wouldn't be needed, for by then Tom might have been persuaded to retract. As the chaise rattled away, Kit entered the narrow alley beside the tea merchant's and went up the wooden steps to the door of the first-floor apartment.

It was opened by Dudley, valet to Mr. John Partridge, whose apartment it was. He was a small, whippetlike man, a former jockey whose career had been ended by a terrible fall from one of the Prince Regent's horses at Newmarket. His wizened face was anxious as he opened the door, but he smiled with relief as he recognized it. "You've come at last, my lord. Do come inside."

Removing his hat, Kit stepped past him into the candlelit rooms. John Partridge was a follower of the fancy, and his taste was immediately evident. There were prints on the walls, a collection of weapons above the mantlepiece, and copies of *Bell's Weekly Messenger* and *Woodfall's Daily Advertiser* on the table, both of which publications were renowned for their accounts of sporting events, especially pugilistic matches. There was no sign of Tom, or of his friend, and Kit turned inquiringly to the valet. "I take it they're both out?"

"Mr. Partridge is away in Scotland, my lord. His father passed away last week. Mr. Cherington is at the Prince of Wales Coffee House."

Kit sighed, tossing his hat on the table. "And how long has he been drowning his sorrows there?"

"Several hours, my lord."

Kit glanced at the clock on the mantelpiece. It was just gone nine. "If he's not here by half-past, I'll go and drag him out."

"Thank you, my lord," said the valet gratefully. "I didn't know what to do, for it's hardly a servant's place to tell a gentleman to come home."

"I'm not sure it's my place either. How is he?" Kit flung himself onto a shiny brown leather sofa.

"Very low, my lord."

"What on earth possessed him to face it out with Rowe, of *all* men?"

"I don't know, sir. He's been a little odd these past few weeks, not at all his usual self."

"In what way?"

"It's hard to say. He seems to have something on his mind, but when Mr. Partridge asked him what was wrong, all he'd say was that he'd failed in his family duty in the past, and was continuing to fail in it."

"Continuing? How can that be when his family's dead?"

"Precisely, my lord. Mr. Partridge didn't know what to make of it; he reckoned Mr. Cherington was in drink."

"And was he?"

"No, sir. Not to my knowledge."

Kit leaned his head back thoughtfully.

"Can I offer you some refreshment, sir?"

"Is there any cognac to be had?"

"No, sir, but Mr. Partridge always keeps a bottle of fine Scotch whiskey in readiness."

"A heathen beverage, but it will have to do."

"Very well, sir." The valet went to a cupboard and took out the bottle and a glass, which he placed on the table by Kit's arm after pouring a generous measure. "Will there be anything else, sir?"

"No, you can get on with whatever it was you were doing."

"I was polishing and cleaning Mr. Cherington's dueling pistols."

"I didn't know he had any."

"I understand they were his father's, sir. The late Mr. Cherington collected such items, and this pair is all that Mr. Tom has left."

Kit smiled a little. "I had no idea that Tom's father collected firearms. It's a strange coincidence."

"Coincidence, sir?"

"My grandfather collects them as well. The walls at Highclare are arrayed with a veritable arsenal, enough to equip Wellington's whole army, I fancy. I spent more than an hour yesterday standing before one particular pair of dueling pistols, while my grandfather saw fit to lecture me about failing in *my* family duty by not marrying before now and producing the required heir." He picked up the glass and raised it to the valet. "Your health, Dudley."

"Sir." The little man gladly withdrew. There were times when he simply didn't understand gentlemen. Didn't understand them at all.

Kit sipped the whiskey and glanced at the clock. The hands were creeping toward the half-hour; no doubt he'd have to go and winkle Tom out of the Prince of Wales.

Carriages were still passing to and fro in the street outside, and he could hear the jingle of spurs as groups of gentlemen strolled along the pavement. Just as the clock struck half-past nine, he heard someone coming up toward the apartment door. It opened and Tom Cherington stepped inside.

He was of medium height and slender build, with the same dark-chestnut hair and gray eyes as the sister of whose existence Kit knew nothing. He wore a rather creased light-brown coat and fawn trousers, and his simple neckcloth boasted neither gold pin nor jewel. His expression was heavy as he entered, but Kit saw immediately that he wasn't very much in drink. His steps were steady and his aim deft as he tossed his top hat onto a hook on the wall.

"Good evening, Tom."

"Kit!" Tom whirled about, his face breaking into a grin. "You're here at last! I thought you wouldn't get my note in time. Thank you for coming, you're the best friend in all the world!"

"I'm overwhelmed by such a warm welcome. Actually, I'd have been here sooner but for the damned weather."

"But you're here, and that's what matters." Tom went to the cupboard to look for the whiskey.

"It's here, dear boy. And should you be indulging?"

"Dutch courage," replied Tom, bringing a glass to the table and pouring himself a liberal helping.

"Dutch courage has a habit of turning into a morning after, and that's the last thing you need."

"I want your company, not your advice, Kit." Tom sat on a chair opposite, stretching his legs out. "I meant it when I said that you're the best friend in all the world, for although we haven't known each other for all that long, I regard you as the stoutest fellow I've ever known."

"Flattery indeed."

"It's the truth. A man needs a good friend at his side at a time like this." Tom swirled the whiskey, smiling in a way that revealed how strained he was. "It was an ill wind that brought the *Mercury* and the *Spindrift* together in the spring. But for that singular misfortune, Rowe would have been safely away in Cowes by now, making it impossible for you and Thea to meet, instead of dawdling back here and having the execrable taste to sit down at the same green baize as me."

"Which brings me neatly to my most immediate duty as your friend and second; that of persuading you not to proceed with this nonsense."

"Rowe was guilty of cardsharping, Kit, and I won't retract a single word of my accusation."

"Is his cheating worth your fool life?"

"My honor is at stake."

"No, Tom," replied Kit quietly, "your life is at stake."

"I saw him cheat, and I won't let it pass this time."

"What's so special about this time? Damn it all, Tom, you've seen him cheat before and it hasn't bothered you. The man's a blackguard of the first order, a maggot, and he simply isn't worth all this."

"I've *thought* I've seen him cheating in the past," corrected Tom, "but I was never absolutely sure."

"Oh, come off it, man. You were perfectly certain before; you were just wise enough to put your neck before your urge to be noble."

Tom hesitated, avoiding his gaze. "Very well, perhaps on those occasions I wasn't as tipsy as I was this time."

Kit gave an incredulous laugh. "Don't try to gull me, Tom. I know you like a glass or two, but you're never soaked. You've got some other reason for charging into this duel, haven't you?"

Tom smiled a little. "You're too damned perceptive for your own good. You're right, of course, I do have a reason, but I'm not about to divulge it, except to say that a guilty conscience is a dreadful burden."

"Guilty conscience? About what? Surely not about turning a blind eye to Rowe's misconduct? If so, then a great many other gentlemen must have the same burden."

"It isn't about Rowe. Don't ask me any more, Kit, I don't want to talk about it."

"As you wish. Perhaps you could give me some details about the duel. I trust it's to be within an hour's reach of dawn, I've sent word for my carriage to be here—"

"It's at Kensington. A secluded meadow on Holland House land. His lordship's away and the house is closed. Rowe chose the place."

"Trust Rowe to know a suitable venue."

"He's a past master at duels." Tom took a large gulp of the whiskey. "How was Cowes?" he went on, changing the subject yet again. "I take it you've deserted the delightful Thea on my behalf?"

"Cowes was a crush, and yes, I've deserted Thea because of you."

"I'll warrant she wasn't pleased."

Kit didn't reply.

Tom glanced shrewdly at him. "How is she?"

'Still very much married to Rowe."

"You should be thanking your lucky stars."

"Why do you say that?"

"Because the lady simply isn't worthy of you."

"I don't wish to discuss it," replied Kit shortly.

"We'd better change the subject yet again," said Tom with a sigh, "Maybe it's safe to inquire after your grandfather?"

"I was with him at Highclare yesterday when your message arrived. He's in his usual fettle. He lectured me endlessly about failing in my family duty by remaining unmarried."

"He's right, you *are* failing in your duty," said Tom candidly. "You have to marry if the Earls of Redway are to continue."

"Don't you start. I'll marry when I'm ready."

"When Thea's ready, you mean. You're a fool, Kit."

"Tom, I'm warning you . . ."

"And I'm warning you. Don't speak lightly or disparagingly about family duty, because there could come a time when you will bitterly regret neglecting it. You could leave these rooms tonight and break your damned neck on the steps. What price your family duty, then? The earldom's future would be snuffed out at a stroke, and your grandfather would be left grieving for what might have been—the great-grandchildren he would have had but for your selfish and nonsensical obsession with a vain and mischievous strumpet who has no intention of leaving her husband for you, but every intention of indulging in an affair because she thrives on the danger of it.''

Kit rose angrily to his feet. "God *damn* you, Tom. Can't you leave Thea out of this?"

"God doesn't have to damn me, Kit, I'm damned already," replied Tom quietly. "And when it comes to spouting knowledgeably about the sorrows caused by neglected family duty, believe me, there's no greater expert in the whole world than my good self."

Kit looked perplexedly at him, remembering what Dudley had said earlier. "Tom, what *is* all this about? You haven't got any family anymore, so how—?"

"Oh, but I have, my friend," interrupted Tom. "I have." He got up and went to a chest of drawers, opening the top one and taking out a miniature, which he held out to Kit.

Kit took it and found himself looking down at the likeness of a pretty young woman, with Tom's hair and eyes. "Who is she?" he asked.

"My sister. Louisa Cherington."

Kit looked incredulously at him. "Your sister? Why haven't you said anything about her before?"

"Because I'm ashamed of having failed her. Look at her. What do you see?"

"A very attractive young lady."

"Yes. She's also sweet, charming, intelligent, and accomplished. With such qualities she had every right to expect an excellent match, but I robbed her of the opportunity because I selfishly frittered away the family fortune at the card table. She's now a governess, to Sir Ashley Lawrence's daughter at Lawrence Park near Brentford. Do you know him?"

"Slightly. I know that he's recently made a monumental misalliance with a woman whose past doesn't bear a close inspection."

"A *chienne* of little real class," agreed Tom with feeling. "Rather like Thea, if you ask me."

"I didn't ask you."

"So you didn't. Well, Louisa isn't a *chienne*, she's an angel, and I've been the very devil to her. And in spite of my sins, she still loves me. I've denied her her chance in society and reduced her to governessing, but she still writes me loving letters and looks forward to the few occasions when we can meet in Brentford. We were due to meet very soon, but I haven't heard from her, so she probably can't have the time off." He paused, meeting Kit's gaze. "I failed in my responsibilities, my friend, and now I wish with all my heart that I hadn't. I went blithely on with my gambling, even when I could see the way things were going, and in recent months my conscience has been very hard to bear. That was how I felt the evening I sat down opposite Rowe, and that's why when I detected his chicanery, it was all just too much. I decided that enough was enough, and it was time I acted honorably for once."

Kit was silent.

"Don't do the same as me, Kit," went on Tom. "Oh, I know your situation isn't quite the same, but you're still shirking your responsibilities."

"Don't bring Thea's name into this again, Tom," warned Kit.

"But I must. It's because of her that you're still unmarried."

"It's impossible to state categorically that I would have married someone else if I hadn't taken up with her," pointed out Kit.

"I think you would." Tom took the miniature again, looking at it for a long, pensive moment. He placed it on the table next to the whiskey bottle and then sat down again, still gazing at Louisa's smiling face. Then he smiled too.

Kit watched him. "I can't imagine what you've got to smile about, my friend," he said, resuming his own place on the sofa.

"It was just a passing thought. A rather ironic one, actually."

"Yes?"

Tom paused, glancing almost speculatively at him. "It occurs to me that there's a way we could both, at one fell swoop, attend to our neglected family duties."

"And what, pray, is this singular thought?"

"That you would marry Louisa."

Kit gave an incredulous laugh. "You sound serious!"

"I am." Tom was a little startled himself at the simplicity of the idea. "Yes, dammit, I *am* serious. Consider it for a moment, Kit. You have to marry to continue the family line; with an ancient title such as yours, it's your particular duty. I should provide for Louisa's future, as her brother it's *my* particular duty. If you marry her, Kit, both problems are immediately solved."

Kit was still incredulous. "Tom, this is quite preposterous. I think you must have had too much at the Prince of Wales, after all."

"I'm not in drink, Kit. Far from it, I've never felt more sober in my life. Look at her likeness. She's everything you could want in a wife. Will you at least think about it?"

Kit drew a long breath. This was all quite unreal. "Tom—" he began.

"Please, Kit. At least consider it as a serious proposition."

"It's progressed to a proposition?"

"Yes. I'm in earnest about this. Will you consider it?"

After a moment Kit nodded. "All right."

Tom smiled. "Thank you."

"I only said I'd think about it."

"That's enough. Common sense will do the rest. By God, you've done me good, I feel hungry for the first time since I crossed Rowe. Where shall we eat?"

"Where do you want to eat?" Kit was still a little bemused.

"I'm a dying man, I need a very hearty meal."

"That wasn't very funny."

"No. Forgive me." Tom looked a little chastened and

got up, draining his glass. "You hold the purse strings, Kit; my pockets are as empty as ever."

"Will Long's do you?"

"What a very foolish question, dear fellow; of course it will do. I've a fancy for deviled soles, and no one does them better."

"I won't argue with that."

Tom smiled a little. "You won't argue with anything I've said, not when you've thought about it."

"Go to blazes," replied Kit amiably.

"At dawn I very probably will." Tom went to take his top hat from the hook and then turned to look at him again. "You can thank your lucky stars you're such a good shot, my friend, because when Rowe eventually finds out about you and Thea—and find out he will—you at least have the comfort of knowing he'll think twice about calling you out."

"I suppose I might as well tell you. I doubt very much that he'll be calling me out, because my affair with Thea is over."

Tom stared at him. "Over? Why?"

"I wanted more than she was prepared to offer. In short, I wanted her to leave him and become my wife."

Tom drew a long breath, doubting very much that it was as definitely over as his friend claimed. "I won't pretend I'm sorry. She was the wrong one for you, I've always thought it."

"And now you think your sister is the right one?"

"Yes, more than Thea ever will be." Tom smiled again, tapping his hat on and then going out into the darkness.

Kit got up and picked up his own hat and gloves, pausing for a moment to look at Louisa's little likeness again. The sweet face smiled enigmatically back at him, revealing nothing of the real woman.

Putting on his hat, he followed Tom outside. Behind him the clock began to strike ten.

7

At Lawrence Park the clocks were also striking ten. Louisa slipped down through the house to keep her appointment with Geoffrey. She avoided the servants and kept well clear of the card party taking place in the drawing room. The sound of laughter and conversation drifted behind her as she crossed the entrance hall and emerged into the darkness.

She paused at the top of the portico steps, looking down at the carriages drawn up before the house. The coachmen and postilions were standing together on the far side of the elegant vehicles, talking and playing dice out of sight of the drawing-room windows. No one noticed Louisa as she went stealthily down, keeping well out of the light of the lanterns that had been suspended between the portico columns.

The night air felt cool as she crossed toward the grounds and the path leading down to the summerhouse and the river. Her white muslin gown was a little too light and flimsy, and she drew her shawl closer. But it wasn't really the temperature that was making her feel cold, it was her deep doubts concerning the wisdom of meeting Geoffrey Lawrence like this.

She halted for a moment by the parterre, looking back at the drawing-room windows where she could see the card party. The gentlemen were distinguished in full evening dress, and the ladies wore silk and jewels, with plumes in their hair. Their reflections moved in the immense gilt-framed mirrors on the rose damask walls, and the chandeliers glittered in the warm air.

Turning, she looked down toward the summerhouse, outlined against the river. All day she'd been filled with misgivings about this meeting, but each time common sense nearly prevailed, her conscience had reminded her of Geoffrey's words that morning: "I behaved monstrously toward you last night, and I'm thoroughly ashamed of the fact. . . . Can you forgive me, Miss Cherington? . . . I want to redeem myself in your eyes. . . . I promise on my honor to behave like a gentleman. . . . You're condemning me out of hand, and what could be more unfair than that? You mustn't deny me the chance to prove that I'm truly repentant. . . ." She'd disliked him from the moment he'd returned to the house; she still disliked him, but her sense of justice decreed that she kept this appointment. Slowly she walked on, passing the croquet lawn and approaching the summerhouse.

She'd almost reached it before she saw him. He was standing at the of the river steps, keeping the little summerhouse between him and the house. Smoke curled from his Spanish cigar as he gazed at the *Cyclops*.

For a moment her nerve almost failed her. Memories of his conduct the previous night came rushing back, and her steps faltered, but then he seemed to sense that she was there, turning quickly to look directly at her.

He dropped the cigar and crushed it with his heel. "Good evening, Miss Cherington."

She didn't go any closer. "G-good evening, sir." The doubts were suddenly stronger than ever. Oh, why hadn't she stayed in the house? Why had she been such a fool as to come out here in the dark? She swallowed nervously, casting around for something innocuous to say. A little self-consciously she nodded toward the cutter. "Will you really have to sell her?"

"Yes. The old boy's sticking to his guns this time. No more funds for wicked gamblers. I think I've solved the problem, though. I've thought of the very man to approach about buying her."

"You have?"

"Lord Rowe. He lost his yacht in the spring and needs another." He smiled inwardly, guessing her thoughts. She'd come here against her better judgment. Now she was nervous, anxious to talk about anything that might deflect him from some ulterior purpose. How lovely she was, so fragile and soft—so alluring in her innocence.

She detected the warmth in his glance and looked a little uncomfortably back toward the house. "Won't you be missed from the card party?"

"Most probably, but I'm not a child to be confined under strict orders." He paused, gauging her. "I'm glad you came," he said softly.

"I shouldn't have."

"Yes, you should. Shall we sit down?" He indicated the summerhouse.

It was too dark in there, and far too private. She shook her head. "I'm sure that what you wish to say can be said out here."

Annoyance flitted through him, but he didn't reveal it outwardly. "As you wish."

"If I'm perfectly honest with you, sir, I don't think there's anything to be gained from this meeting. I have accepted your apology about last night, and I believe that that ends the matter."

"But I wish to know you better, Miss Cherington."

"I'm a governess, sir, and you are my employer's son and heir, which means that there's absolutely no point in getting to know each other better. Besides . . ." She broke off, decidedly against what she'd been about to say.

"Yes?"

"Nothing."

"Please say what you were about to, Miss Cherington."

She colored a little in the darkness. "I was going to say that there was also no point because I don't want to know you any better."

For a second his outward air of calm friendliness was breeched, allowing the real Geoffrey Lawrence to gaze coldly out from his brown eyes, but then he dissembled again with a smile. "You cannot mean that, Miss Cherington. If you do, why on earth have you come here tonight?"

"Because it is as you said, I owe you the courtesy of a hearing."

There was an aloofness about her that told him she meant every word. She was immune to his charm and indifferent to any soft words he might choose to employ. If he wanted to possess her—and he did—then he'd have to force her. But first she must be lulled into a false sense of security, so that even if she didn't find him irresistible, she did at least trust him to conduct himself correctly.

He smiled again, looking toward the *Cyclops*. "I'll be very sorry to see her go, but maybe if I choose my words carefully, I'll be able to persuade Rowe to invite me to Cowes with him. I'd dearly like to see the race between Highclare and Grantham, it's all the talk. I was entertaining hopes of taking Highclare on myself with the *Cyclops*, but that's not to be now."

"Lord Rowe hasn't bought her yet," she replied, relieved that he'd apparently accepted what she'd said.

"He will, I'm sure of it." He pretended to admire the cutter. "What do you think of her figurehead, Miss Cherington?"

"Figurehead?" She glanced at the vessel's sleek prow. She thought the carved cyclops very ugly indeed, but could hardly say so. "It—it's very handsome."

"And very clever, don't you think?"

"Clever? I don't understand."

"Haven't you noticed? No, evidently you haven't, or you'd know straightaway what I was talking about. Come here, and I'll show you." He smiled reassuringly. "Don't be nervous, I won't bite you."

Slowly she went closer, but not too close.

"I doubt if you'll see even from there," he said,

pointing toward the figurehead. "It's the cyclops' eye. Can you see?"

She shook her head. "No. What is there to see?"

He laughed a little and with seeming innocence moved over to her, gently taking her arm and pointing again. Then he shook his head. "No, you still can't see, you'll have to step over here." He maneuvered her to where he wanted, so that the summerhouse stood between them and the house.

She was very aware of his hand holding her arm, and aware that he stood very close to her. Too close. Distrust rose sharply in her, and her breath caught as she glanced up and suddenly saw the truth written large upon his handsome face.

What a fool she'd been! Panic almost seized her, but with a superhuman effort she remained calm. He mustn't guess that she'd seen through him—he must be made to believe she felt at ease with him—but her heart was pounding almost unbearably and she knew she was totally defenseless. He had her at his mercy.

He didn't know he'd alerted her. "Now can you see the figurehead's eye, Miss Cherington?" he inquired reasonably. "From wherever you look at it, it seems to be staring directly at you. Can you see?"

"Y-yes," she replied, trying to quell the tremble in her voice. "You're right, Captain Lawrence, it is indeed very clever."

At that moment, to her immense relief, a new sound broke the silence of the night: the sound of voices and laughter as the card party emerged from the house to indulge in the amusing diversion of playing croquet by lantern light.

Geoffrey gave a low curse, whipping around as the party came into view beyond the summerhouse, their lanterns bobbing. The ladies' jewels winked and flashed in the moving light, and there was a great deal of hilarity as they discussed what forfeits should be paid for losing.

Louisa didn't need bidding; the moment his attention was diverted she wrenched herself free and gathered her skirts to fly toward the shelter afforded by some shrubs on the far side of the croquet lawn. She knew he wouldn't dare pursue her, not when his parents and their guests were so nearby, and her only thought was to reach the safety of house.

Geoffrey could only watch her flee. For a moment his thwarted desire made him savage. God damn her, she'd been within his grasp but was free yet again without his thirst being slaked. He'd been too sure of himself and he'd misjudged her. Bitter fury darkened his eyes and made his lips a thin, cold line. He wasn't used to being denied, especially not by a woman he regarded as little better than a servant.

Taking a deep breath to try to regain his calm, he took another cigar and lit it, watching the party on the croquet lawn. He'd promised himself success with the governess before he left for London in the morning, but now there was no hope of that; she'd seen through him once and for all. Suddenly the thought of remaining at Lawrence Park tonight wasn't to be tolerated. He wasn't in the mood to be amiable to his father's guests, and he certainly wasn't in the mood to endure Anne's clinging jealousy. The cigar smoke curled into the night air. He'd leave for London straightaway and amuse himself at a certain house of ill repute in Covent Garden, where there was a golden-haired demimondaine whose charms would placate him for the disappointment with the governess; and after his business in town tomorrow, he'd return by way of the Green Dragon Inn in Brentford, where one of the plump serving girls could be relied upon for a night of pleasure. Drawing on the cigar, he began to walk toward the croquet lawn to tell his father of his change of plan.

Anne watched him approaching. The diamonds in her hair flashed in the lantern light, and the sequins shimmered on her mauve silk gown. An elegant feather boa was draped idly over her arms, and she toyed with her closed fan. Her face was very still, her eyes bright with jealousy. She'd seen Louisa fleeing from the

summerhouse, and now she knew that Geoffrey had
been with her. She'd feared his interest in the governess
for some time; now she knew beyond a doubt that she'd
been right. The jealousy intensified, burning through
her like a flame. Louisa Cherington had to go, and the
sooner the better.

Geoffrey sensed nothing as he approached his father,
who turned irritably. "Geoffrey, where the devil have
you been?"

"I merely took a stroll."

"I'd appreciate it if in future you informed me of
your whereabouts. I dislike having to make excuses
when my guests ask after you."

"I'm sorry. I didn't think."

"You seldom do," retorted his father caustically.

"Well, it so happens that I've been thinking tonight,
about my appointment in the morning. It occurs to me
that I might be cutting it a little fine by leaving after
breakfast, and that it might be wiser to go to town
tonight. It wouldn't do to be late for Lord Palmerston
and the War Office. I can stay at Long's, or at the
club." He smiled a little blandly.

"Very well, leave tonight if you wish."

"Thank you. I'll bid you good night, then."

"Good night." Sir Ashley returned his attention to
the croquet.

Geoffrey walked quickly away toward the house, and
Anne could only watch. To hurry after him now would
look questionable, especially as it was almost her turn to
play. The jealousy still consumed her. Where was he
going? To the governess's room? Was he going to be
that blatant?

After a while she heard hooves and looked toward the
stable in time to see his curricle being led out. Her lips
parted. He was leaving the house tonight! That at least
meant he couldn't be with the governess. As she
watched, the groom halted the light vehicle before the
house, and then Geoffrey emerged, dressed for
traveling. He vaulted easily into the curricle and took up

the reins. A moment later he was driving swiftly away toward the lodge and the London road; before he reached the capital, he'd pass through Kensington, where unknown to him, the duel was to take place at dawn.

It was some time before the party broke up and Anne was at liberty to inquire about his plans. She didn't ask her husband; she went directly to the man who'd have been told the absolute truth—the butler. Geoffrey would have left precise word with him about his whereabouts, in case of an emergency; he'd only have told his father what he wanted him to know.

She found the butler in the drawing room, supervising the clearing away of the supper tables. "Ah, there you are," she said lightly, waving the other servants away. "Sir Ashley and I have been left rather in the dark as to Captain Lawrence's plans. Where exactly will he be tonight?"

He colored a little, not wanting to divulge the truth.

"I'm waiting," she said, her fan tapping impatiently.

"He'll be at—at . . ."

"Yes?" She raised a cold eyebrow.

He capitulated. "He'll be at an, er, establishment in Covent Garden tonight, my lady, Jerry's Coffee House, and tomorrow he'll be at his club or keeping an appointment with Lord Palmerston at the Horse Guards. He intends to spend tomorrow night at the Green Dragon in Brentford."

She said nothing, turning abruptly on her heel and walking away, her skirt rustling. So, he'd be in Brentford, would he? What a coincidence that it was in Brentford that the wretched governess had wanted to meet her brother. Her *brother* indeed! No doubt she hoped to be able to sneak away from her duties, after all, so that she could join him there and spend a cozy night *à deux!*

Anne's mouth was set in a spiteful, malevolent line. It was time to sweep the house clean of governesses and spoiled brats; both would be gone before the end of the week, or Ashley's life wouldn't be worth living.

Trembling with inner rage, she went to her private apartment. The governess wouldn't at any price be allowed to leave Lawrence Park tomorrow, and when dear Geoffrey arrived at the Green Dragon, he'd find a very different ladylove waiting for him!

8

Long after the lights at Lawrence Park had been extinguished and Geoffrey had arrived at Covent Garden to commence his night of debauchery, Tom Cherington was still sitting up in the apartment above the tea merchant's writing a letter to Louisa. Dudley had retired to his small bedroom at the rear of the building and Kit had fallen asleep on a couch close to where Tom sat. A single candle illuminated the room, the pale light creating dark, dense shadows in the corners.

Tom put the quill down and sanded the paper. The candle flame reflected in his gray eyes as he read the letter, anxious to be sure he'd worded it so that his sister would do exactly as he wanted. He glanced at her little portrait, which he'd placed on the table before him. "Oh, Louisa," he murmured, "you must do this for me, you're meant to be Lady Highclare and the next Countess of Redway, I know you are."

Folding the paper, he held a stick of sealing wax to the candle and then allowed several thick blobs to fall on the fold. He pressed his signet ring into the wax and then sat back, drawing a long breath. He'd failed her in so many ways until now, but he was going to do right by her now, even if he had to do it from beyond the grave.

Behind him the room was quiet. Kit was deeply asleep, exhausted after the arduous journey from Cowes. His fair hair was tousled, giving him an almost boyish look, and his neckcloth was crumpled. Tom got up and went to look down at him as he slept. Kit had to give his solemn word to marry Louisa, and he had to promise to arrange the ceremony as quickly as possible, for any delay might see Thea's return to complete favor. Tom felt no conscience about putting pressure on his friend, for he was convinced that the marriage was the perfect answer to everything. Thea might still linger in Kit's heart, but she would become a mere memory once Louisa had entered his life, for Louisa Cherington was everything that cold, arrogant Thea was not.

Outside, New Bond Street had yet to stir. The street lamps cast pools of light over the deserted pavements, and the bow windows of the shops opposite were brightly illuminated. A carriage was approaching. Tom went to the window and looked down as Kit's town coach drew up at the curb.

A cold, sinking fear passed through him, and he turned sharply from the glass, his tongue passing nervously over his lips. "Kit? It's time."

Kit stirred, and then sat up quickly. "Deuce take it, I didn't mean to fall asleep."

"It's as well you did, one of us needs to have his wits about him this morning." Tom's light tone belied the awful apprehension he felt within. He picked the letter up and gave it to Kit. "This is for Louisa. Will you be sure to give it to her if things go against me?"

"You know that I will."

"And, Kit . . . ?"

"Yes?"

"Remember what I suggested about her." Tom pressed the miniature into his hand as well.

Kit nodded. "I'm a man of my word. I'll give it my consideration."

"I know."

Kit put both items into his pocket. "Tom, you know there's still time to get out of this mess, don't you? You can retract your accusations, and Rowe's so-called honor will be satisfied."

"No." The single word was uttered quietly, but firmly.

"Please, Tom."

"No."

Kit drew a heavy breath and said nothing more.

Dudley had heard the carriage as well, and came into the room carrying the case of pistols. He wore a long gray coat and a low-crowned hat, and he looked pale and unhappy, avoiding Tom's eyes.

A minute or so later the three left, descending the steps to the alley and emerging by the waiting carriage. As the other two climbed in, Kit instructed the coachman to drive to the Horse and Groom Inn, Kensington, from where they'd go on foot to the meadow.

The team's hooves clattered on the cobbles, echoing sharply around the silent street as the carriage drew away, moving south toward Piccadilly, and then west in the direction of Kensington. They passed through the turnpike at Hyde Park Corner and then drove along the southern boundary of the park to the Knightsbridge turnpike. With this behind them, they passed on toward the little village of Kensington.

Tom gazed out the carriage window. This was the same road he'd taken in the past to Brentford to meet Louisa; now he knew in his heart that he'd never see her again.

Kensington was quiet as they drew up in the yard of the Horse and Groom in the village's straggling main street. Lord Rowe's blue barouche was already there, but there was no sign of either him or his second; they'd already proceeded to the meadow on Lord Holland's land. At one time it had been the custom for duelists to drive boldly up to their chosen site, but recently there'd been an outcry about duels, with citizens alerting the Bow Street Runners or the constables, and so now it was the practice to prudently leave carriages at nearby inns, where they wouldn't attract much unwelcome attention.

The first faint light of dawn was staining the eastern sky as the three alighted and walked north up a small lane between dark, silent houses. There were fields and enclosures ahead, and in the misty gloom the tall

Jacobean chimneys of Holland House could be seen among the trees. Stepping through an open gate into a field, they quickly crossed the wet grass to a gap in a high hedge, and then they were in the secluded meadow chosen by Rowe. It was a silent place, with ghostly trees looming beneath a slowly lightening sky, and in the distance there was a large pond that glinted like steel. The air was cool, and there was the promise of more rain before long.

Rowe was waiting with his second, Jasper Dillington, a lisping fop who always dressed extravagantly, this morning in lilac satin. With them was a local surgeon, Mr. Thomson, who looked decidedly uneasy about the whole business. William, Lord Rowe, was forty years old, and of slim, aesthetic appearance. His face was refined and aristocratic, but very cold and hard, and he was dressed in black. He had thinning dark hair, graying at the temples, and his eyes were a chill pale-blue; these eyes swung toward the newcomers the moment they appeared, giving them a calculating, malevolent glance that spoke volumes of the loathing he felt for them, especially Kit, because of the *Mercury*. He said not a word.

Leaving Tom standing with Dudley, Kit went to confer with Dillington. The main purpose of this preliminary discussion was to see if the duel could, with honor, be abandoned, but as the fop struck a pose and exuded an air of ennui, Kit knew that there was no hope of this.

"I thay, Highclare," lisped Dillington, flicking open his snuffbox, "can't we get thith wetched bithneth over and done with ath thoon ath pothible? I confeth I'm devlish hungwy, and the Horth and Gwoom do a thplendid beef pie."

"A plague on your stomach, Dillington," snapped Kit. "This is much more important."

The fop was offended. "Ath you wish, of corth, though let me thay thwaightaway that me fwend here ith thet on eight patheth at the motht."

Kit was appaled. "Eight paces? Convention demands twelve, no more and no less. I won't agree to anything else."

"But—"

"Twelve paces," insisted Kit, determined not to allow Rowe any more advantage than he already had over poor Tom.

Dillington closed the little box with a snap. "Vewy well, twelve patheth, if you inthitht. It don't thignify much anyway, your fellow'th ath good ath dead."

"There's no need for anyone to die, Dillington. All you have to do is get Rowe to admit he was a little slippery-fingered, and then we can *all* toddle off to the Horse and Groom for beef pie."

"Your fellow'th at fault, Highclare, *he'th* the one who mutht weetwact."

"If that's what you believe, sir, we have stalemate."

The fop affected to stifle a yawn. "Thith ith gettin' tediouth, Highclare. Shall we pwotheed?"

"Very well, but at twelve paces."

"Whatever you thay," drawled Dillington, turning and strolling back to Rowe and the surgeon.

Kit returned to Tom and Dudley. Tom smiled a little nervously. "It's all set, then?"

"I'm afraid so. God damn it, Tom, why won't you retract? To go ahead with this now is to throw your fool life away!"

"If I step back from this, Kit, I'll never be able to look anyone in the eye again. I have to go through with it, no matter what the price."

"None of this is worth your life."

"It is to me." Tom looked urgently at him then. "Kit, you must give me your word you'll marry Louisa."

Kit was startled. "Tom, I can't just—"

"Of course you can. Please, for it means everything to me." Tom knew he was being grossly unfair, begging such a thing when the circumstances were so very dire, but he was absolutely convinced that the marriage was the answer to everything. "Your word, Kit. I implore you."

Kit didn't want to promise anything, but the urgency in Tom's eyes was very hard to resist. Reluctantly he nodded, hardly able to believe it was his own voice replying. "Very well, Tom, you have my word, but only if she wants such a match."

Tom thought of what he'd written in the letter and smiled. "She'll want it, you have my assurance of that. Marry her quickly, my friend, don't give yourself time to fall back into your old ways. Thea will give you nothing, my sister will give you everything. Promise me you won't delay. I want no respectful but pointless mourning for me, I want the marriage to take place immediately."

"You're not dead yet," said Kit uneasily. He was being cornered and didn't much care for it.

"Your word on all I ask, Kit. Please."

Kit nodded. "Very well."

Tom's eyes cleared then. "Thank you, Kit. I know I'm not being fair, but it's too important."

"No, you damned well aren't being fair, but you've got what you wanted, I've given my word and I'll stand by it."

"I know you will."

Rowe was taking up his position in the center of the meadow, and Tom went to join him, followed by Dudley with the open case of pistols. The morning light was pale and translucent, shimmering in the middle distance as dawn began to break fully. The two duelists selected their weapons, and Dillington and Kit tossed a coin to see who would call the commands. Kit won, and the fop retreated to join the surgeon, who was glancing nervously around, half-expecting to see the Bow Street Runners appear through the gap in the hedge. Duels were risky for everyone these days, not just the two principals.

Rowe and Tom stood with their backs to each other. The meadow was very quiet, except for the first blackbird singing in a tree nearby. In the distance a dog began to bark, the sound seeming to carry too clearly. Tom's face was pale and strained, but Rowe's already bore an expression of anticipatory confidence.

Kit breathed in heavily, reluctant to issue the first command, but he knew he had to. "Twelve paces, if you please, gentlemen."

They obeyed.

"Turn and cock your pistols."

The sounds clicked horridly over the meadow.

"Take your aim."

Slowly the barrels were raised; Rowe's was steady and remorseless, but Tom's was trembling and uncertain.

With a supreme effort Kit brought himself to utter the final command. "Fire!"

Two reports split the silence, reverberating through the trees toward Holland House. A cloud of rooks rose screaming into the sky, and every dog within a mile seemed to set up an immediate clamor. The noise was deafening.

Rowe gave a sharp cry, whipping around and dropping his pistol to clutch his left arm, where a stain of crimson blood was suddenly visible on the costly black cloth.

Kit and Dudley stared at him in astonishment, as did Dillington and the surgeon. Against all the odds, it seemed that Tom had emerged the victor. But then the little valet gave a dismayed cry, tugging Kit's arm and pointing toward Tom, who was slowly sinking to the ground.

As Dillington ran to Rowe, who was still standing, the others hurried to Tom, who lay motionless on the grass. A bloody wound on his chest marked the place where Rowe's ball had found its deadly target.

The surgeon knelt to examine him. Tom's face was ashen, and he made no sound or movement. "He's still alive," said the surgeon, "but only just! We'll have to get him away from here, the law will be upon us within minutes!"

Rowe and Dillington were already making good their escape, and Kit looked anxiously at the surgeon. "But should we move him?"

"Would you have him arrested and flung into jail? Listen, the whole neighborhood's been aroused. The alarm's already been given, you may count upon it! If we can get him to my house, we'll avoid detection, and I can tend him as best I can."

"Will he come through it?"

The surgeon shook his head. "He won't see another dawn."

There were shouts coming from the village now. The surgeon was anxious. "Please, sir! We must get away from here!"

Kit nodded then and helped the man to lift Tom's unconscious body. Followed by Dudley, who'd rescued the pistols, they moved as swiftly as they could back out into the lane and toward the village, where there were lights in many windows now. They reached the sanctuary of the surgeon's house without anyone seeing them and were safely inside as the first Bow Street Runners ran past.

9

As the morning progressed, the early sunshine was replaced by rainclouds, and before noon it began to rain heavily, with now and then the familiar roll of distant thunder.

It was quiet in the bedroom at the surgeon's house as Kit stood looking out of the rain-soaked window at the chimneys of Holland House across the fields. The change in the weather had swiftly dampened the enthusiasm of the Bow Street Runners and constables who'd swarmed over the meadow, and they'd soon abandoned their search for the guilty parties who'd met at dawn on Lord Holland's land.

Rowe and Dillington were long since back in London, having evaded the hue and cry by managing to reach the barouche and driving off before the alarm had been fully raised. Now they were ensconced in Rowe's fine Berkeley Square house, where a fashionable physician had deftly attended to his lordship's unfortunate "hunting" wound.

Looking out of the rain-soaked window, Kit couldn't help marveling that poor Tom had been carried safely back to this house without detection. Mr. Thomson's residence stood close to the Horse and Groom, in full view of many of Kensington's dwellings, and yet no one had seen the furtive little party slipping back through the dawn light, carrying a mortally wounded man.

Kit turned, looking at the bed where Tom lay, still clinging to life. His face was gray and there was fresh blood oozing onto the dressing the surgeon had placed over his wound barely a minute before. His life was ebbing slowly and inexorably away, and there wasn't anything his friends could do but stand helplessly by.

Dudley's thin little face was sad as he stood by the door, watching as Mr. Thomson leaned over the dying man again.

Kit went closer to the bed. "How is he?"

The surgeon shook his head. Unexpectedly Tom stirred a little, his lackluster eyes flickering and opening.

Kit sat on the edge of the bed, taking one of his cold hands. "Tom? Can you hear me?"

The weak fingers moved barely perceptibly. "I hear you." The once-strong voice was a shaky whisper, only just audible.

"Is there anything you wish me to do for you?"

"My-my affairs . . ."

"I'll settle everything."

"Kit . . . ?"

"Yes?"

"You gave your w-word."

"I know."

"Don't let me down."

"I won't."

"I l-love my sister, Kit. You-you'll soon love her too."

Beads of perspiration dampened the dying man's forehead, and the effort of speaking seemed to have drained him of his final strength. Kit felt the weak fingers begin to relax, and then they were completely still. He looked anxiously at the ashen face. "Tom?"

But the gray eyes were lifeless. Tom Cherington was dead.

There seemed no end to the rain as Kit drove back to London with Dudley. Thunder growled dismally across the low heavens, and the two in the carriage said nothing; they were both lost in their own private thoughts and memories of the man who'd so needlessly left them forever. They'd both miss Tom Cherington very much indeed, and they were both aware of a perverse, unspoken anger, directed not at Rowe for killing him, but at Tom himself, for having gone so willfully into the duel. That willfullness now thrust an awful sadness upon those he'd left behind.

As the carriage drove past wet Hyde Park, Kit looked out and saw some stalwart gentlemen riding in their fine clothes, ignoring the dreadful weather. He watched them without really seeing, because all he seemed able to see in the rain-washed glass was the reflection of Louisa Cherington's smiling face. He'd given his word; he'd promised to marry her without delay.

Leaving the valet at the lodgings in New Bond Street, Kit went about his remaining sad duties as Tom's second. He settled all his outstanding bills and made arrangements for his funeral in two days' time at fashionable St. George's, Hanover Square. The interment would take place at the burial ground in Uxbridge Road, near Tyburn, because St. George's didn't possess a graveyard.

Word of the duel hadn't got out fully over Mayfair; there were just whispers that there might have been one. If Rowe's fashionable physician had his suspicions about the so-called hunting wound, then for the moment he kept them to himself, and Kit explained Tom's sudden death were as the unfortunate result of a terrible fall from his horse. But there were still whispers, and it wouldn't be long before names were circulating.

It was the early evening when Kit at last returned to his house in Grosvenor Square to change out of his tired clothes and take a well-earned bath. The house was a handsome four-story property built of red brick and occupying a prime corner location. It was reckoned one of the finest in the square, and certainly had the most handsome facade.

As Kit entered, he felt very low-spirited and tense. He needed to relax, but too much had happened, and too much had yet to happen, not least of which was that he had to go to Lawrence Park and seek what had to be a very painful interview with Louisa Cherington.

It felt good to take off the clothes he'd been wearing since leaving the Isle of Wight and step into the hastily prepared hot bath. He then took an early dinner, a cold chicken salad, which he ate at the gleaming mahogany table in the elegant dining room. Outside, the rain continued to fall. Thunder rolled from time to time, fitting weather for such a harrowing day.

He debated whether to go out to Lawrence Park tonight. The weather was very bad for traveling, and it would be late when he arrived, but he wanted to see Louisa Cherington and break the sad news to her of her brother's death. He also wanted to get his first meeting with her over and done with. He didn't know what he was expecting, he only knew that sooner or later he had to face her; he'd prefer it to be sooner, because his resolve might weaken.

The light was fading fast as he emerged once more into the rain to climb into his carriage. The roads were running with water as he drove again along the highway to Kensington. He didn't look out as he passed the Horse and Groom, nor could he bring himself to glance up at the curtained bedroom window of Mr. Thomson's house. The rain made the light deteriorate quickly, even though it was August, and Holland House was a vague outline in the gathering gloom as the carriage left Kensington behind and drove on toward Brentford.

The road was worse than he'd anticipated, with so many deep puddles that the coachman dared not proceed with much speed. The flashes of lightning were becoming more frequent, stabbing the darkness with brilliant white light that was swiftly followed by threatening rolls of thunder. The carriage lamps barely pierced the murk, and the downpour shone silver as it sluiced past their light. By the time Brentford was at last visible ahead, Kit knew that he wouldn't be able to reach Lawrence Park that night, after all; he'd have to take a room at one of the town's many inns.

Lowering the glass, he shouted above the noise of the rain. "We'll go no farther tonight. Stop at the first suitable hostelry in Brentford."

"Yes, my lord." The coachman thankfully touched his dripping hat.

Brentford was the end of the first stage out of London, and consequently boasted many fine inns. Driving slowly along the High Street, the coachman glanced at the line of swaying signs: the Pigeons, the Catherine Wheel, the Green Dragon . . . The Green Dragon seemed a more handsome establishment than the rest, and therefore more suitable. Clicking his tongue, he maneuvered the tired team into the inn yard.

As the carriage came to a standstill, some grooms came out to attend to the horses, and Kit alighted quickly, stepping through the rain toward the taproom door, above which there was a sign: "Under New Ownership Today."

There was a drone of conversation in the taproom. A number of men sat playing cards, while others talked over their ale. The innkeeper was a burly, red-faced, rather harassed-looking man wearing a round-skirted, sleeved fustian waistcoat, with a starched white apron tied around his thick middle.

"Good evening, sir. Welcome to the Green Dragon. May I inquire if by any chance you are Captain Lawrence?"

Kit looked a little testily at him. England was at war with Bonaparte's France, and all military personnel were required to wear uniform at all times. Here he was, wearing a claret-colored coat and white corduroy trousers, with a jeweled pin of very unmilitary fashion reposing in his neckcloth, and this fool asked him if he was a captain! "Do I *look* like a Captain Lawrence?" he inquired dryly.

The man was covered in confusion. "Er, no, sir, of course you don't. I wasn't thinking. I've been rushed off my feet today and don't know whether I'm coming or going. It's my first day here," he added by way of explanation.

"Do you hope to survive to a second?"

The innkeeper cleared his throat, his face redder than ever. "How—how may I be of assistance to you, sir?"

"By providing me with your best room for the night."

"I'm afraid the best room is already taken, sir, by the lady who is expecting Captain Lawrence. I have other rooms, though, all of them very fine."

"Then I'll take one of them."

"Very well, sir. Do you wish to dine?"

"No, but you can bring me a bottle of your best Burgundy—unless, of course, the same lady has taken that as well."

The man looked as if he wished the ground would open up and swallow him. Everything that could go wrong had gone wrong today, and now he had to have a swell with a sarcastic sense of humor. "A bottle will be brought to you immediately, sir. If you will come this way, I'll show you to your room." Picking up a lighted candlestick, he led Kit toward a low door, beyond which rose a steep wooden staircase.

At the top, the door of the principal bedroom faced them, easily identifiable by its intricately carved architrave. A little farther along the passage was the room selected for Kit.

The candlelight flickered and swayed as the innkeeper flung open the door. Apart from an immense, brocade-hung four-poster, so high off the floor that a small flight of steps was required to climb into it, the room was furnished with a wardrobe, a chair, a washstand, and a small table. Before the innkeeper set down the candlestick and went to draw the curtains, Kit saw that the window looked out over the rain-drenched main street outside.

The man turned to look at him. "I'll have the Burgundy sent up directly, sir. Will there be anything else?"

"No. Thank you. I'd like to be called before nine in the morning."

"Very well, sir. Good night."

"Good night."

The door closed and Kit was alone. With a heavy sigh he removed his top hat and gloves, tossing them on the table. Then he took out Tom's letter and the miniature of Louisa. He looked at the latter for a long moment. This was the face of the woman he'd promised to marry. But as he stared at it, the features and colors became blurred, and it was Thea that he saw.

A maid tapped at the door and came timidly in with a tray on which stood a glass and the promised bottle of Burgundy. She slipped hurriedly out again, evidently having been told that the gentleman in this room had a particularly acid tongue.

Kit poured himself a glass of the wine and then sat down in the chair. He seldom stayed in inns, and when he did, he loathed it. The rooms were so impersonal. Suddenly he became aware of voices in the adjoining room. The lady expecting Captain Lawrence was talking to her maid, and the wall was so thin he could hear every word.

"That will be all, Johnson. Be sure not to return until I send for you in the morning."

"Yes, my lady."

"And remember, not a word of this is to get out. As far as Sir Ashley and everyone else at Lawrence Park is concerned, I've been visiting Lady Dales, who's sick. Is that clear?"

"Yes, my lady."

"And see to it that fool of a coachman knows it too. One slip and I swear I'll have you both dismissed."

"We won't say a word, my lady."

"You may go."

The door opened and closed, and Kit heard the maid's footsteps as she descended to the taproom.

Kit looked thoughtfully at the adjoining wall. The lady had to be the new Lady Lawrence, for she'd referred to Sir Ashley and to Lawrence Park. And here she was, waiting in an inn for a certain Captain

Lawrence. Was it possible that she was actually keeping an assignation with her stepson?

Kit sipped the Burgundy. Yes, from what he'd heard of both of them, it was only too possible that this was what was happening, for neither of them appeared to possess many commendable qualities.

10

As Kit sat pondering what he'd heard in the next room, Geoffrey Lawrence was driving through the darkness and rain toward Brentford. He was wet and uncomfortable, and knew he'd have shown more wisdom by remaining in town for another night, but he'd promised himself the serving girl at the Green Dragon. The demimondaine had provided him with something of a diversion, but he hadn't been able to put Louisa Cherington out of his mind; maybe the more rustic charms of a tavern wench would go some way toward slaking the thirst the governess had aroused in him.

He'd had a good day, apart from the discomfort now caused by the atrocious weather. His interview with Lord Palmerston had gone so well that he'd been promised promotion, and he'd sold the *Cyclops* to Rowe for a handsome-enough price to see the duns off. It had been as he'd guessed: Rowe was so anxious to get even with Highclare over the loss of the *Mercury* that he hadn't quibbled at all over the asking price.

Rowe had been in a sour mood when Geoffrey had first called, and seemed to be in considerable pain from an arm wound, the result, so he said, of an unfortunate hunting mishap. Geoffrey hadn't been entirely convinced, for there'd been something a little odd about Rowe's manner, as if he was concealing something. It seemed more likely that the wound was the result of a duel; there'd been whispers about a duel on Lord Holland's estate in Kensington that very morning. Still, what did it matter how he received the wound? He'd bought the *Cyclops*, and the duns could be paid off.

Geoffrey grinned to himself as he tooled the horses on through the rain. Yes, things had gone well, even to the point of his having dared to ask Rowe if he could accompany him to Cowes for the regatta, and so pleased had Rowe been at the prospect of gaining revenge upon Highclare that he'd readily agreed. Geoffrey cracked the whip, urging the horses to greater effort. If he'd managed to conquer Louisa Cherington the night before, he'd have been completely satisfied; but there was time yet, maybe he'd still be able to have his way with her.

At last he reached Brentford and soon saw the Green Dragon's sign ahead. Slowing the team, he turned the light curricle into the inn yard, reining thankfully in. If the damned serving girl wasn't here, he supposed he'd have to take a room for the night, the weather was too foul to consider continuing to Lawrence Park.

Alighting, he thrust the reins into the hands of a groom and then approached the taproom door, noticing as he did so the sign fixed above it. New ownership? He trusted that wouldn't hamper his plans.

He entered the inn and glanced around for the serving girl. The new landlord espied him immediately. A beam spread across the man's face, and he came quickly over to Geoffrey. "Captain Lawrence?" he inquired.

Geoffrey stared at him, caught off guard. How did the fellow know his name? "Yes?"

"Welcome to the Green Dragon, sir. The lady awaits you in the principal bedchamber. If you will come this way?"

"Lady? What lady?" Geoffrey was wary. What was all this about?

The landlord was a little puzzled. Didn't he know who he was meeting? It was a little irregular. "She didn't give a name, sir, but she said that she was expecting you and that when you arrived you were to be shown up to her. She's ordered a very handsome cold supper and some champagne."

Geoffrey's wariness increased. "No one's *expecting* me. There must be some mistake."

The landlord was fast becoming tired of the whole matter, but he kept his smile. "The lady *is* expecting you, sir. Very definitely so."

"Could you describe her to me?"

The man gaped. "Describe her, sir?" How many ladies could there be who might risk staying at an inn on his account?

"Yes, dunderhead! Describe her."

"Well, she has black hair and is what I'd call very beautiful indeed. She's dressed handsomely—quite the tippy, in fact. She's most certainly a lady, sir."

It had to be Anne. "Did she come in a dark-red landau?"

"Yes, sir."

It *was* Anne. Geoffrey's lips pressed angrily together. No doubt she'd sunk so low as to quiz the damned butler!

The landlord looked uncertainly at him. "Do—do you wish to be shown up to her, sir?" he inquired, picking up a lighted candlestick.

"Just tell me which room she's in," replied Geoffrey, almost snatching the candlestick from him.

"But, sir—"

"Which room is it?" snapped Geoffrey impatiently.

"The one facing you at the top of the stairs," replied the man quickly, indicating the low doorway.

Without another word, Geoffrey strode toward it, the candle flame streaming and smoking. His spurs jingled on the steps and his shadow swayed over the walls. He paused when he reached the top. The door was right in front of him. His eyes were dark with anger and his lips a thin line as without ceremony he flung the door open and went in.

Anne sat up with a startled gasp. She'd been reclining on the sumptuous four-poster bed with its crimson, gold-fringed hangings. Her curvaceous figure was outlined by her soft, lemon muslin wrap, and her raven hair was brushed loose. The cold supper and champagne the landlord had mentioned had been set out on a small table, lighted by a solitary candle, and the draft caused by his entry made this flame to sway wildly, sending gyrating shadows leaping around the room.

She recovered a little. "Don't you know you should knock first?" she said softly.

"What are you doing here?" he demanded, kicking the door to behind him.

"I'm waiting for you, of course."

"I don't like being snooped upon, Stepmama." He knew she hated it when he addressed her in this way.

Her eyes flashed. "Don't call me that!"

"Why not? It's what you are." He put the candlestick down and then stood looking coldly at her, his hands on his hips.

She got up from the bed, her shapely legs revealed for a moment as the wrap parted. "Don't be peevish, dear," she murmured, going to the table. "Have some champagne, it's surprisingly good for a mere inn." She poured a glass and brought it to him.

Her perfume drifted over him, warm and flowery. Once it had stirred him, but now it was cloying. He ignored the glass. "I don't want to see you, Anne."

"No, I'll warrant you don't," she replied, an edge to her voice. "I suppose you're disappointed *she* isn't here."

"She? What are you talking about?"

"Your dear Miss Cherington, of course."

He stared at her. Somehow she'd found out about the summerhouse last night. He gave a derisory laugh. "My dear Anne, if I *had* been expecting Miss Cherington to be in this room, I would indeed be damned disappointed to find only you, for you're a very poor substitute."

Her breath caught and she tossed the champagne at him. "How dare you!"

He wiped his face, his eyes coldly furious as he looked at her. "You're a tiresomely obvious woman, Anne. You've made yourself too available, and I find that boring. Louisa Cherington, on the other hand, is very *un*available, and that makes her much more intriguing and exciting.''

Bitter jealousy burned on her face. "Indeed? Well, perhaps you'd like to know that she's soon to leave Lawrence Park. Your father's agreed to send Emma to school in Kensington, which means that there won't been any need for your precious Miss Cherington.''

"I don't believe you. My father would never agree to send Emma away.''

"He consented this morning, after another execrable display of indiscipline from the precious brat.''

"What did you do to her this time?'' he inquired dryly.

"Very little.'' Anne's smile was tight and cool. "She's to be told tomorrow morning that she's being sent to school in Kensington before the end of the week. She'd know already were it not that your father had business to attend to all day, and it is his wish that he and I tell her together what has been decided on her behalf.''

"*Her* behalf? Methinks you exaggerate, Stepmama,'' he said mockingly.

"She'll be leaving Lawrence Park very shortly,'' she went on, as if he hadn't spoken, "and so will her wretched governess, for whom there will no longer be any requirement.'' Her eyes glittered. "Poor Miss Cherington, how pinched she'll be to find her clever plans thwarted at the eleventh hour. I rather think she had notions of becoming the next Lady Lawrence, but instead she's to remain a mere governess. What a shame. Or is there sufficient of the trollop in her for her to be satisfied with just being your mistress? What's the price she sets on her favors, Geoffrey, dear? A little house in some reasonable street in town? Or is she holding out for a ring?''

"I don't think it's the governess who's pinched, Stepmama; it's your good self. I'm flattered that you're so jealous of my every move that you're prepared to go to such lengths. What a pity your activities have all been in vain, for nothing you've done is going to stop me enjoying Louisa Cherington, you may be sure of that.''

She flushed again. ''No? I wonder what your father would say if he found out about your advances toward a mere governess? His son bedding a servant? Ashley wouldn't approve at all, and I'm quite prepared to tell him, make no mistake about that.''

''And I'd be quite prepared to tell him about us, my dear. Dare you risk that? I doubt it.'' His scornful glance moved toward the supper table. ''What a waste,'' he murmured, ''for, to be sure, you'll have to eat it all yourself. I came here tonight to enjoy feminine charms, but certainly not yours, and I still intend to enjoy myself. Good night, dear Stepmama.'' Picking up the candle again, he strode out, slamming the door behind him.

Anne remained where she was. She was quivering with fury, so angry that for a moment she couldn't move. Then she went to the table, furiously sweeping everything off. The candle was knocked over and the room was immediately engulfed in darkness.

Kit listened to the commotion. He'd heard every word from the moment Geoffrey had entered. So that was the way of it at Lawrence Park; the question was, how innocent—or guilty—was Louisa Cherington?

He swirled his glass of wine. Was he making a grave mistake in honoring his promise to Tom? What manner of creature was he going to find waiting at Lawrence Park in the morning? Was she a virtuous damsel in danger of falling into the evil clutches of a practiced libertine? Or was she a scheming, conniving fortune-seeker with ambitions of one day becoming the mistress of Lawrence Park?

Kit leaned his head back. He'd have to rely on his own judgment when the time came, and unfortunately it had always been Tom's contention that where the fair sex was concerned, Christopher, Lord Highclare, was a very poor judge.

11

The next morning was cool and unsettled. Low clouds scudded across the sky, and the wind soughed through the trees as Anne's dark-red landau splashed through the puddles on its way to Lawrence Park. Geoffrey still languished in the obliging arms of his plump serving girl as Anne gazed coldly out of the carriage window. She'd been humiliated last night, and he was going to pay dearly. She'd bide her time, like a cat stalking its prey, and when the chance presented itself, she'd pounce. He'd rue the day he'd chosen to two-time her.

The landau reached Lawrence Park, and she alighted quickly. The plumes in her sky-blue velvet hat fluttered as she paused, looking icily beautiful in a blue sprigged muslin dress and matching pelisse. She directed a cold gaze down toward the summerhouse and the river steps, where Louisa and Emma were walking, their mantles flapping in the damp summer breeze. Their laughter carried faintly to her and she gave a tight smile. Let them laugh while they could, for very shortly they'd have little to laugh about. Gathering her skirts, she continued into the house, going directly to the breakfast room, where she knew she'd find Ashley lingering over his newspaper. She didn't intend to allow him an inch, he had to be held precisely to his word of the day before, and his daughter and the governess were to be faced with their respective fates the moment they returned.

By the summerhouse, Louisa had no notion of what was about to happen. The brim of her gypsy hat tugged in the wind, and the wide ribbons fluttered beneath her

chin. Her beige linen mantle billowed as the breeze
swept up over the river steps, and the hem of her pink-
and-white checkered gown beneath was revealed now
and then. She felt in oddly low spirits, although she was
endeavoring to hide it. She'd dreamed about Tom the
night before, and it had been a sad dream, the sort that
was forgotten the moment one awakened, but that left a
very depressing atmosphere.

Emma's spirits weren't low, she was enjoying the
rather unladylike pastime of tossing stones into the
narrow strip of water between the *Cyclops* and the foot
of the steps. A few raindrops were carried on the wind,
and she looked up as Louisa called to her that they must
return to the house. "Oh, must we? Can't we sit in the
summerhouse?"

"No, we must go back to the schoolroom and get on
with your lessons. Your stepmother has returned; I saw
her landau a minute or so ago."

Emma's face became surly at the mention of her stepmother, but she left the river steps and came to slip her
hand in Louisa's. They began to walk back through the
grounds, but then the rain became heavier and so they
ran. Emma laughed at the rain, and Louisa began to
laugh too, but as they dashed up the portico steps and
into the entrance hall, their laughter was immediately
silenced, for Anne and Sir Ashley stood waiting for
them.

Sir Ashley wore his green paisley dressing gown and
tasseled cap, and he looked decidedly unhappy. Beside
him, Anne was spitefully triumphant; the moment had
come at last, and she was going to enjoy every vindictive
second.

Emma moved instinctively closer to Louisa, knowing
that something awful was about to happen. Her large
eyes fled from Anne to her father. "Papa? What is it?"

"Go to the schoolroom, Emma."

"But, Papa . . ."

Anne's eyes flashed. "Do as your father tells you,
missy," she snapped.

Emma flinched, but obeyed. Louisa went to follow her, thinking that they were both in disgrace for having indulged in a promenade rather than morning lessons, but Anne's hard voice halted her.

"We wish to speak to you, Miss Cherington. Please wait in the library."

Slowly Louisa turned. The light in the other woman's eyes told her that it had happened at last, Sir Ashley had given in to all the pressure about sending his daughter away. Without a word, Louisa went to the library.

The library was on the ground floor, facing north toward the lodge and the London road, and was a dark, cheerless room. Its walls were lined from floor to ceiling with shelves laden with fine volumes, all of them bound especially for Sir Ashley in brown gold-embossed leather. There were dark-green velvet curtains at the tall windows, and a vast marble fireplace above which was a portrait of Sir Ashley as a young man. A large cut-crystal bowl of pink roses stood in the hearth before a Chinese lacquered fire screen, and the smell of old leather was heavy from both the hundreds of books and the deep armchairs and sofa.

Louisa took off her damp mantle and gypsy hat and went to stand by the rain-spattered window, staring across the park toward the highway. A stagecoach was driving westward, its outside passengers huddled against the inclement August weather.

The minutes ticked away and no one came. She glanced at the golden, glass-domed clock on the mantelpiece. What was happening? Why hadn't anyone come? Suddenly she heard faint cries echoing through the house. It was Emma, and she sounded frightened and distressed. Dismay flooded through Louisa. Emma needed her! Gathering her skirts, she began to hurry to the door, but even as she did so, it opened and Anne came silently in, closing it behind her.

"I trust you weren't about to leave the room, Miss Cherington, for you were expressly instructed to wait here."

"I thought I heard Emma crying."

"You did, but she's no longer any concern of yours."
Anne went to the sofa and sat down, arranging her
sprigged muslin skirt very carefully and then clasping
her hands coolly in her lap.

Sir Ashley's steps could be heard approaching, and
then he too came in, but unlike his wife, he looked pale
and upset, having found Emma's great distress a considerable strain. He glanced at Anne's coldly set lips and
chill eyes, and knew that he had to see this through to
the very end, otherwise his life would be made
unbearable. He went to the fireplace, standing with his
back toward it as he looked at Louisa. "Miss
Cherington, we've been giving Emma's well-being a
great deal of thought in recent weeks, and it is our
decision that she be sent to the seminary in Kensington.
The move will take place without delay."

Emma looked at him in consternation. "Sir Ashley,
you must not do it. Emma needs to be here with you."

Anne raised a disapproving eyebrow. "Are you
presuming to question our decision, Miss Cherington?"

"It—it's just that . . ." Louisa's voice died away.
Yes, she *was* presuming to question the decision,
because it was a very bad decision indeed for a child like
poor little Emma.

"It rather seems, Miss Cherington," went on Anne,
"that you are more concerned about yourself than you
are about Emma. Am I not right?"

"No, Lady Lawrence," replied Louisa, endeavoring
to hide the anger this unwarranted charge aroused.
"I'm thinking of Emma, who will be utterly miserable if
she's sent away from Sir Ashley." She looked
imploringly at Emma's father. "Please, sir, reconsider
your decision. Send me away if you're displeased with
my services, but don't send your daughter away, she
loves and needs you."

He shifted uncomfortably. He didn't like the
decision—second thoughts had beset him from the

moment he'd made it—but to have it questioned by the governess merely made him feel obliged to dig his heels in. "Miss Cherington, the decision has been made for Emma's good, her recent behavior has been far from acceptable."

Louisa defended her absent charge. "She—she's merely a little exuberant, Sir Ashley," she said, darting an accusing look at Anne, whose fault all this was.

Anne had had enough. With a gasp of outrage, she looked expectantly at her husband. "Are you going to stand there and allow a servant to question what you decide? Dismiss her immediately!"

Sir Ashley gave a start, as if she'd jabbed him with a pin. He looked sternly at Louisa. "I won't be taken to task by an employee, Miss Cherington. Your services are dispensed with from this very moment. I want you to leave Lawrence Park straightaway, and so I suggest that you repair immediately to your room to pack your belongings. You will not be given a reference, since you don't deserve one, but you'll be paid whatever is owed to you, and a pony and trap will be provided to convey you to Brentford. What you do and where you go after that is no concern of mine."

Anne smiled with cold satisfaction. "And don't think of speaking to Emma before you go, Miss Cherington, for I rather think you've done enough damage already. The sooner she forgets all about you, the better." She was about to say something more, when suddenly her eyes fled past Louisa toward the window. A fine carriage was approaching, its team of handsome grays stepping high through the wind and rain.

Sir Ashley saw it too. "Good heavens, who can this be?" he murmured, going to the window to peer rather shortsightedly out. "Can't say I know the drag. Do you know it, my dear?"

"No, but whoever it belongs to must be a person of some standing." Anne rose to her feet, gesturing impatiently to Louisa. "Please go to your room to pack,

Miss Cherington, I wish you to be gone within the hour.''

Numb, Louisa left the library. She'd feared this ever since Geoffrey's return had caused such jealousy, but now that it had finally happened, it had still hit her like a bolt out of the blue. She'd been concerned about Emma's welfare, but now she must think of her own. What would become of her? She'd been dismissed without a reference, and who would want to take someone on who'd apparently left under something of a cloud? Destitution was staring her in the face, and all because of an unscrupulous rake who thought any woman he fancied was fair game, and a spiteful, vindictive creature whose thoughts were only of herself.

She hurried across the entrance hall to the staircase, going swiftly up just as the carriage drew to a halt outside. She'd reached the top when the caller knocked at the front door. She looked back. Her view was obscured by the columns and chandeliers; she could only see the gleaming black-and-white-tiled floor. The butler crossed it and opened the unseen door. She heard a gentleman's voice. "My name is Highclare, I wish to speak to Miss Louisa Cherington.''

Her eyes widened and she leaned over the balustrade to look down, but still she couldn't see anything. Highclare? *Lord* Highclare? The gentleman whose yacht had caused the *Mercury* to founder? But what on earth would he want to see her for? There had to be some mistake.

Anne thought so. Emerging from the library, she went toward him. "Do come in, Lord Highclare, but I'm sure there must be an error, for Miss Cherington is only the governess.''

"There's no error, Lady Lawrence, it is Miss Cherington that I've called to see.'' The door closed and at last he came to where Louisa could see him. He was tall and superbly attired, Bond Street to the tip of his elegant fingers. His blond hair was wavy, and the jeweled pin in his excellent neckcloth flashed as he moved. She thought him the most handsome man she'd ever seen.

He bowed over Anne's hand, but in such a way as to convey a certain dislike. "Good morning, Lady Lawrence. I trust that I will be able to see Miss Cherington?"

"I . . . Well, I really don't know, sir," she replied, a little confused by his manner.

"It's important, Lady Lawrence. I would have called yesterday, but I was delayed by the weather and forced to spend the night at the Green Dragon in Brentford. Do you know the establishment?" His eyes were piercing as they held her startled gaze.

Guilty color flooded into her cheeks and her glance fled toward her husband, who had also now emerged from the library. "The Green Dragon? I—I believe I've noticed it in passing, sir."

As Louisa watched, the gentleman smiled. "I'm sure you have," he murmured. "It's an excellent hostelry, but cursed with rather thin walls."

Anne gave a sickly smile and went to link her arm through Sir Ashley's. "Lord Highclare has called to see Miss Cherington, my dear."

Sir Ashley was taken aback. "The governess?"

"So it seems. It will be in order, won't it?"

"Of course." Sir Ashley nodded, bowing toward the gentleman. "Your servant, sir."

"And yours, sir." The gentleman sketched a graceful bow as well.

"The butler will show you to the library, and Miss Cherington will come to you directly."

"Thank you." With a faintly mocking smile, the gentleman followed the butler, his gleaming boots echoing on the tiled floor.

At the top of the staircase, Louisa drew slowly back, afraid that someone might glance up and see her. She couldn't imagine why a gentleman like Lord Highclare would call upon her. But then she hesitated, an awful icy finger touching her spine. Tom! It had to be something to do with Tom! Echoes of her dream moved over her. Something dreadful had befallen her brother.

12

Kit stood by the library window. His thoughts were mixed as he heard light footsteps approaching. What was his first impression going to be of the woman he'd agreed to make his wife?

Louisa came hesitantly in, her face pale and anxious. Her pink-and-white-checkered gown was oddly bright in the dull room. He was struck immediately by her likeness to her dead brother; she was her portrait come to life. Her dark-red hair was piled up into a soft knot, and a single long curl tumbled down over her left shoulder, as if it had but a moment before come free of its pins. It was a very becoming coiffure, soft and very feminine, and it made her large gray eyes seem very lovely indeed. He had to admit that his first impression was very favorable, but he mustn't forget what he'd overheard at the Green Dragon, for maybe this delightful book couldn't be judged from its enchanting cover.

She came closer and then halted, her hands twisted anxiously. "You—you wished to see me, sir?"

Her voice was light and as softly feminine as the rest of her. He continued to look at her for a moment and then cleared his throat. "Yes, Miss Cherington, I do."

"It's about Tom, isn't it?"

"Partly."

The gray eyes searched his face, and then she put a trembling hand on a chair. "What—what's happened?"

"Perhaps you should sit down, Miss Cherington."

Dread flooded through her and her breath caught.

"Please tell me," she whispered, her face draining of all color as she prepared for the worst.

He didn't know how to break it gently. "I'm very much afraid that Tom died yesterday."

She gave a sharp intake of breath, flinching as if he'd physically struck her, but as he went instinctively toward her, she shook her head fiercely. "No! No, I'll be all right."

He could see how she struggled to contain the hot tears stinging her eyes. Her body was shaking, but she strove to overcome the grief that rushed to overwhelm her. After a moment she managed to look at him again. "How did he die, sir?"

"He was fatally shot in a duel."

She stared at him. "A duel? Tom? But he was no shot."

"I know, but he was unfortunate enough to fall foul of Lord Rowe."

She was bewildered. "The Lord Rowe of the *Mercury*?"

"Yes." Of course she'd know about the *Mercury*; Geoffrey Lawrence's interest in yachting would have seen to that. He found himself searching her face. What was the truth about her? Was she really as sweet and innocent as she seemed?

She spoke again. "You said he was fatally wounded. Does that mean that he didn't die immediately?"

"Not immediately, but he was mostly unconscious and wasn't in pain."

She nodded. Her eyes were hollow, as if something had been extinguished in them. "Will you tell me why there was a duel, Lord Highclare? What happened?"

"I believe Tom detected Rowe cheating at cards."

"Oh." Cards. Tom could never resist the green baize.

"He asked me to be his second, and I returned to London the day before yesterday to try to persuade him not to proceed. I didn't succeed and the duel took place at dawn yesterday, on Lord Holland's land in Kensington. Tom actually managed to wound Rowe in the arm, but was fatally struck himself. He died yesterday afternoon in the house of the attendant surgeon."

She closed her eyes for a moment, but the hot tears that had rushed to the surface a moment or so earlier had gone, stifled completely by the firm grip she'd taken on herself. "My poor Tom," she said quietly. "What shall I do without you?"

The quiet strength with which she held herself in check impressed him, and somehow he couldn't believe she was an adventuress. And yet . . . What did he really know about her? Nothing. Nothing at all.

She looked at him again. "Where is he now?"

"In the care of the undertakers. The funeral is arranged for the day after tomorrow at St. George's, Hanover Square."

She was alarmed. "But I cannot possibly afford so fashionable a church, Lord Highclare. I am—was— only a governess."

Was? So the vicious Lady Lawrence had plunged the dagger in already, had she? "You don't have to afford it, Miss Cherington, the responsibility is mine."

"Yours?"

"As both his second and his friend. I've undertaken to meet whatever costs arise."

"Oh." She lowered her eyes for a moment, obviously unsure about something important. "Lord Highclare, will I be able to attend?"

The question took him aback. "Of course. There's absolutely no question of you not attending. Why do you ask?"

"St. George's is very Mayfair, sir, and circumstances have reduced me to being little more than a servant."

"You're Tom Cherington's sister, and you're a lady, Miss Cherington. That's all that matters." He hesitated. "Tom loved you very much, and he was conscience-stricken that he'd failed in his duty toward you."

Her eyes fled to his face. "But I didn't blame him for anything, Lord Highclare."

"He knew that." He took the letter from his pocket. "He wanted me to give you this."

Slowly she took it, looking for a long moment at the impression of her brother's ring in the hard wax. Then she broke the seal and began to read.

My dearest Louisa,

I hope with all my heart that you can forgive me for leaving you like this, but if you regard it as little more than further proof of my shabbiness, then I shall not be able to blame you. I've been a poor brother, too unmindful of my duties and responsibilities, and too preoccupied with my own selfish pleasures. I'm ashamed of myself, and that shame has led me to remain silent about your very existence. Those who knew our family in the past were led to believe that you'd perished along with our parents; those who knew nothing about us, we left in ignorance. Kit knew nothing until I told him tonight.

She looked up. "You—you are Kit?"

He nodded.

She read on.

My conscience has been weighing more and more heavily in recent weeks, and has become a burden that has driven me to belatedly attempt to right the wrongs I've done you. You must do as I ask, Louisa, otherwise I shall not rest in peace. Accept my good friend Kit, become Lady Highclare and the future Countess of Redway. Do this, and you'll permit me to at last have done my duty. Be happy with him, my dearest, and remember me sometimes.

Your loving and repentant brother,
Tom

She stared at the letter. Accept his good friend Kit? Become Lady Highclare and the future Countess of Redway? It was too much to take in. Slowly she folded the letter again. She felt as if she were asleep and caught up in a nightmare; but it wasn't a nightmare, it was all only too real.

Kit belatedly realized that Tom had taken the initiative from him by mentioning the match in the letter; he could see it in her face.

She swallowed. "Lord Highclare, I don't know what all this is about. Indeed, I think my brother must have made a mistake."

"Mistake?"

"Yes." Taking a long breath, still needing to hold on to her composure, she met his gaze. "Thank you for coming to see me; it was very kind of you."

So she was going to terminate the interview without even mentioning it. Hardly the action of a fortune-seeker. "Miss Cherington, I have much more to discuss with you than Tom's death."

"More?"

"Yes, and now that you've read his letter, I rather think you know what I'm about to say."

She stared at him, gradually realizing what he was saying. "You mean that what Tom said about . . . ?" She couldn't finish it, it was too preposterous. What possible reason could a man like this have for marrying a penniless governess?

"Yes, Miss Cherington, I've come here to ask for your hand in marriage," he said quietly, watching the expression flitting across her pale, strained face.

She was totally at a loss. "Lord Highclare, I don't know what you and Tom agreed together, but I assure you that you aren't under any obligation to marry me. I gladly release you from any promise you may have made, for I'm well aware that I'm totally unsuitable as a future countess. I'm a governess, and as far as society's concerned, I'm not even a competent one, for I've been dismissed without a reference, so I know full well that I'm the very last person you should want as a wife. I'd be an encumbrance, and I've no wish to be that to anyone."

Again hardly the reaction of an adventuress. "It doesn't matter to me that you've been reduced to your present circumstances, Miss Cherington. I still wish to make you my wife."

Her large gray eyes searched his face, and then she shook her head a little, as if she thought she was imagining it all. "Lord Highclare, I find this quite incredible, for when I look at you I see a gentleman of very distinguished appearance, a man of rank and fashion who must be very sought after indeed, and yet you come here to offer for someone like me. I have to ask myself why you'd do such a thing."

"I've already explained."

"Yes, you say it's a matter of duty."

"That is correct."

"If your family duty matters so much to you, sir, why haven't you married before now?" Her gaze was unexpectedly penetrating.

He smiled a little. "I can see that nothing less than the truth will do. Very well, I'll tell you. I've remained single because the woman I wanted to marry was already married to someone else." He didn't elaborate, for he didn't want to mention Thea by name and he certainly didn't want to risk mentioning Rowe again so soon after bringing the news of Tom's death. He found himself wishing that Thea was married to anyone in the world other than William, Lord Rowe, for he felt distinctly uncomfortable about asking Louisa Cherington to be his bride when his mistress was married to the man who'd dispatched Tom Cherington into the hereafter.

She'd looked away when he'd answered. She felt oddly clearheaded. So much that was painful had happened this morning, and now there was this, but somehow she felt extremely perceptive. It was as if her senses had been heightened by the strain of all that had gone before. He spoke of the other woman in his life as if she were in the past, but she knew that that wasn't so, this other woman was very much part of him still. She looked at him again. "Lord Highclare, do you really, in your heart of hearts, wish to proceed with such a match?"

"Yes."

She didn't reply, for she could see that he meant what he said, no matter what his feelings were for this other woman.

"Miss Cherington, what is your answer? Will you marry me?"

"I don't know," she said, almost in bewilderment. "I really don't know what to do." The clearheadedness seemed suddenly to desert her.

"What does the alternative hold for you? I stayed at the Green Dragon last night, as did Lady Lawrence and Captain Lawrence, and so I know full well why you've been dismissed."

"Oh." A little dull color stained her cheeks as she wondered exactly what he'd heard said of her, for she had no doubt that Geoffrey Lawrence would taunt her stepmother.

"If you don't accept my offer, Miss Cherington, you face penury, don't you? You've been dismissed without a reference, and so you'll find it virtually impossible to find another position. What, then? What options are open to a young woman in desperate need, especially a young woman as attractive as you? I don't think I need to elaborate, do I?"

"No." The color had heightened on her cheeks now.

"Marry me and you'll lack for nothing, you'll move in the highest circles in the land, be mistress of a fine house in Grosvenor Square, and chatelaine of an even finer one on the Isle of Wight. Maybe I'm not offering you a love match, but I'll show you every respect and consideration, and no one in society will ever know that ours isn't an affair of the heart." He smiled slightly. "Society has a habit of looking down upon calculated contracts, Miss Cherington, and I wouldn't wish that on you; on the contrary, I'd do all I can to protect you from such unpleasantness."

She lowered her glance for a moment, trying to assimilate everything, but the clarity of earlier had seemingly gone forever. "What does your family think about all this, Lord Highclare?"

"I haven't any family, except my grandfather, the earl, and he's spent so long recently trying to persuade me to do my duty by tying the knot that he'll be only too pleased that I've at last done just that."

"He'd be pleased at such a misalliance?"

"I don't regard it as a misalliance, Miss Cherington."

"Nevertheless, sir, that's exactly what it is. You could have your pick of brides, but you've chosen to ask me. I can't really believe your grandfather will be delighted, no matter how much he wants you to do your duty." She was silent for a moment. "When would you wish such a marriage to take place?" It wasn't until this question slipped out that she realized she was seriously considering the proposition.

"Two days after Tom's funeral."

She stared at him. "So soon? But what of a respectable period of mourning for Tom? I couldn't possibly . . ."

"Tom didn't want you to go into mourning; he wanted us to marry as quickly as possible, and by my calculation I could arrange for a special license for that day at the earliest. A swift marriage would be the wisest move, Miss Cherington, for it would bolster a tale of a love match, and it would mean taking on all the gossip in a short period of time. There will be gossip, you know, for such a match is bound to cause a sensation. First of all, society will learn of your very existence, then you'll be Lady Highclare, and it will be a nine days' wonder. If your name is attached to mine for a long time before the wedding, then the less agreeable elements in society—and there are many—will feel at liberty to discuss your character *ad infinitum*. That wouldn't be a very desirable state of affairs, as I think you'll agree. An early marriage would confound them, and that *would* be a desirable state of affairs. I have to return to the Isle of Wight soon because I've engaged to take part in an important yacht race against Lord Grantham, and if you accept my proposal, we could be man and wife before I leave London.'' He paused. ''Have I been anticipating too much? Maybe you've already decided to turn me down.''

''There's something I must know before I answer you, Lord Highclare.''

''Yes?''

''Will I encounter the woman you wanted first?''

''You're bound to.''

''Where is she now?''

''Attending the regatta at Cowes.''

''Does she know about me?''

''How can she? I didn't know about you myself until a short while ago.''

''Did you love her very much?''

''Yes.''

She lowered her eyes. ''Then I must ask if she's really in the past, Lord Highclare.''

He hesitated. ''Yes, she is.''

''You don't seem very sure, sir.''

''I'm sure.'' But was he? In his heart of hearts he really didn't know, for how could it be possible to be completely over someone in so short a time? Especially someone like Thea.

She looked down at Tom's letter, now rather crumpled in her hand. ''Lord Highclare, we've talked of your duty, and of my brother's, but perhaps we should also mention mine.''

''Yours?''

''To Tom. He wanted me to marry you, and he wouldn't have urged me to do so unless he thought it was the right thing. I loved him very much, and if it was his duty to do right by me, then it's also mine to do as he wished.'' For a moment he thought her tears would overwhelm her again, but after a moment she continued. "He said that our marriage would mean that he could rest in peace, Lord Highclare, and so I will accept you."

"You do me a great honor, Miss Cherington."

"We're strangers, sir. We're to be man and wife, but we're strangers."

"Time will rectify that."

"But will time also make us regret our actions?"

He smiled. "I don't think so. Now, then, are you ready to face your former employers?"

"I—I think so."

"If you need to compose yourself . . ."

"I'm ready."

He drew her hand over his arm. Her fingers were cold and they trembled a little. He left his own hand gently over hers. It was a comforting gesture, and was all he felt able to do. She was right: they were strangers.

13

A little later, as Kit conveyed Louisa to London and her astonishing new life, the atmosphere they left behind at Lawrence Park was stunned, to say the least.

Sir Ashley was appalled that he'd been persuaded to so summarily dismiss the future Countess of Redway, and he blamed Anne for having forced it upon him with her constant importuning. He didn't give his own weakness a second thought; he put it all down to her. He was acutely embarrassed at the thought of the stories that might soon circulate in London, for he was sure that Louisa would use her new position to paint a dark picture of her former employers. And why shouldn't she? She been dealt with very unfairly. She'd been told to leave immediately without a reference, and she'd been blamed for Emma's misconduct, misconduct that, if he were honest with himself, was really Anne's fault.

Maybe there wasn't much Sir Ashley could do to stop Louisa saying what she wanted, but at least he could deny her the opportunity of spreading monstrous tales of little Emma's banishment to school. His daughter would remain at Lawrence Park, where she belonged, and there wasn't anything Anne could do about it. Informing his furious wife of his decision, he retreated to the safety and privacy of his rooms, where he reflected that life had been very fraught ever since his second marriage. Standing by the window, gazing out at the rainswept park, he dwelt wistfully upon the calmer, more pleasant days of his widowerhood.

Anne was in a rage about everything. Nothing had

gone as she wished, nothing at all! First there'd been
Geoffrey, and now this. Not only was Emma to stay,
after all, but Ashley had had the temerity to stand up to
the wife he'd never denied anything before. And last,
but certainly not least, the governess hadn't been
reduced to penury, after all; she'd instead somehow
emerged with the prospect of one of the most enviable
matches imaginable! Louisa Cherington had pre-
sumptuously reached out of her station toward
Geoffrey, but she hadn't been punished for her im-
pudence; instead, she'd been rewarded with the
infinitely more glittering prize of Lord Highclare.
Anne's jealous frustration was boundless, as was her
capacity for malevolent spite, and just as she'd sworn to
play a waiting game if necessary in order to have her
revenge on Geoffrey, so she now promised the same for
Louisa.

Up in her bedroom, Emma wept hot tears in her
pillow. She was immeasurably relieved that she'd wasn't
to be sent away to Kensington, after all, but she was
heartbroken that her beloved Cherry had gone away
forever and hadn't even been permitted to say good-bye
properly. There'd never been another governess as
loving, sweet, kind, and thoughtful as Cherry, *never!*

Geoffrey returned to the house to find the astonishing
news waiting for him. At first he was dumbfounded.
Louisa Cherington was soon to become Lady Highclare? It simply wasn't possible. But he'd soon had to
accept that it was true, and with that acceptance had
come an initial savagery that his prey had eluded him.
Then the savagery had gone, to be replaced by his
former burning anticipation, for he could pursue the
governess when her new husband took her to the Isle of
Wight. A new life wouldn't be the only thing she'd find
there; her old life would be swift on her heels. He smiled
to himself. He'd possess her yet; she wasn't going to
escape that easily.

Kit's carriage bowled along the London road, passing
through Brentford and then approaching Kensington.

Louisa's thoughts returned fleetingly to Lawrence Park. She wouldn't miss anything about it, except Emma. She wished she'd been allowed to see the child before she'd left, but permission had been very firmly refused. Lady Lawrence had suffered too many setbacks to be in any mood to change her mind about that as well.

Staring out at the passing countryside, Louisa determinedly pushed all thoughts of Tom to the back of her mind. She didn't dare think about him, for, if she did, then she would give in to the tears that she'd been keeping barely in check. She'd never been one to show her emotions in front of strangers, it was alien to her; this man was a stranger. She couldn't succumb to her awful grief just yet. Not just yet.

Forcing memories of her brother to the recesses of her mind, she glanced at Kit. What was he really like? She knew nothing of his character or temper, but outwardly he was breathtakingly handsome, at once rugged and manly, and yet refined and elegant. There was something very nordic about his sunburnt complexion, blond hair, and vivid blue eyes, but he was an English aristocrat to his fingertips. There was immense strength in his firm chin and finely chiseled mouth, and as he lounged on the seat opposite, she was very aware of his athletic grace. He was dressed impeccably in clothes that were the very best London could provide, and he wore them with dashing style. But what was he really like behind all that perfection?

She looked away. He was a brilliant catch, and society was going to be very shocked indeed when it learned that he was going to take such a very unlikely bride. Not only that, it would be much intrigued that the wedding was to take place so very quickly. There was bound to be considerable speculation as to whether the bridal pair had anticipated their vows. She was going to be notorious, and every time they looked at her, they wouldn't see Lady Highclare, they'd see a governess. She felt suddenly very alone and vulnerable, for this marriage was going to be based soley on duty. What if

Kit should suddenly wish he hadn't observed that duty? What if he wished to resume his affair with his former love? And what if that lady would suddenly become free?

Unknown to her, Kit was secretly observing her as well. His first impression still lingered, for she was a book with a most enchanting cover, but if he turned the pages, what would he really find? Was she as absolutely innocent as she seemed? Geoffrey Lawrence was a handsome man, with a reputation as a lover, and if he cast his amorous eyes in her direction, would she really have completely resisted such an accomplished admirer? Wouldn't she, as a penniless governess, have been flattered by his attentions? Faced now with a direct question about Lawrence, could she with complete honesty say she'd never welcomed his advances? The question hung on his lips for a long moment, but as he looked at her demure profile, so sweet and pure, his doubts died away again. It was impossible to think ill of her.

The carriage drove on, passing through the outskirts of London, where Hyde Park was bathed in sunshine as the clouds sped by, leaving blue skies in their wake. The elegance of Mayfair surrounded them as at last they entered Grosvenor Square, drawing to a standstill before Kit's fine town house in the corner.

Louisa waited nervously as he alighted and then held out his hand to her. Hesitantly she accepted, her skirt whispering as she stepped down to the sunny pavement. She glanced around. In the center of the square there was an oval railed garden covering at least six acres, and in its middle there was a gilded equestrian statue of George the First as a Roman emperor. There were trees, shrubs, and flower beds, and a spaciousness that was most appropriate for this most-sought-after part of Mayfair.

She turned to look at the house then, taking in the handsome red brick facade and pedimented doorway. It was very beautiful, but very intimidating. She'd known a life of comfort at Cherington Court, but that life seemed very far away now, and the thought of being mistress of a London property of such exclusivity was very daunting. She froze for a moment. The sounds of Mayfair drifted over her, from the clatter of hooves and rattle of fine carriages, to the calls of a pretty flower girl on the corner of Duke Street. A laughing group of ladies and gentlemen emerged from a house opposite, paying little attention to the carriage outside Lord Highclare's residence as they entered a waiting landau and drove smartly away.

Kit sensed her trepidation. "Whenever you're ready . . ."

"I'm ready now."

He still held her hand, drawing it gently over his sleeve. They proceeded toward the door, which opened as if by magic as the watchful butler anticipated their steps precisely. He was very like the butler at Lawrence Park, boasting the same full-skirted, light-brown coat and beige silk breeches. His thin face was dominated by a large nose, and his hair, whatever color it may have been, was hidden beneath a white powdered wig. He was so well disciplined that if he was surprised to see an unknown lady entering with his master, he gave no sign of it whatsoever. "Good morning, my lord. Madam."

Kit led her into the hall, removing his top hat and gloves and handing them to the man. "Good morning, Miller. I trust all's well?"

"It is, sir. The Marquess of Hertford called, and so did the Earl of Eldon. There is also a note from Devonshire House inviting you to be a guest there next month."

"Very well, I'll attend to it all in due course."

"Yes, sir."

"Miller, perhaps it's best to inform you straightaway that my situation, and therefore the situation of this house, is about to change considerably. This is Miss Cherington, and she is very shortly to become my wife."

The butler's great experience hadn't prepared him for such a bold announcement. His jaw dropped and he gaped at Louisa for a moment, before recovering his customary serenity. "May I offer you my congratulations, sir. Madam."

Kit nodded. "She is to reside here until the wedding, which will take place very shortly, and I therefore wish the main guest room to be made ready immediately. And would you have, er, Pattie, come here straightaway?"

"Yes, sir." The shaken butler bowed and withdrew.

Louisa had been glancing around the entrance hall. It had very pale ice-green walls, with little white niches containing statuettes of Greek gods and goddesses, and the doors opening off it had surrounds of particularly decorative gilded plasterwork. The floor was black-and-gray-tiled, and the staircase rising from the far end was of black marble, with a graceful, gleaming handrail. Glittering chandeliers were suspended from the high ceiling, and shining, gilt-framed mirrors adorned the walls above the white marble fireplace and the solid console tables. She glanced at her reflection in one of the mirrors. She looked so pale and drawn. It was like looking at herself in a dream.

Light footsteps approached from the kitchens, which lay beyond the staircase. A neat maid came quickly toward them. She was dressed in a gray seersucker dress, with a white apron and muslin mobcap, and she had fair hair and a round-cheeked face with bright, hazel eyes. The butler had evidently broken the news about the sudden advent of a future Lady Highclare, for as she bobbed a respectful curtsy, the maid's glance moved curiously toward Louisa. "My lord. Madam."

Kit looked at her. "Pattie, I seem to recall that you were once a lady's maid."

"I attended Mrs. Hancock of Oxford when her maid was indisposed, sir, but I wasn't exactly a lady's maid."

"But you know how to go on?"

"Oh, yes, sir."

He glanced at Louisa. "Will she suit to be your maid?"

"Yes, of course."

The maid's eyes lit up at such unexpected promotion. "Oh, thank you, madam."

Kit surveyed her a little sternly. "Being a lady's maid requires discretion at all times, Pattie. See that you remember it."

"I will, sir."

Kit returned his attention to Louisa. "Forgive me if what I'm about to say sounds a little blunt, but I take it the rest of your wardrobe is like the clothes you're wearing now?"

She flushed self-consciously. "Yes, sir. A governess can hardly expect to keep up with Mayfair."

Pattie stared. A governess?

Kit smiled a little. "I realize that a governess is hardly a person of means, but Lady Highclare most certainly is, and will accordingly be expected to dress in the very latest modes. I'll send for Madame Coty immediately, instructing her to bring with her any items that may recently have been left on her hands. Unpaid bills frequently mean undelivered goods. The dressmaker will also be useful when it comes to putting word around about our match. She can be told exactly what we wish her to be told and thus determine what story goes the rounds."

Louisa was silent. Madame Coty was the most-sought-after couturiere in England, and not even when at Cherington Court had she ever dreamed of possessing a wardrobe by her; only the cream of society aspired to Madame Coty, and the Cheringtons, respectable and well-off as they'd been, had never been the cream of society.

Her unexpected silence concerned him a little. "If Madame Coty isn't acceptable . . ."

"She's very acceptable indeed, sir."

"Good. I'll mention in the note that the funeral is the day after tomorrow and that if she has anything that might do, she's to be sure to bring it."

The funeral. It sounded so very final. She looked quickly away, biting her lip.

He found her determined composure a little disconcerting. She was obviously devastated by grief, and yet apart from the first moments, she'd controlled her tears. He couldn't help but compare her with Thea, whose tears would by now have been a veritable flood and whose lack of composure would have been audible all through the house. Thea had always indulged to the full in theatricals, picturing herself as a dramatic heroine; Louisa Cherington was evidently cast in a much more subtle mold. He touched her arm. "If you'll go with Pattie now, she'll show you to the main guest room. Luncheon will be served in"—he glanced at his fob watch—"about half an hour in the dining room. You may join me if you wish, or you can have something served to you in your room if you'd prefer."

"I'll join you."

She followed the maid up the staircase. The main guest room was at the front of the house, on the second floor overlooking the square. It was a fine room, exquisitely decorated and furnished. Its walls were paneled alternately with pink floral Chinese silk and tall mirrors, and its ceiling was coffered in pink and gold. The magnificent French four-poster bed was draped with golden silk, tasseled and fringed, and on the floor there was a specially woven Wilton carpet that matched the ceiling design exactly. There were elegant chairs and a sofa, and a dressing table laden with little porcelain dishes and pots. The wardrobes were cunningly concealed in the walls, their doors formed by the Chinese silk and mirrored panels, and so the room seemed very spacious and uncluttered. The fireplace had beautiful ormolu decorations, and on the mantelpiece there was an ornate gilded clock supported by plump cherubs, and some graceful silver-gilt candlesticks.

Some maids were still busy inside as Louisa followed Pattie in. The windows had been hastily thrown open, and the bed was being made up with lavender-scented sheets. Finishing their tasks, the maids lowered the windows again before respectfully retiring, closing the door behind them.

Almost immediately it opened again, and a footman carried in Louisa's solitary valise; then he too retired, leaving her alone with Pattie. The maid relieved her new mistress of her gypsy hat and plain mantle, and then efficiently attended to the unpacking of the valise.

Louisa stood by the window, gazing down at the garden in the center of the square. How different a view it was from that at Lawrence Park. There was no parterre, no croquet lawn, and no river, just the elegance and grandeur of one of London's foremost squares.

Pattie finished her tasks and came shyly toward her. "Begging your pardon, madam, but is there anything you wish me to do for you?"

Louisa turned, giving her a quick smile. "No. Thank you."

The maid hesitated. "I—I'll try to serve you well, madam."

"I know you will, and I'll try to be a good mistress."

"Miss Cherington . . . ?"

"Yes?"

"Was Mr. Tom Cherington your relative?"

"My brother."

Pattie's eyes were compassionate. "We were all very sorry to hear what happened, madam. He was a very fine and kind gentleman, always ready with a smile."

"Thank you, Pattie."

The maid bobbed another of her neat little curtsies and then went out.

Louisa returned her attention to the scene outside in the square. Tears shimmered in her eyes, but she blinked them back; she wasn't ready for tears.

14

Louisa took luncheon with Kit, but what conversation there was, was stilted, and by the end of the meal she knew very little more about him than she had at the beginning. The fault lay mostly with her, and she knew it. She felt ill at ease and a little overwhelmed by the amazing changes in her life in this single day.

In the afternoon Madame Honorine Coty's well-known light-blue carriage drew up at the door, bringing the dressmaker, several assistants, and a surprisingly large selection of beautiful garments. Madame Coty was not usually available at a moment's notice, not even to ladies of such rank as the Duchess of York, who only the week before had been most put out when the dressmaker had declined to attend her at home, but such was the careful wording of Kit's brief note that she sallied forth to Grosvenor Square immediately.

Louisa was resting in her room when the dressmaker's carriage drew up, and Kit received the caller in the library, the French windows of which looked out over a narrow walled garden at the rear of the house.

Madame Coty was a diminutive, bustling Parisienne, always perfectly turned out in charcoal taffeta gowns with blond lace fichus. She had straight brunette hair, which she wore pushed up beneath a large day bonnet, and she spoke perfect English, although with a very heavy French accent. With an imperious gesture to her attendants to wait in the entrance hall, she followed the butler to the library.

Kit rose to his feet the moment she entered. "Ah,

Madame Coty, how very good of you to come."

She gave him a gracious smile, always prepared to be obliging to a gentleman as handsome and charming as this one. "Milord, how could I possibly resist such a mysterious note? Provide a wardrobe for the lady who is disgracefully soon to become Lady Highclare, and be rewarded by being the first in town to know all about what is bound to be the most-talked-of match for months to come? Sir, you have the measure of me, I think."

Yes, he did. The dressmaker's capacity for gossip was legendary; indeed, she was frequently used as a means of spreading tales, and so he knew that receiving such a note as his would be bound to prove too great a temptation to ignore.

He went to her, drawing her hand dashingly to his lips. "Madame, I know that you are the personification of generosity and that you'll help me if you possibly can, and in return I think I can promise you the sort of interesting information that will give you an immense advantage in conversation for weeks to come."

She smiled, tapping his arm a little reprovingly. "Milord, you are wicked to tempt me so. I'm ashamed to say that I'm most definitely at your disposal. I've brought all the clothes I have in stock, but since your note gave no indication of the lady's, er, proportions, it is not easy for me to say if the garments will do or not. Is she slender? A little embonpoint?"

"Slender, and not too tall."

"Ah, then I'm sure I can accommodate, sir." She surveyed him then. "But first, milord, you have to tell me all about it."

He led her to a chair. "Very well, madame. The lady's name is Miss Louisa Cherington, and she is the sister of the late Mr. Tom Cherington, of whose sad demise you've no doubt heard."

"I have indeed, milord," she replied in some surprise, "but I did not know he had a sister."

"Nor did I, until the night before last."

She stared at him. "You did not know her until then, and yet you are now to marry her?"

"Yes. Affairs of the heart are so unpredictable, madame, but then you are from Paris, you understand such things."

She smiled and fluttered a little. "I do indeed, sir. Oh, how romantic your story is. Love at first sight."

"Indeed so. Perhaps you will find it even more so if I tell you that until this morning Miss Cherington was the governess at Lawrence Park."

She blinked. "A-a governess? *Mon dieu!* And she will one day be the Countess of Redway."

"She's under my protection—in the most proper sense of the word, of course—and will be residing here until we leave for Cowes toward the end of next week. Before then she'll attend her brother's funeral with me."

"And when will you marry, milord?"

"That has yet to be decided, but it will be before we leave."

"But her reputation . . ."

"Will be protected. She's a lady, madame, without a stain on her character, and it is my wish that we marry as quickly as possible, so that her reputation does not suffer unfairly."

She sat back, totally bemused by what she'd been told. She'd expected to hear his fiancée was an heiress or a rich widow, she certainly hadn't expected *this*. "As you say, milord, it will be a talked-of match. Lord Highclare and a governess."

"And a lady of gentle birth," he corrected. "Her family fell on hard times, madame, and she was reduced to seeking a position. But you understand such things, don't you? You are a lady too, a lady of considerable breeding, but circumstances conspired to thrust you into the world of business. You've risen magnificently, and now you're the undisputed queen of London fashion. I admire your talent and spirit, madame, and certainly don't think you less of a lady because of your situation.''

She blushed, very susceptible to such praise. "You're so right, milord. I understand such things only too well. Miss Cherington must not be judged as a governess, but as a lady who has suffered misfortune.''

"I knew you'd understand, and that is why I do not hesitate to entrust you with the story. You'll tell it as it should be told, madame, because you're the soul of discretion." May God forgive him such a monstrous fib, for the woman wasn't in the least discreet.

The dressmaker knew nothing of his thoughts. She smiled warmly at him. "Rest assured, milord, for I will see that all the chatter is *sympathique.*''

"You're too kind, madame," he murmured. "Now, then, I won't waste any more of your valuable time in idle conversation. I'll have the butler show you up immediately to Miss Cherington." He rang the bell.

When she'd gone, he sat down again, leaning back in his chair to gaze thoughtfully at the walled garden outside. It was a peaceful place: long and stone-flagged, with an elegant classical temple at the far end. A raised lily pond adorned the center, with a stone dolphin from the mouth of which a fountain played, and the whole was dappled with leafy shadows from the cool willows draping their fronds low over the ground.

He was well and truly set upon his promised course now, for by telling the dressmaker he'd made certain of a fanfare over town. The Frenchwoman might or might not attempt to see that the story was told sympathetically, but was bound to repeat his claim that the match was a matter of love, and nothing less. He wanted the furore to be over and done with as quickly as possible, and if that meant causing a sensation, then so be it. Let them make what they would of Louisa's sudden appearance on the scene, of her improper residence beneath his roof, of their marriage only a day or so after Tom's funeral—at the end of it all she'd be his wife and society would accept her as such. So would Thea.

He drew a long, heavy breath. Thea seemed to hover close to his thoughts all the time. No doubt word of his marriage would reach the Isle of Wight before he and his new bride did.

Leaning forward, he unlocked a small drawer in a table. Inside lay a sheaf of letters bound with ribbon. He extracted one and began to read it.

My dearest, most beloved Kit,

It's only an hour since I was in your arms, but it seems a lifetime. I cannot believe that such ecstasy exists, but exist it does when I am with you. You're my life and soul, my adored Kit, and only the thoughts that one day I'll be free of my mockery of a marriage to be with you forever sustains me through each day.

Come to me again soon.

My love forever,
T

He smiled bitterly. What a sham her words were, for she'd never had any intention of leaving Rowe. Tom had been right, it was the thrill of an illicit affair that she wanted, and that was all.

Crumpling the letter, he tossed it angrily away. It rolled across the floor, coming to rest behind one of the curtains at the French windows. Then he locked the little drawer again.

There was a discreet knock at the door. "My lord?"

"Yes, Miller? What is it?"

"Sir Reginald Carruthers has called, sir."

A spontaneous smile broke across Kit's face. Reggie Carruthers? The very man to brighten any dark mood. "Show him in, Miller, and be so good as to bring a bottle of my best cognac."

"Very well, sir." The butler's steps went away.

Kit rose to his feet. It wasn't often that Reggie sallied forth from the wilds of Devon, and when he did, it was always a pleasure to receive his company. His arrival would also solve a certain problem, that of finding a suitable groomsman for the wedding, which was so soon to set London by the ears.

Reggie entered, striking a pose in the doorway. He was a tall, angular bachelor of about Kit's age, with a pale, freckled face, soft brown eyes, and a frizz of mousy hair. He was much given to wearing blue, and today he had on a sky-blue coat, a sapphire-blue silk neckcloth, and trousers of such an indefinite gray that they too could have been taken for blue. He flicked open his snuffbox and took a pinch or two before surveying his friend. " 'Pon me soul," he drawled languidly, "what a wreck of a fellow you are. Sink me, but you've a strange air about you. What's afoot?"

Kit grinned. "Reggie, my lad, you've no notion of what a dark horse I am. Come, take a pew."

Reggie flung himself on a sofa, carefully flicking back the lace spilling from his cuffs. "I heard about Tom Cherington. A bad business."

"Yes." Kit said no more, for at that moment Miller brought the cognac, setting the tray on the table from which Kit had a short while before taken Thea's letter. When the butler had withdrawn again, Kit poured two large glasses and handed one to his friend.

Reggie swirled the amber liquid, sniffing the bouquet and smiling appreciatively. "You keep the best French brew in town, and that's the only reason I keep in with you."

"Thank you very much."

"Not at all." Reggie sipped the cognac and then settled back, looking shrewdly at Kit. "I'm ready for anythin' now. So what makes you a dark horse, my dear fellow?"

Kit embarked upon the tale, being careful to tell him the same version he'd told the dressmaker, namely that his match with Louisa was an affair of the heart.

Reggie listened in astonishment and then whistled. " 'Pon me soul, you *have* been busy! But I can't believe you mean to go through with it. Tom Cherington may have been a stout fellow, but that don't make his sister suitable for you. Dammit, Kit, she's a governess! I hardly imagine that will make her acceptable to your grandfather.''

"He's been badgering me for years to do the right thing.''

"Yes, but . . .''

"I'm going to marry her, Reggie.''

"All right, marry her if you must, but do you have to do it so damned hastily? Don't rush into it like this, give yourself a little time. If it's a matter of a chaperone for Miss Cherington, I know my aunt would be only too delighted to come up from Devon to do the honors . . .''

"Thank you, but, no, Reggie. I intend to marry Louisa Cherington before I return to Cowes next week. All I need from you is your presence as my groomsman. Will you do that for me?''

Reggie smiled and nodded. "You know I will. Sink me, but she must be quite a girl to have so completely turned your fool head like this. The great Kit Highclare, *the* catch, and he's gone to a little governess!''

"Dine with us tonight and judge for yourself.'' Kit grinned as Reggie raised his glass in acceptance.

While the two friends took their glasses of cognac amicably together in the library, Louisa's room on the second floor had been virtually taken over by Madame Coty and her assistants. Pages of sketches lay on the dressing table, and a half-finished list of the various accessories a lady of the future Countess of Redway's standing would require had been left casually on the windowsill. It was a long list, comprising patent shoes, satin bottines, ankle boots, overshoes, reticules, fans and gloves, hats, bonnets, shawls, boas, and mantles.

Beautiful garments were scattered everywhere: on the bed, draped over chairs, lying on the floors like rags, and sometimes hanging neatly on the picture rail. Each garment had a story attached to it, and the dressmaker made certain that Louisa knew every word. The peach morning gown had been ordered by the Duchess of Blyss, who'd then been inconsiderate enough to visit hot climes and succumb to some fatal foreign fever. The blue silk evening gown should have been worn at Carlton House by the Marchioness of Holworthy, but she'd been caught deceiving her enraged husband, who'd refused point-blank to pay any of her bills, including those outstanding to Madame Coty. The wine velvet traveling cloak had been intended for the famous and much-respected actress Mrs. Siddons, but she'd been overheard criticizing a gown of which Madame Coty was particularly proud, and so had been refused delivery of any further garments. And so the stories went on, each one recounted in detail as Louisa was assisted in and out of the succession of beautiful clothes.

Louisa was a little overwhelmed. She still could hardly believe her life had changed so completely since the morning, and she was a little in awe of the dressmaker, but not so much in awe that she couldn't detect sly questions intended to extract interesting snippets of gossip. She gave nothing away, and a disappointed Madame Coty knew she'd have to be content with what Kit had told her.

With a sigh, the dressmaker snapped her fingers at a waiting assistant, who immediately stepped forward with a very fine oyster silk evening gown trimmed with heavy lace. Its skirt was split, to reveal an underskirt stitched with thousands of tiny glass beads. As Louisa was helped into it, the dressmaker regaled her with the story of its intended owner, despicable Lady Codrington, who'd gone on for far too long without even attempting to pay her outstanding bills. The voice with its heavy French accent seemed to drone. Louisa looked at her reflection in the mirror. It was like looking at a stranger.

Madame Coty was holding up yet another gown, this time a dazzling white taffeta slip with an overgown of rich silver lace stitched with sequins. It had a very high waistline marked by a silver drawstring, and little petal sleeves adorned with a shivering silver fringe. "Perhaps mademoiselle would prefer this one? It was intended originally for the Countess of Lawton, but she ran away to Gretna Green with a very unsuitable young man and hasn't been heard of since." Madame Coty tilted her head thoughtfully, surveying Louisa's reflection. "*Non*, I think the one you have on now is much more suitable for the occasion in question."

"Occasion?"

"Your wedding, mademoiselle." The Frenchwoman looked at her in surprise.

"Oh. Oh, yes." Louisa felt color flooding into her cheeks.

"You do not like the gown?" asked the dressmaker, a little offended.

"It's very beautiful, I just have so much on my mind."

"Oh, *pardon, mademoiselle*, on such a sad day for you I should not be rattling on about happy occasions." Madame Coty snapped her fingers at yet another assistant, who stepped forward with some somber but beautiful black clothes. The dressmaker quickly helped Louisa out of the wedding gown and into a mourning gown instead. Trimmed with chenille, it had a matching three-quarter-length pelisse, which was to be worn unbuttoned to show off the gown's exquisite high waist and jet-studded belt. To go with it there were long black gloves, a hat with a heavy, chenille-trimmed veil to keep out prying eyes, and little black shoes. The dressmaker rattled on in her usual way, relating the story of the original person for whom it had been ordered. A certain Mrs. Carrington-Haltrop had intended to wear it at a relative's funeral, but had then fallen out with the whole family and elected not to attend, after all, leaving the garments on the dressmaker's hands. So ill-mannered!

Never again would the dreadful Mrs. Carrington-Haltrop know the joy of wearing a Coty creation.

The words flowed over Louisa. Her black image stared sorrowfully back at her from the glass. This was how she'd look when Tom was laid to rest . . .

"Mademoiselle?"

Louisa turned quickly. "Yes, madame?"

"Is there anything else you particularly wish me to provide for you?"

"No. I'm sure you've been most thorough."

"For a lady such as you it is a pleasure, mademoiselle. You have an excellent figure, and my clothes could have been made just for you. I shall be much honored to know that the, er, famous new Lady Highclare is wearing my garments." The dressmaker smiled. She'd been about to say the astonishing new Lady Highclare, but had thought better of it. "I shall gather together everything on the list and send it to this address, and when I am ready for you to take fittings of the garments I have sketched for you, I shall send word."

"Thank you, Madame Coty. I don't deserve such kindness."

The dressmaker beamed. "Anyone who is loved by such a man as Lord Highclare deserves everything, mademoiselle. You are the most fortunate of ladies."

"I am indeed," murmured Louisa, managing to return the smile. Loved by such a man as Lord High-clare? She wondered what the dressmaker would have said had she known the truth about the Highclare match.

15

By the morning of Tom's funeral, the Highclare story was all over fashionable London. As Kit expected, the fact that Louisa had been a governess and was residing unchaperoned under his roof proved to be of consuming interest. Society accepted his claim that it was a love match, but delighted in discussing the bride's character —or lack of it—at great length.

Reggie Carruthers proved staunch in his friend's support, having formed a favorable impression of Louisa when he'd dined at Grosvenor Square. He'd found her a little quiet and withdrawn, strained even, but had put it all down to her understandable distress about her brother. She was, Reggie confided afterward in Kit, a quite delightful little thing, and would make a creditable Lady Highclare. Kit privately trusted that his friend's judgment was going to prove correct, for Louisa Cherington was an unknown quantity who might yet turn out to be the greatest mistake he'd ever made.

An hour before the funeral service was to commence at St. George's, the streets nearby became thronged with carriages, as the *monde* turned out to pay its last respects to Tom Cherington; at least, that was its professed purpose, the truth was that everyone was anxious to see the intriguing Miss Cherington.

Louisa was ready to leave. The clock was creeping toward eleven, and she stood by the window of her room, looking down at the sun-drenched square. The weather was beautiful and quite at odds with her low spirits as she pulled on Madame Coty's costly black gloves. Behind her veil, her face was more pale and drawn than ever, and there were shadows beneath her eyes. She had yet to break down and cry.

Kit's carriage entered the square and drew up at the curb. The horses' bridles were fixed with black rosettes, and the coachman wore a black gauze scarf around his hat.

Kit entered the room. He wore a black mourning cloak from which fluttered long weepers, and beneath it a plain black coat and gray trousers. She went to pick up her little reticule and he saw her hand trembling. "Are you up to this?" he asked.

"Yes."

"It will be a considerable ordeal for you."

"I know, but I must go. It's my duty."

A light flickered through his eyes. "That's a word I seem to have heard a great deal lately."

"It's an important word," she said quietly. "It's the reason we're marrying."

"So it is." He offered her his arm. "Shall we go?"

Her skirts rustled as they descended the staircase, and when Miller opened the front door, a light summer breeze played with her veil. It was warm outside, and she could hear birds singing in the garden in the middle of the square.

It wasn't a long drive to the church, but it seemed endless. Louisa kept her eyes lowered to the reticule lying on her lap, for every time she looked out of the window, all she could see was the rose garden at Cherington Court, and two children, a brother and sister, playing hide-and-seek.

The carriage drew up at last outside St. George's, having maneuvered through the crush of similar vehicles conveying the astonishingly large congregation of mourners. As Kit alighted and assisted Louisa down, she was aware of all eyes being upon them. She was glad of her heavy veil, for she could hide behind it. She was glad, too, of Kit's presence at her side. His black-gloved hand rested protectively over hers, and his fingers were firm and reassuring. She still barely knew him, he was a stranger, but she needed him now.

She glanced up at the church's magnificent portico, which had six Corinthian columns, but then her attention was snatched away by the arrival of the hearse with its team of black-plumed horses. Tom's coffin was draped with a velvet pall, and on top of it rested a large wreath of creamy white lilies. The flowers quivered as the bearers lifted the coffin and raised it to their shoulders.

For a moment Louisa's resolve almost failed her. The sight of her brother's coffin was just too much, and she felt suddenly weak. Her fingers closed convulsively beneath Kit's, and her breath caught.

He steadied her. "Don't proceed with this if you don't feel able," he said.

"I must go through with it. He is—was—my brother." Was. It had to be the past tense now.

"I'll be with you," he said gently.

She didn't reply, but behind the veil her eyes were grateful. She took a deep breath and moved with him to take up their position behind the coffin, then they followed it up the steps beneath the portico and into the packed church. The sound of slow, sorrowful organ music drifted over them, and the perfume of lilies seemed to fill the air. She hardly knew it, but now her fingers had coiled tightly around Kit's, her nails digging through her gloves.

A stir passed through the congregation as the coffin was carried down the aisle, followed by the chief mourners. Everyone watched as Kit assisted Louisa into a pew at the very front. Many noted how he held his future wife's hand and how considerate he was toward her, and there wasn't a person present who didn't wish Louisa would turn back her veil and reveal her face.

She sat quietly, her hands clasped in her lap, her head bowed as she whispered a prayer for Tom. Then she raised her eyes to look at the church. It was one of

Wren's most beautiful, its interior giving the impression of simplicity and light. There were plain white walls and a ceiling picked out in gold, and behind the altar there was a painting of the Last Supper.

She found the funeral service harrowing. Time after time her unwilling gaze was drawn to the velvet-draped coffin. Her beloved Tom was in there. The solemn hymns washed over her, as did the clergyman's voice, for all she could hear were the sounds of the past: childish laughter in the rose garden at Cherington Court.

She was only vaguely aware of the service coming to an end. Suppressed emotion almost overcame her, and unshed tears shone in her eyes as she watched the men taking up the coffin again, for its final journey to the burial ground near Tyburn.

Kit touched her arm, assisting her to her feet. His hand was steady and reassuring at her elbow as they followed the coffin out into the sunshine again. The rest of the congregation streamed out behind them, determined to see Tom Cherington being laid to rest, and determined, too, to gain an introduction to his sister if they possibly could.

The slow procession of carriages moved westward through Mayfair to Tyburn, and then along the northern boundary of Hyde Park to Uxbridge Road. Louisa remained tightly composed, giving no outward sign of the distress she felt as the bearers conveyed the coffin to the freshly dug grave. Incongruous thoughts entered her head. If she'd still been at Lawrence Park, she and Emma would have been taking their luncheon in the schoolroom now; and if life had gone on at Cherington Court, she and Tom would have been seated at the white-painted wrought-iron table on the terrace, where they'd always sat on such beautiful summer days.

She steeled herself to scatter a handful of earth over the coffin's gleaming wood. She was aware of all eyes being upon her, and she sensed the continually raised quizzing glasses and gloved hands hiding whispering lips. She knew they were hoping to speak to her when this final part of the ceremony was over, and the thought filled her with dread. She found herself wondering how many of them took Lord Rowe's side where the duel was concerned. Rowe. She'd hardly thought of him since first she'd heard of Tom's death, but now she had to think of him, for as far as she was concerned, he'd murdered her brother. He'd known he was by far the superior shot, and yet he'd still called Tom out. It had been murder.

To her relief Kit did not expect her to endure introductions just yet, and the moment everything was over, he escorted her back to the carriage. She leaned her head back as the vehicle drew away, but then something made her glance behind to the burial ground again. Beyond the gaggle of black-clad people she could see the grave. Some men with spades were filling it in, closing Tom Cherington off from the daylight forever.

Suddenly she felt her steely grip deserting her, slipping inexorably away and leaving her at the mercy of her grief. Behind the veil her eyes shimmered with tears again, and her lips trembled. With a supreme effort she managed to hold back the sobs, but the moment the carriage drew to a halt in Grosvenor Square, she alighted, her black skirts rustling as she hurried into the house ahead of Kit. She fled up the stairs, a choked sob catching in her throat, and the tears almost blinded her as she reached the sanctuary of her room and closed the door behind her, leaning weakly back against it, her whole body shaking as the sobs of misery had their way at last.

The anguish of bereavement surged over her, the hot tears coursing down her cheeks. She had no strength left, and she moved slowly toward the bed, where she collapsed, her face buried in the soft coverlet as she gave vent to the awful grief she'd bottled up over the past days.

Kit followed her into the room, standing by the doorway for a moment as he watched the sobbing, crumpled figure on the bed. Then he went to her, bending to take her hand and draw her into a sitting position. He raised her veil, pushing it back over her head, then he pulled her to her feet and into his arms, holding her very close as she continued to sob.

She was so engulfed in sorrow that she was only vaguely conscious of him.

He stroked the nape of her neck, dislodging a heavy lock of dark-red hair so that it tumbled down from its pins beneath her little hat. The warm tress fell against his hand, its touch sensuous and oddly affecting. He was aware of how vulnerable and utterly feminine she was, and of how her body quivered in his arms. The fullness of her grief moved him, and he was conscious of being far more drawn to her than he'd expected.

"It's all right, Louisa," he murmured, instinctively using her first name, "It's best that you cry it all out."

She was aware of him now, for how could she not be? Part of her drew back from such intimate contact with a man she hardly knew, but the other half wanted to cling to him, needing so desperately to be comforted that all thought of impropriety was forgotten. Her arms moved timidly around him and she hid her face against the fine frills of his shirt. She could smell costmary on the soft lawn, a clean, sharp smell that seemed to envelop her; and she could feel the steady beat of his heart close to hers.

16

She'd recovered her composure a little later as she went down to the library, where Kit was waiting to speak to her. Pattie had combed and pinned her hair again, and she still wore the black mourning gown.

He was standing before the fireplace, looking up at his grandfather's portrait, and he turned as she entered. "I trust you're feeling better now," he said, coming to conduct her to one of the chairs.

"Yes, much better. Thank you." Her black skirt rustled as she sat down.

He watched as she arranged the rich skirt. Clothes of such quality became her very well, bringing out her fine-boned daintiness and emphasizing her natural grace. He resumed his position by the fireplace. "I know that this isn't really the time to discuss such things, but we should talk about the wedding."

She nodded. "Yes."

"Under the circumstances I hardly imagine you want it to be a grand affair, but if you do——"

"No," she interrupted quickly, horrified at the thought. "No, I'd prefer it to be quiet."

"It can be completely private if you wish."

"What would you prefer?" she asked.

"I'll go along with whatever you want, Louisa." He smiled then, conscious of having again used her first name. "Perhaps we should be less formal with each other. Please call me Kit; after all, we are shortly to be man and wife."

Warm color blushed on her cheeks. "I—I'll try to remember."

"Kit," he prompted.

"Kit."

"To the wedding again, then. I think we can assume that it is to be a private occasion, can we not?"

"Yes."

"The next point has to be where it's to take place. I'll obtain a special license, which means we can marry either in church or here in this house. Have you a preference?"

She hesitated. "I realize this may sound a little foolish," she said, "but I wouldn't feel properly married unless it was in a church."

"Why should that sound foolish?" he asked, vaguely amused.

"Because we aren't embarking on a love match; we're marrying solely because of duty."

"It's still a marriage," he pointed out.

"In name, maybe."

He was silent for a moment. "What makes you say that?"

"Well, I . . ." She couldn't reply. The color heightened on her cheeks and she was suddenly covered in confusion.

His eyes were very blue as they held hers. "You're going to be my wife in every way, Louisa. I thought you realized that."

She felt very hot now, her hands clasping and unclasping in her lap. "F-forgive me, but I really hadn't given it any thought, I just imagined . . ."

"That it was to be a purely platonic arrangement? You imagined incorrectly." He paused, a little embarrassed himself then. "Louisa, if this makes a difference . . ."

"No. No, it doesn't make any difference. I'm still prepared to marry you." She met his eyes. "I accept that you'll be my husband in every meaning of the word."

"Intimate strangers?" he murmured, raising a slightly wry eyebrow.

"We can hardly be anything else, sir."

"Kit."

"Kit." She lowered her glance. "Do—do you think we're doing the right thing?"

"You have doubts?"

"I'm filled with them."

"Do you want a completely honest answer?"

"Of course."

"Then I have to admit that it is as much a leap in the dark for me as it is for you, but I also have to admit that although we don't know each other very well, what we do know cannot be said to be disagreeable. I find you very pleasing, Louisa, and if I had reservations before we met, I don't have them now. I'm content that you're going to be my wife."

"Content?" She searched his face. "How can you say that when your heart is given elsewhere?"

"It *was* given elsewhere." But the reply lacked real conviction.

"I think we both know that this other lady is still very much in the present for you."

"She still isn't going to wear my ring, is she?" he said softly. "She has no place in this discussion, for it's of *our* wedding that we talk, yours and mine. Now then, where were we . . . ? Oh, yes, we'd agreed that it was to be a church ceremony. Tell me, did your family have a connection with a particular church in London?"

"No. Please don't suggest St. George's," she added quickly.

"I wouldn't dream of it. My family has always worshiped at the Grosvenor Chapel in South Audley Street, and I'm well acquainted with the present incumbent. Would that be acceptable to you?"

"Yes."

"Which brings me to the matter of a bridesmaid. Reggie is to be my groomsman, but I don't know if you have anyone you particularly—"

"There isn't anyone. I've lost touch with those near Cherington Court, and when I was at Lawrence Park there wasn't an opportunity to make friends."

"But a bride must have a bridesmaid." He hesitated. "I know that a maid is only a servant, but perhaps Pattie would suit?"

She smiled. "Pattie would do very well, sir."

"Kit," he insisted.

She colored. "I'm sorry, I just find it immensely hard to speak to you as if I've known you for a long time."

"Soon you will know me very well indeed," he said softly.

The confusion overtook her again, flaming on her pale cheeks.

He smiled a little. "And I trust you won't forget that as far as society is concerned, we are in love. Nothing was expected of you today—it was hardly the occasion—but when we do sally forth in public for the first time after our marriage, we will be expected to behave as lovers do."

"We—we will?"

"Of course."

She drew a long breath. She really hadn't considered any of this; she'd been too wrapped up in simply coping with all that had happened.

"Louisa, if we don't conduct ourselves like that, we'll be exposing the marriage to very unwelcome comments, and I'm sure you don't want that. I haven't embarked lightly upon this. I've made a decision and I intend to stand by it. You'll be my wife, you'll receive every consideration from me and not be treated as a mere chattel." He watched her for a moment. "Do you have any lingering doubts concerning the nature of what I'm offering?"

"None at all."

"Then I'll attend to the special license without delay and we'll be married within days. Louisa, a moment ago I mentioned going out together in public for the first time. It's something that should be got over and done with—the gossips and scandalmongers have to be faced.''

"I understand that.''

"I wondered if a visit to the Italian Opera House would be the very thing. I have a private box there, and Catalini's singing in *Così Fan Tutte* at the moment. I think we should attend the day after the wedding.''

"Poor Madame Catalini, she'll have her thunder stolen when we appear,'' she said a little wryly.

"I've no doubt of it.''

"Kit . . .''

"Yes?''

"About appearing in society for the first time. I know that I'm bound to come face to face sooner or later with Lord Rowe.''

He nodded. "That can't be avoided.''

"Must I meet him? I'd prefer not to.''

He drew a long breath. "It might be exceeding difficult to avoid it, Louisa.''

"He murdered Tom.''

"You and I may think that in private, but we can't say it in public. Whatever the truth of it, one fact remains; Rowe obeyed all the unwritten rules as far as duels are concerned, and that places him beyond accusation.''

She looked away. "I can't see it in that light, Kit, and if I'm faced with him, I don't think I can be polite.''

"Maybe it's a bridge that is some way away from being crossed.'' He trusted so, for there was an edge to her voice that told of the strength of her feelings. He took out his fob watch then. "If I'm to obtain a special license, there are several gentlemen I have to run to ground as quickly as possible. Is there anything else you wish to ask me before I go?''

"Just one thing.''

"Yes?''

"When will you next see . . . her?''

"She'll be at Cowes when we arrive.''

"Are you ever going to tell me who she is?''

"I don't think there would be any point, do you? It's over, Louisa, and you needn't concern yourself about her."

"So, I could be talking to her, maybe even laughing with her, and not know that she's the one you really wanted as your wife?"

He held her gaze. "I suppose that could happen—indeed, it probably will—but will it really matter? She isn't the only woman I've ever kissed and made love to; there have been many others who've warmed my bed, for I cannot by any stretch of the imagination be called a monk. Will you then wonder if every woman you meet has meant something to me in the past?"

"No, because I know that only one woman fully matters: this one woman you won't name."

"How many men have kissed you, Louisa?" he asked suddenly.

"None!"

"None at all? Are you going to tell me that Geoffrey Lawrence never kissed you?"

Her breath caught. "He took a liberty," she said, caught off guard. "How . . ."

"Thin walls at the Green Dragon. He made his interest in you very clear indeed, much to Lady Lawrence's chagrin. How am I to know that you didn't really return that interest?"

"You have my word."

"And you have mine. The woman I refuse to name no longer has any place in my life. I do not deny that I'm not entirely free of her, but each day makes it easier, and I shall certainly not succumb to any second thoughts." He smiled then. "So will it really matter that one day you might fall into conversation with her?"

"No, I suppose not." But it did matter, it mattered very much. She knew she had no right to expect anything more from the match than he'd promised, but she couldn't help herself. She hardly knew him, but what she was beginning to know she liked very much. She couldn't believe that in the midst of the turmoil and grief that beset her she could have emotion enough left to be drawn to him, but it had begun to happen. If she'd colored at the mention of consummating their marriage, it hadn't been because she was filled with virtuous alarm at the thought of such violation, it was because the prospect of surrendering to him filled her with an unexpectedly warm sense of anticipation.

Startled at how she felt, she said nothing more as he went quietly out, closing the door behind him. As his footsteps died away, she got up, going to the French window to watch the water playing from the stone dolphin's mouth. A light breeze whispered through the willows, moving their fronds sensuously to and fro and casting dappled shadows over the stone flags.

Out of the corner of her eye, she noticed something white behind the curtain, close to her feet. It was a crumpled piece of paper.

She bent to pick it up, straightening it out. The opening words leapt out at her: "My dearest, most beloved Kit . . ." She knew she shouldn't read any more, but the temptation was too much.

Each loving, tender word stabbed her with foolish pain, and as she finished, the letter slipped from her fingers. There was always going to be a side of Kit's life in which there was no place for his wife, only a place for the mysterious lady who signed herself T. He might claim that he was almost over her, but how could he be over someone with whom he'd quite obviously shared such burning passion? He'd honor and respect his wife; he'd love the mistress who'd refused to leave her husband for him.

17

The special license enabled Kit to arrange the wedding ceremony outside canonical hours, and so it was late evening when Louisa dressed in the beautiful gown once intended for despicable Lady Codrington. The August sun had almost set, and the lamplighter and his boy were attending to the work in the square.

The bead decorations on the underskirt of the oyster silk gown glittered like ice in the light of the candlestick on the dressing table as Pattie fixed a little knot of white rosebuds to the twist of dark-red curls at the back of Louisa's head. A posy of the same rosebuds lay on the dressing table, its white satin ribbons spilling prettily over the edge. There was a drift of perfume in the air from the Yardley's lavender water dabbed on her wrists and behind her ears. She wore no jewelry because she didn't possess any, but the gown was rich enough on its own.

Pattie had already dressed for the occasion. Louisa had given her the clothes she'd brought from Lawrence Park, and tonight the maid chose to wear the pink-and-white-checkered dress Louisa had been wearing when Kit saw her for the first time in the library there.

Louisa felt strange. She was a bride, about to give her vows to one of London's most handsome and eligible men, and yet she didn't know what her feelings really were toward him. It shouldn't upset her that he was so in love with his beloved T, but it did. And it shouldn't matter to her that when he spoke lovingly to her in public, it would be a sham, but it did. She'd known him for such a short time that everything about him was still new to her, but when he smiled at her, she liked it very much. Yes, she liked it very much indeed.

"It's time to go down, madam," said the maid, glancing out of the window at the sound of a carriage drawing up at the curb. She picked up the gauze veil draped over the back of a chair, arranging it over Louisa's carefully dressed hair.

Kit was waiting in the library with Reggie Carruthers, whose penchant for blue most definitely extended to wedding attire. He was clad in blue satin from head to toe, and looked very much the dandy. A quizzing glass swung between his elegant fingers, and he raised it immediately as Louisa entered.

" 'Pon me soul," he murmured, "the lady's a veritable vision of loveliness. I've a mind to take your place, dear boy."

Kit turned, his glance taking her from head to toe. He looked very distinguished in a high-colored dark-gray coat that fitted very tightly. It boasted gleaming silver buttons and ruffled cuffs, and its cut was quite superb. He wore white silk breeches with silver buckles, white stockings, and black shoes with buckles to match those on the breeches. his lace-filled shirt protruded through his partially buttoned white satin waistcoat, and a particularly fine diamond pin flashed in the intricate folds of his neckcloth. His eyes were very blue as they met hers through the veil. He smiled, taking her hand and drawing it to his lips. "You look very beautiful indeed, Louisa."

"It would be difficult to be ugly in such a gown," she replied, slowly taking her hand away. She was uneasily conscious of how contradictory her feelings were where he was concerned. She wanted to be indifferent, untouched by emotion, so that his love for someone else wouldn't matter, but she wasn't indifferent, and her emotions were stirring in a way she'd never experienced before. She couldn't be falling in love with him, she couldn't be. She was mistaking her feelings because of

Tom's death. Yes, that must be what was happening. Kit had been kind and gentle, and in her unhappiness she was confusing gratitude for something much more.

Reggie glanced at his fob watch. "*Eh bien, mes enfants*, it's time to toddle along to church."

Kit offered her his arm and the small wedding party left the library, the bride and groom in front, the bridesmaid and groomsman following. Miller and the rest of the servants were waiting in the entrance hall to wish them well, and the butler spoke for them all.

"My lord, Miss Cherington, our warmest thoughts go with you."

Kit smiled at him. "Thank you, Miller."

They emerged into the darkness. The streetlamps cast their light over the waiting carriage, shining on the panels and on the team's harness. The air felt fresh and cool.

The drive from Grosvenor Square to the chapel in South Audley Street was short, but to Louisa it seemed very long indeed. The chapel was a plain brown brick and stone structure, built less than a hundred years before. It had a classical facade and a spire that looked very elegant when viewed by the approach from Hyde Park, along Aldford Street, but looked less than impressive from South Audley Street.

There were few people about, but those who were, halted with interest on seeing the wedding party alight from Lord Highclare's carriage. Kit took Louisa's trembling hand and drew it over his arm. The light breeze lifted her veil, almost revealing her face as they stepped into the chapel.

Inside, it was candlelit, the soft glow falling warmly on austere white walls. The chapel was second only to St. George's as far as high society was concerned, and so the gold plate on the altar was appropriately grand. Above the sanctuary there was a beautiful domed ceiling of brilliant blue and gold. The rows of pews were deserted, as was the fine gallery, and the only person present, apart from the organist who played softly in the background, was the clergyman.

The smell of candles hung in the air as the wedding party moved slowly down the aisle. The ribbons on Louisa's posy fluttered as she gave it to Pattie. Her heart was beating so loudly that she was sure they'd all hear it above the soft sound of the organ.

Suddenly all was quiet, and the clergyman began to speak. "Dearly beloved, we are gathered together here in the sight of God, and in the face of this congregation, to join together this man and this women in holy matrimony . . ."

The time-honored words echoed over the chapel. As the moments passed, an air of unreality filled Louisa, and it was with a start that she realized Kit had already repeated his words and it was her turn. The clergyman addressed her. "Wilt thou have this man to thy wedded husband, to live together after God's ordinance in the holy state of matrimony? Wilt thou obey him, and serve him, love, honor, and keep him in sickness and in health; and, forsaking all other, keep thee only unto him, so long as ye both shall live?"

"I will."

Everything was a dream. She was aware of Kit's hand being placed over hers, and she heard him repeating his vows. Then it was her turn again.

"I, Louisa Elizabeth Mary, take thee Christopher Matthew Charles, to my wedded husband, to have and to hold from this day forward, for better for worse, for richer or poorer, in sickness and in health, to love, cherish, and to obey, till death us do part . . ."

Then Kit was slipping the ring on her finger. The gold felt so very cold. "With this ring I thee wed," he said quietly, "with my body I thee worship . . ."

His words were somehow changed in her head: With this ring I thee wed, but with my body I someone else worship, someone whose name begins with T . . . Louisa was forced to remember that all this was a pretense, a matter of duty. His duty to his grandfather and to Tom. Hers to Tom.

The clergyman was speaking. "Those whom God hath joined together, let no man put asunder."

And no woman put asunder either . . . Unbidden, the extra words sounded within her, and with sudden sharp clarity she knew that she wasn't mistaken about her feelings for Kit; she wasn't merely grateful to him, she was falling in love with him. The realization was unnerving, making her sway a little, and she barely heard the clergyman's final words.

"Forasmuch as Christopher Matthew Charles and Louisa Elizabeth Mary have consented together in holy wedlock . . . have given and pledged their troth . . . I pronounce that they be man and wife together . . ."

Still shaken by her inner thoughts, Louisa turned hesitantly toward Kit. Would the deception now begin in earnest? Would he kiss her lovingly, to convince those around them that the story of a love match was the truth? She held her breath and there were tears shining in her large gray eyes. Slowly he raised her veil, draping it back over her dark-red hair, then he cupped her face in his hands and kissed her softly on the lips.

Her mouth trembled beneath his, and a weakening fire flamed through her veins. A wanton side of her nature suddenly surged to the surface, a side she'd never dreamed existed, and it prompted her to wish with all her heart that he'd sweep her into his arms with all the passion he felt for his secret love. There was no modesty in such feelings, no modesty at all, and she drew quickly back, flushing. Had he guessed? Had he been able to tell how she felt?

Then Reggie was stepping forward to congratulate them both, and Pattie was shyly offering her felicitations as well. Louisa smiled and tried to appear light and happy, but in reality she was in turmoil.

Kit's hand rested gently over hers shortly afterward as they walked back toward the door of the chapel, but just as they were about to go out, he suddenly halted, turning to her. He wanted to tell her he felt more for her than he'd revealed hitherto. He hesitated.

Puzzled, she looked up into his eyes. "What is it?" she asked, thinking for a breathless moment that he was about to kiss her again.

Suddenly he couldn't say it. The time wasn't right, they should be alone together for such a confession. He'd wait until tonight. Smiling a little, he drew her hand to his lips. "It will wait. Come, let's brave the crowd that has undoubtedly gathered outside. Word travels like wildfire in Mayfair."

Slowly they walked on. She wondered what he'd been on the point of saying. Whatever it was, it hadn't been part of the pretense, for Reggie and Pattie had already gone outside, and the clergyman was otherwise engaged.

He was right about the crowd, for South Audley Street seemed to be suddenly filled with fashionable people, all eager to catch a glimpse of the most sensational bride and groom for several seasons. There was a hum of interest as they emerged from the chapel and entered the carriage, which soon pulled away in the direction of Grosvenor Square, where a small wedding breakfast awaited them.

At the house, Miller and the servants were still waiting, giving a cheer as their master and his new bride entered. The butler beamed. "Congratulations, my lord. My lady."

My lady. How strange it sounded. She wasn't Miss Cherington anymore, she was Lady Highclare. She was suddenly aware of the ring on her finger.

Miller went to the console table and picked up a tray on which lay a small package. "This was delivered a short while ago, my lady." He held it out to her.

She took the package a little curiously. It was indeed for her, Miss Louisa Cherington, care of this address, but she didn't know whose hand had penned it. Slowly she undid it, finding inside a slender leather box of the sort used by the more exclusive jewelers. She opened it and her breath caught, for there, nestling on a lining of pure white silk, was a beautiful golden locket on a chain. Surely it was from Kit. Was this what he'd been about to say in the chapel? She turned inquiringly to him.

He shook his head. "I have to confess I know nothing about it, Louisa. I only wish I did."

His reply took her a little aback, for who else would send her such a thing? She took the locket from its bed of silk, and as the light caught it, she suddenly saw it bore an inscription. She read it, stiffening with angry amazement. "To my beloved Louisa, Geoffrey." How dared he do such a thing!

Kit realized something was wrong, and he took the locket from her, seeing the inscription for himself. His face became very still and his glance suddenly cool. So he'd been mistaken about her, after all; behind her outer innocence lay a creature of deceit who'd managed to hoodwink him with her clever demureness. Just as he'd begun to feel so much for her, he was forced to see that she'd lied to him about her relationship with her former employer's handsome son. When he spoke, his voice was measured and clipped. "Shall we proceed to our wedding *repas*, madam?"

She stared at him. Madam? He believed the inscription to signify her guilt! He believed there to be something between her and Geoffrey Lawrence! "Kit . . ." she began hesitantly.

"Shall we proceed, madam," he interrupted, "or would you prefer to linger here?"

A dull flush entered her cheeks and she was only too conscious of all eyes being upon them. Slowly she accepted the arm and they proceeded toward the dining room. As they passed the console table, Kit tossed the locket down.

Behind them the servants began to whisper together, and Pattie looked on in dismay. Reggie hesitated a moment, clearing his throat awkwardly, then he followed the bride and groom. The wedding meal suddenly promised to be a rather strained affair.

The moon had risen and the house was quiet. Louisa

sat in the window of her darkened room. She'd
extinguished the candles, preferring the shadows. Her
hair was brushed loose, and she wore a flounced white
nightgown tied at the throat with pink ribbons. The
square was bathed with silver light. Reggie had long
since departed, and the servants were in the kitchens
enjoying their own wedding feast.

Kit hadn't said very much to her, and when she'd
come up to her room, he hadn't indicated when he
would join her, or even if he would at all. His whole
manner toward her had changed. She'd told him the
locket was simply spite on Geoffrey's part, but he'd
remained cool.

Her hands twisted nervously in her lap, and her
wedding ring caught the moonlight. She heard his steps
approaching at last. Her heartbeats quickened and she
rose expectantly to her feet.

He knocked. "Louisa?"

"Yes?"

He came in, his tall figure silhouetted from behind by
the light in the passage. He still wore the clothes he'd
had on for the wedding. For a moment he couldn't say
anything; he just looked at her, thinking that in spite of
her deceit she was still very lovely indeed, still so very
attractive to him. He wanted to spend the night with
her, but pride wouldn't permit him. He was glad now
that he hadn't confessed the truth to her in the chapel,
for at least she'd never know how close he'd come to
making a fool of himself. At last he spoke. "I came to
wish you good night," he said quietly.

She stared at him, a myriad emotions crossing her
face. Anger and hurt swept through her: anger that he
so obviously believed her guilty where Geoffrey
Lawrence was concerned, and hurt that he could so
easily treat her like this. She raised her chin defiantly.
"Good night," she replied.

He inclined his head and went out again, closing the
door softly behind him. The room was once more
engulfed in darkness.

18

She was embarrassed as well as unhappy as she went down to breakfast the next morning, for she knew that her lonely wedding night would be common knowledge belowstairs; they'd be talking of little else. She felt low, and the prospect of the opera that evening was daunting.

She wore a high-waisted light-green muslin gown by Madame Coty, with a dark-green velvet ribbon tied beneath her breasts. Rows of dainty lace on the hem swung richly as she descended the staircase. Her hair was pinned up beneath a little day bonnet, with soft curls framing her face, and there was a light cashmere shawl draped over her arms. She wasn't looking forward to facing Kit, for the hurt still lingered deeply that he had so swiftly believed ill of her; it was a hurt tinged with resentment, for even if she'd behaved wantonly with Geoffrey Lawrence—which she hadn't—did that make her any worse than Kit himself, who'd been bedding another man's wife?

The dining room lay at the back of the house, next to the library, and had French windows overlooking the same walled garden. Outside, the sun was shining, catching brightly on the dolphin fountain. The room itself was decorated with blue-and-cream-striped silk wallpaper, and a soft sapphire-blue carpet almost completely covered the floor. A great sideboard ranged down one wall, the silver-domed dishes supervised by Miller, and Kit sat at the oval mahogany table reading *The Times*. The white tablecloth was very bright in the morning light, and the smell of coffee and toasted bread hung in the warm air.

Kit rose as she entered. He was wearing a dark-red silk dressing gown over a shirt and cream cord trousers, and his blond hair was a little ruffled. His eyes were impenetrable as he spoke to her. "Good morning, Louisa."

"Good morning."

Miller hastened to draw out a chair for her.

Kit waited until she was seated and then sat down again himself. "I trust you slept well."

She flushed, her glance flying toward the butler, who was bringing some freshly made toast to the table. "Yes, thank you. Quite well," she replied.

He nodded toward the newspaper. "*The Times* speaks highly this morning of Catalini's performance in *Così Fan Tutte*. I think we can be assured of an excellent evening."

"Indeed?" It was dreadful making idle conversation about things that really didn't matter when so many unspoken words hung almost audibly in the air. It was made even worse by the butler's hovering presence.

Kit glanced at her, his eyes still veiled. "Aren't you looking forward to tonight?"

"It doesn't exactly fill me with eager anticipation."

He studied her for a moment and then nodded at the butler. "That will be all for the moment, Miller."

The butler bowed and withdrew.

Kit looked at her again. "You appear to have something on your mind, Louisa."

"Is that really surprising?"

"I suggest you tell me whatever it is."

Her eyes flashed. "You say that as if you expect me to confess to a passionate affair with Captain Lawrence! I'm sorry to disappoint you, because I'm not about to confess to something that isn't at all true!"

"You told me yesterday that you were innocent of misconduct. I accept your word."

"Do you? Then why have you been so cold toward me since?"

"I haven't been cold, I've been very civil."

"That, sir, is a monstrous untruth, and you know it. Before I received that odious locket, you were very agreeable, but since then you've been disagreeable in the extreme. You imagine me to be guilty of considerable indiscretion, and you consequently treat me badly. I don't imagine you to be guilty of indiscretion, I *know* you are, and that, sir, makes you something of a hypocrite." She was reckless because he'd caught her so much on the raw.

"Does it indeed?" he replied shortly. "I think you've said more than enough, Louisa."

"I've only said what needed to be said. I refuse to be unfairly condemned, especially by someone as patently guilty of double standards as you." The rashness still gripped her.

"I said that was enough, Louisa, and I meant it." There was an edge to his voice, and his eyes were angry. "You may be my wife, but I won't be spoken to in that tone. Is that quite clear?"

"Oh, it's perfectly clear, sir," she replied in a quivering tone. "Do you now expect me to sally forth to the opera house tonight and dote upon you as if we're a love match? To do that I'll need to be a veritable Mrs. Siddons!" She didn't know why she was blundering on, but she couldn't help herself. He'd touched a very sensitive nerve, arousing her considerable hurt and indignation.

"Madam," he said quietly, "if Lawrence had any reason to send you that locket, as far as I'm concerned you already *are* a Mrs. Siddons. I vow your act of sweet innocence was breathtakingly convincing."

Her breath caught as if he'd physically struck her.

Slowly he rose to his feet. "Absorbing as this conversation is, I fear I must bring it to a close as I have much to attend to. I intend to be out all day, but I'll return in time for the opera. Good day to you, Louisa.''

She didn't reply, and as the door closed behind him, she remained motionless in her chair, devastated with hurt that he could say and think such things.

She had a lonely day, spent mostly reading in the garden temple. She'd found a book about Highclare and the Isle of Wight in the library, and as it contained several illustrations of the house that she would soon be seeing, she was very interested. It looked very beautiful, with grounds sweeping right down to the Solent, but as she looked at it, she wondered what awaited her there. What would the earl have to say about his grandson's undoubted misalliance? Her gaze moved away from the book to the dancing waters of the dolphin fountain. Maybe it was all academic anyway, for things had gone so very wrong that Kit might already be contemplating having the marriage set aside. He now believed her to be less than virtuous, and he hadn't spent the night with her. She wasn't yet really his wife.

When evening came, she went to her room to dress for the opera, having first taken a lonely dinner in the dining room. For her first appearance in society as Lady Highclare, she selected one of Madame Coty's finest gowns, a creation in lilac silk with an overgown of plowman's gauze sprinkled with small silver spots. It had a very low, scooped neckline decorated with silver embroidery, and dainty little puffed sleeves made of the gauze alone. Its high waistline was marked by a silver drawstring diectly beneath her breasts, and its hem was adorned with more of the fine silver embroidery. Pattie piled her hair up into an intricate knot, teasing wispy curls around her face, and then looped silver ribbons through the knot, allowing them to tumble down to the nape of her neck.

She heard Kit return, but he didn't come to her room. Pattie must have been curious about the strange coolness between the newlyweds, but she gave no outward sign of it. She brought her mistress's silver-threaded shawl and lilac velvet reticule, and then her long white gloves and ivory fan. A few moments later, Louisa was ready to go down. With a last look at her reflection in the cheval glass, she left the room.

The drawing room was a large, elegant chamber on the first floor, its tall windows overlooking the square. Its walls were pale peach, with white-and-gold niches containing marble busts and statuettes. The furniture was upholstered in gray brocade, and the specially woven Axminster carpet picked out the gray, peach, and beige design on the beautiful ceiling. Three chandeliers gleamed in the fading evening light, and they moved just a little in the draft of cool evening air drifting in through the open windows. The room was deserted as she went in, for Kit had yet to come down.

Outside, a carriage was passing, and a church bell was striking the half-hour. Was it the bell of St. George's in Hanover Square? For a moment her thoughts threatened to return to Tom, but she struggled to prevent that happening. She needed her composure if she was to face society, for there wouldn't be a veil to be behind this time.

At last she heard Kit approaching. The white-and-gold double doors opened and he came in. He was dressed in the very formal attire required of gentlemen attending the opera, his appearance completed by a dress sword and cocked hat, both of which were *de rigueur* for such occasions. His fair hair shone in the fading light, and there was still a shadow in his eyes as he came toward her. "Good evening, Louisa," he said coolly.

"Sir." She responded to his reserve, but her heart tightened within her. Nothing had changed since this morning: he still thought ill of her.

He looked her over from head to toe. "You're looking particularly lovely tonight."

"Thank you." She wished she could take pleasure in the compliment, but she knew it meant nothing.

He went to a painting on the wall, and to her surprise she saw that it concealed a cupboard set flush into the plasterwork. Taking a key from his pocket, he unlocked it and lifted out an elegant silver casket, which he brought to a table. With yet another key, he unlocked the casket, and she saw inside a magnificent collection of jewelry. He looked at her. "These are the Highclare jewels, given to each new Lady Highclare. They are therefore now yours."

She stared at them and then at him. "Do you really want me to have them?"

"You're Lady Highclare now, Louisa, and therefore you have the right to them."

"But what if I don't remain Lady Highclare?" she asked hesitantly, unable to help herself because of her thoughts in the garden temple earlier in the day.

"Why wouldn't you remain my wife?"

She looked into his eyes. "Because you could want to set me aside."

"Is that what you think I intend?"

"I can't deny that it's crossed my mind."

"Then let me assure you that you're wrong. You are my wife and will remain so."

"In spite of what you think of me?"

"I have your word that you're innocent where Lawrence is concerned."

"But you don't believe that word, do you? You've made that only too clear."

"You're my wife," he said again, in a tone that closed the subject. He looked through the jewels for a moment and then selected a silver circlet set with three very large amethysts. He raised it to her head, resting it gently around her forehead. "The finishing touch, I believe," he murmured.

"Kit . . ."

"When society sees that circlet," he interrupted, "it will know beyond a doubt that you are my wife, for it's well-known as part of the Highclare collection."

"Kit, I haven't done anything of which I'm ashamed. Captain Lawrence has never meant anything to me, I swear he hasn't."

He met her gaze for a long moment, then he offered her his arm. "Shall we go?"

Renewed hurt surged through her, but she said nothing more, accepting his arm.

They went down to the entrance hall, where Miller waited to open the front door, then they emerged into the gentle evening air to go to the waiting carriage.

19

The Italian Opera House, also known as the King's Theater, stood at the foot of the Haymarket. It was an impressive building, its ground floor graced by a lamplit arcade, behind which were the brightly illuminated bow windows of little shops. Madame Angelica Catalani was always a great attraction, and tonight was no exception. A constant flow of fine coaches arrived and departed outside the main entrance.

Louisa grew more and more apprehensive as she sat opposite Kit in the town carriage. Her heart was pounding as the vehicle swayed to a standstill, and Kit alighted, turning to assist her. Her gown rustled richly as she stepped down, and the silver spots on the plowman's gauze shone in the light from the lamps in the arcade. It was almost completely dark, the sunset a stain of dull red on the western horizon.

She'd barely alighted when another carriage drew up, and Reggie Carruthers got out, accompanied by a slender young man with receding auburn hair. They were both clad for the theater, although Reggie was as always in blue. He saw Louisa and Kit and came over immediately, his friend at his side. "*Mes enfants*, I trust you've kissed and made up."

She hardly dared glance at Kit, but he was smiling. "A lover's tiff, dear boy, no more and no less," he said.

"I'm glad to hear it. Mind you, with a wife as glorious as this, I can't wonder you got into a jealous pet." Reggie grinned at him and then drew Louisa's hand to his lips.

148

Kit was looking at the other man. "Good evening, Harry. How goes Almack's and the War Office these days?"

"Both go very well," the other replied. He had an agreeable face, with a high forehead, and he looked at Louisa, waiting to be presented.

Kit hastened to effect the introduction. "Harry, this is my wife, Louisa. Louisa, allow me to present Harry Temple, Lord Palmerston, our disgustingly youthful Secretary of War."

The man Geoffrey Lawrence had had an appointment with. She made herself smile. "Good evening, Lord Palmerston."

He kissed her hand. "*Enchanté, madame*. I trust I'm one of the first to have the honor of meeting you."

"The second, sir. Mr. Carruthers was the first."

"Wretched fellow, always pushing in." He smiled at her. "I must confess that the stir you've created hasn't prepared me for your beauty."

"You flatter me, I think."

"On the contrary, for such a small compliment doesn't do you justice. Actually, by a strange coincidence I was speaking only the other day to Captain Geoffrey Lawrence, the son of . . ." He broke off in some embarrassment.

"Of my former employer?" she finished for him, her heart sinking that Geoffrey's name had been mentioned.

"Forgive me, I didn't mean to speak out of turn."

She was aware of a barely discernible reaction from Kit. Outwardly he was as affable as before, but she'd felt the tightening of his gloved hand over hers. She managed a light smile. "You haven't spoken out of turn, Lord Palmerston, for there's no gainsaying that I was employed as a governess at Lawrence Park."

"But nevertheless, I'm sure you don't wish to be reminded of the fact. Please forgive me, and say that when we next meet you'll kindly forget my blunder and allow me to begin again."

"There's nothing to forgive, sir, but if it will please you to hear me say it, then of course I'll forget."

Another carriage was drawing up, and he seemed to find it rather interesting. "If you'll excuse me, there's someone I wish to speak to." He bowed over her hand again, nodded to Kit, and then hurried away to the other vehicle.

Reggie lingered for a moment more. "I say, I trust mentionin' that toad Lawrence isn't goin' to make you two fall out again. That dashed prank of his with the locket really ain't worth squabblin' over, you know."

"I know," answered Kit, "and we won't fall out."

"Good. Well, I suppose I'd better toddle along, then. Harry's dead set on joinin' the Jerseys in their box. It's damned embarrassin', if you ask me." Drawing Louisa's hand to his lips again, he took his leave of them, strolling over to join Lord Palmerston, who stood talking with the lady and gentleman who'd alighted from the other carriage.

The lady was very beautiful, but seemed a little imperious, and she glittered with jewels, from the dazzling comb in her hair to the rhinestones adorning every inch of her yellow taffeta gown. She looked about twenty-five years old, and her husband, if husband he was, looked about forty. Unlike his wife, he had a pleasant, easygoing countenance, his face breaking into a pleased smile as he saw Reggie approaching.

Louisa was anxious to forget Geoffrey Lawrence; she glanced at Kit. "The Jerseys? Does that mean the Earl and Countess of Jersey?"

"Yes, and if you wonder what Reggie's cryptic remark about embarrassment implied, it's because Harry Temple is merely the latest in a long, long line of Sarah's lovers. Her long-suffering husband has been heard to declare that he refuses to defend her honor, for if he did, he'd have to call out nearly every gentleman in London."

Louisa stared at the little group. The earl was speaking to Lord Palmerston now, and was giving no sign of resenting him. "Does the earl know about Lord Palmerston?" she asked.

"Of course. Sarah isn't one to keep her amours a secret."

"Oh." Louisa was a little taken aback.

"I detect a certain note of disapproval, but then I suppose that's only to be expected, since you dislike such double standards."

She flushed a little, remembering their breakfast conversation. "You're quite correct, sir, I do dislike them."

"And yet you've quite willingly entered into a marriage based solely on those double standards," he said softly. "Shall we go in?"

"By all means," she replied coolly, wishing that all the awkwardness and mistrust could be dispelled and their place taken by the gentleness and understanding that had existed before.

They proceeded into the theater, but their progress to Kit's private box was a very slow business, because they encountered a great many of his friends and acquaintances, all of them eager to make her acquaintance at last. The whole of society appeared to be buzzing about the astonishing match, and was consumed with speculation as to why she'd become Lady Highclare quite so swiftly.

For her it was every bit the ordeal she'd been dreading, and was made even worse because of the false attention Kit was so assiduously paying her. No one watching could have known that he wasn't in love with her, or that each smile he awarded her cut through her like a knife. The memory of the kiss in the Grosvenor Chapel seemed all around her, for it had awakened a desire that burned like a flame. She wished she could protect herself by being indifferent to him, but she couldn't, she was falling more and more in love all the time.

She managed to remain outwardly calm as she was presented to face after face. Her fan wafted almost lazily to and fro, and she parried their questions with an ease she didn't know she possessed. It seemed a lifetime before they at last reached the sanctuary of the box.

She sat in one of the blue velvet chairs, gazing around the huge auditorium, where the drone of refined conversation seemed like the hum of a million bees. The auditorium was horseshoe-shaped, with five tiers of boxes, a gallery, and a pit where fops and dandies displayed themselves, rattling their canes and snuff-boxes, and talking in loud tones. Over three thousand persons could be accommodated in these magnificent surroundings of Bourbon blue and silver, and tonight it seemed that that many were present.

Almost directly opposite, she could see the Earl and Countess of Jersey's box, with Lord Palmerston and Reggie Carruthers among its occupants. She watched them for a moment, still a little astonished by the earl's amazing forbearance where his unfaithful wife's *amours* were concerned. Glancing at her own wedding ring, she reflected that she'd never sit knowingly with Kit and his beloved T; unwittingly she might fall into the trap, but never knowingly.

Kit had noticed her looking at the other box. "You'll encounter many such double standards in society, Louisa."

"And so I might as well get used to them?"

"Something of the sort."

"Maybe you're right, where others are concerned," she replied, looking at him, "but where we're concerned it's different. Lord Jersey is free to sit amicably with his wife's latest lover if he wishes, but I'll never sit knowingly like that with you and your mistress."

His gaze became cold. "If you think I'd expect such a thing of you, you don't know me very well."

"That's right, I don't know you very well, but I do know that soon we'll be leaving for Cowes, and then you'll see her again. You may claim that it's over between you, but we both know it isn't. What's going to happen when you see her again? What am I to expect?"

"Nothing will change, I'll still treat you with the consideration due to a wife. Now, if you don't mind, I'd prefer not to discuss it further."

"Very well." She returned her attention to the rest of the auditorium. The brief exchange had upset her, although she endeavored not to show it. Why had fate had to deal her such a cruel hand? Why had she had to fall in love with him?

Her glance moved along the tiers of boxes opposite, coming to a halt suddenly on two gentlemen seated alone together. One was of coldly aesthetic appearance, his dark hair graying prematurely at the temples. His left arm was in a sling, and his chill glance was fixed upon her as he lounged in his chair. His gaze was steady and unsmiling, and it sent an unaccountable shiver through her, making her look quickly at his companion instead. With a jolt she found herself staring into Geoffrey Lawrence's slyly smiling face. Her breath caught as he inclined his head to her.

Kit saw and his eyes narrowed angrily. "The fellow seems set to haunt us, does he not?"

She didn't reply. The last thing she wanted was for Geoffrey to once again become a bone of contention. She gazed with resentment across at the other box, despising the man whose spite had made such a horrid difference to her relationship with Kit. Determined to talk about anything but him, she gave further attention to his companion. "Who is the other man?" she inquired.

He hesitated. "Lord Rowe," he said reluctantly.

The name fell into the air like ice. Lord Rowe, the man who'd killed Tom. The color went from her cheeks, and suddenly the sounds of the theater were deadened.

Kit put a warning hand over hers. "Don't show your feelings so clearly, you're like an open book. Everyone now knows about the duel and so they know your brother died at Rowe's hand, they'll be watching you."

"How can you expect me to hide my feelings when

I'm faced with my brother's murderer?'' she breathed.

"That's too strong a word to use in public," he said sharply. "Behave with decorum, for Tom knew full well what he was doing when he embarked upon that duel, and you'd do well to remember that."

"Would you have me smile at him? I cannot believe even you would be guilty of *that* double standard!"

"Lower your voice, madam. You're no longer a governess and this isn't the schoolroom."

The words brought her up sharply, just as he'd intended. "How—how kind of you to remind me," she said stiffly.

There wasn't time to say any more, for at that moment the curtain rose and the performance began. Catalini was brilliant, with a charming, vivacious manner and a rich, harmonious voice. She held the audience enthralled throughout, but Louisa would have enjoyed it far more had it not been for the presence opposite of two men she loathed so much: the one who'd set out to rob her of her virtue and Kit's kindness, the other who'd robbed her of her brother.

When the performance was over and everyone began to leave, she and Kit waited for most of the crush to pass before they quit their box, but somehow she knew that they'd still come face to face with Geoffrey and Rowe. It happened at the head of the staircase, and there were still a number of people there to witness it.

Kit saw them first and took her elbow to firmly steer her past, but Rowe stepped deliberately into their path, determined to force a meeting. "Good evening, Highclare. Madam." His cold eyes moved speculatively over her.

Kit gave a cool response, but she was trembling with loathing, knowing that her feelings were very close to getting the better of her, and so she didn't acknowledge either man.

Rowe smiled a little at achieving such a reaction from her, but Geoffrey decided to try to provoke her into a response. "Good evening, Miss Cherington," he said, affecting to bow gallantly. "Ah, forgive me, it's Lady Highclare now, isn't it?"

She met his eyes, looking straight through him, thus delivering a very deliberate snub.

All those watching—and there were quite a few because all interest was directed at the noteworthy new Lady Highclare—couldn't help recognizing her action for what it was. A stir passed through them all.

Geoffrey was a little uneasy, not having expected her to make her feelings quite so publicly clear, but Rowe wasn't deterred in the slightest; on the contrary he seemed to find it rather amusing, challenging even. "Well, now, Highclare," he murmured, "aren't you going to introduce me to the lady who has all town *en emoi*?"

Kit's fingers tightened warningly over hers as he saw how stormy her eyes were, then he looked at Rowe with deep dislike. "Do you really think such an introduction is entirely appropriate at the present time?"

"My dear fellow, manners are always appropriate," came the smooth reply.

It was too much for her; she couldn't hold her tongue a moment longer. "I refuse to be introduced to you, sirrah," she said, her tone loud and clear.

A pin could have been heard to drop in the ensuing silence. Rowe's unpleasant smile froze. "It seems, madam, that for a governess you stand in strange need of a lesson in civility."

Kit replied sharply to that. "Have a care, Rowe, for it's to my wife that you speak, and therefore to me."

"Does she then think for both of you?" inquired Rowe softly.

Before Kit could reply, she spoke again, her bitterness spilling over into each angry word. "I speak for myself, sir, and for myself alone. I trust that one day you'll pay the full price for having killed my brother, and I also trust that in the meantime you'll suffer every torture imaginable from the wound he inflicted. I find you beneath contempt, sirrah, and I wouldn't stain Tom's memory by agreeing to make your despicable acquaintance.''

There were shocked gasps at this, and she knew she was guilty of great impropriety, but she wasn't repentant. Nothing, *nothing*, would ever make her take back her words.

Rowe's face was now white with fury. ''Highclare, I sincerely trust you'll deal appropriately with a wife capable of such misconduct.''

''I fail to see why I should chastise her,'' Kit replied.

There were more gasps, and Louisa's eyes flew disbelievingly to his face. She'd disobeyed him—ignored his warnings and made a scene—and yet he was defending her?

Rowe's lips parted in momentary surprise, but then his eyes hardened like flint. ''Don't provoke me, Highclare,'' he warned.

''And don't make the mistake of thinking I go in awe of you, Rowe. I know you better than you think, enough to be certain that you're too fond of your elegant hide to risk challenging me. You prefer to restrict yourself to opponents you can be sure of bettering.''

From pale rage, Rowe's face now suffused with dark color. His lips became a thin, malevolent line, and Louisa noticed how his fist briefly clenched. ''You're wrong if you think I shrink from calling you out, Highclare, for believe me, given good cause, nothing would delight me more. For the moment, however, I'll content myself with congratulating you upon your misalliance—you richly deserve such a bride. I'll further content myself by warning you that I'm about to take appropriate revenge for the loss of the *Mercury*. I've bought Lawrence's yacht and I'm going to extinguish you at Cowes.''

''You're welcome to try.''

''Oh, I will, you may be sure of it,'' breathed the other. Then he gave a chill nod of his head and turned to quickly descend the staircase.

Geoffrey had been standing awkwardly by throughout, and for a moment he was caught unawares by Rowe's sudden departure. But then, as he made to follow his new friend from the scene, Kit's hand suddenly shot out to seize his arm. "Not so fast, Lawrence. I want to have a few words with you."

Geoffrey tried to pull his arm free. "I say, Highclare, there's no need . . ."

"Any more tricks like yesterday's, and I swear you'll soon be breathing your last. Do I make myself clear?"

Geoffrey stared uncomprehendingly at him. "Tricks? What tricks? I don't understand."

"The locket. Just stay well away, or you'll regret it."

"I—I don't know anything about any locket!"

"Just remember you've been warned," said Kit releasing him contemptuously.

Geoffrey rubbed his arm a little, for Kit's grasp hadn't been gentle. For a moment he looked as if he'd protest his innocence again, but then he thought better of it, swiftly following Rowe down the staircase.

Among the intrigued, entertained onlookers, there were more astonished whispers as Kit steered Louisa down as well. Louisa felt both defiant and dismayed, for things couldn't have gone more wrong had they tried, and she knew that by morning the whole sorry tale would be in full circulation.

Their carriage was brought immediately, and a moment later they were driving swiftly back through the lamplit streets toward Grosvenor Square.

Kit's eyes were dark with anger as he sat opposite her, and he didn't utter a word. At last she couldn't bear the heavy silence. "I—I went against you in every way, and yet you defend me. Why?"

"You left me precious little choice. I could hardly stand by and let him insult you at will. What possible purpose do you think was served by that lamentable display of yours?"

"I thought I behaved with honor," she replied stiffly.

"You behaved foolishly," he snapped. "And what's

more, you chose to do it as publicly as possible. Rowe may be a snake, Louisa, but he didn't break the rules, and how many times must I tell you that Tom knew perfectly well what he was getting himself into? You were wrong to behave as you did tonight, no matter how justified you may have felt, and I'd thank you if in future you conducted yourself with infinitely more discretion, for to be sure at the moment I feel I've made a great mistake in marrying you.''

Yes, a great mistake, for the wife he'd at first believed to be perfect and for whom his feelings had so misguidedly begun to turn toward love, was proving to be very flawed indeed. Jealousy and anger swung through him as he looked at her, and the shadow of the locket seemed to cloud his vision. He looked away.

She was glad of the darkness, because it hid the tears that sprang to her eyes. She stared out of the carriage window, and not another word was said. When they reached Grosvenor Square, she hurried straight to her room.

20

Several hours later Rowe and Geoffrey returned to the former's town house in nearby Berkeley Square, having first spent some time at a gaming club in St. James's. A losing streak had done little to improve their mood, and Rowe's wounded arm was causing him considerable discomfort.

They repaired immediately to the candlelit drawing room on the first floor, a fine cream-and-gold chamber decorated very fasionably in the style of ancient Rome. The chairs and couches were upholstered in fringed velvet, and the low tables exquisitely inlaid with silver, ivory, and mother-of-pearl. There were cabinets designed to resemble temple facades, and an escritoire that might have come from the villa of Julius Caesar himself. Marble busts of emperors stood on pedestals around the walls, and there were handsome murals of scenes from Roman life.

Above the scrolled white marble fireplace, there was a portrait of Thea as the goddess Diana. She held a bow and arrow in her graceful hands, and there was a wreath of oak leaves and mistletoe in her shining golden hair. Her white robe dipped low over her full, flawless bosom, and her violet eyes gazed haughtily down from the canvas as the two men entered.

The windows stood open to the cool night, and the breeze rustling through the plane trees in the square outside moved the long velvet curtains. On the corner nearby stood the premises of Gunter's, the extremely fashionable confectioners, who remained open until all hours at this time of the year. Laughter drifted in from an open landau drawn up beneath the trees as a party of ladies and gentlemen enjoyed some ices. The sound grated on Rowe, who was in a very sour humor after the encounter at the opera house and the subsequent lack of good fortune at the club gaming tables. He went to close the windows before crossing to one of the classical cabinets and taking out a decanter of maraschino. He poured two glasses, one of which he handed to Geoffrey, who'd flung himself on a couch; the other he carried to the fireplace, where he stood looking up at Thea's portrait. "Not the most rewarding of evenings," he murmured, draining the glass in one gulp. "Damn Highclare and his *chienne* of a bride. I won't let tonight's insults pass, you may be sure of that. No damned governess is going to speak to me like that and get away with it." Abruptly he returned to the decanter to pour himself another very large measure.

Geoffrey said nothing. His encounter with Kit had shaken him. He didn't know anything about a damned locket, but he was beginning to realize who did—his dear stepmother. Before leaving Lawrence Park she'd warned him that she'd pay him back for humiliating her at the Green Dragon and that she'd pay Louisa back for her barefaced presumption. This business of the locket smacked of her hand. It was a neat way of hurting both of those she'd sworn to punish; Louisa's chastity was called into doubt as far as her new husband was concerned, and that husband's dangerous anger was directed at Captain Geoffrey Lawrence. Geoffrey drew a long resentful breath. Damn Anne, how he wished he'd never amused himself with her, for she was proving far more trouble than she'd ever been worth.

Rowe went to sit down, rubbing his sore arm for a moment and then looking speculatively at him. "You've got very little to say for yourself, considering the high-handed snub the governess dealt you tonight."

"I've got a lot on my mind."

"Such as?"

"After you'd gone, I was warned off her in no uncertain terms."

Rowe lowered his glass in surprise. "What do you mean?"

Geoffrey explained the incident at the opera house. "I didn't know what he was talking about. I hadn't had anything to do with any locket, but now I think I'm beginning to see the light. Do you recall what I told you about my, er, dealings with my stepmother?"

"Dear boy, I could hardly forget."

"Well, I fancy this is her doing."

Rowe smiled a little. "Heaven has no rage like love to hatred turned, nor hell a fury like a woman scorned," he murmured.

"She'll soon rue her meddling, of that you may be sure," replied Geoffrey darkly. "And as to those who've been scorned, let me remind you that the governess had the temerity to refuse me, and I don't take kindly to such treatment."

"I take it that Highclare's warning hasn't had the desired effect, for your lust for the lady hasn't diminished."

Geoffrey hesitated. "I'm not a fool, Rowe, and tonight was sufficient to convince me that Highclare isn't a man to tangle with."

"Faint heart," taunted the other.

"You didn't see the look in his eyes."

"On the contrary, I see it every time I meet him. He and I cordially loathe each other, or had you forgotten?" Rowe swirled his glass thoughtfully. "The governess has spirit, I'll grant her that, and while she may not be a beauty in the mold of my wife, she still has a certain *je ne sais quoi*. A man could take infinite pleasure in dominating her, could he not?"

Geoffrey nodded, a faraway look in his eyes. Yes, a man could indeed know such a pleasure with a woman like Louisa Cherington. Hadn't he dreamed of it, promised himself it ever since he'd first seen her?

Rowe watched the expression on his face. "Forget

Highclare's threats and bluster, my friend. Take her if you want her. We should make a pact.''

"Pact?"

"Yes. I'll take care of Highclare himself while you take your pleasure with his wife. It's quite clear to me now that you intended to pursue her once we arrived at Cowes, and I don't think your plans should change simply because Highclare feels provoked."

Geoffrey gave an incredulous laugh. "You can't be serious! After what he said to me tonight, you still think I should attempt to seduce his wife right under his nose?"

"Not seduce—take. From what I saw of the lady tonight, she'll never be receptive to your overtures, you'll have to be a little, er, forceful. And you'll have to see to it that she thinks better of telling her husband afterward, which shouldn't be difficult; she'll want to hold on to him. I'd say things weren't going too well between them so far."

"Not going well? How can you say that when he stood up for her the way he did?"

"He was obliged to defend her. Trust me, my dear fellow, and you'll soon be enjoying those charms you so evidently crave."

"Rowe, I don't think I—"

"Don't tell me you shrink from danger. A fine, dashing officer in Wellington's army? That won't do, it won't do at all."

Quick color touched Geoffrey's cheeks. "I'm not afraid, I promise you, nor do I have scruples about forcing myself upon that damned governess."

"Good, I was beginning to think I'd gravely misjudged you."

Geoffrey finished his glass and got up. "It's gone one, I should be leaving."

"And being the perfect host, I'll see you to the door." Rowe got up as well, pausing to rub his aching arm. God damn Tom Cherington's lucky aim.

They proceeded from the drawing room and down the

grand staircase toward the spacious entrance hall, which was lit only by a few candles, the butler having decided that his master and his guest would be up until dawn.

As they descended, Rowe reminded Geoffrey about the *Cyclops*. "I need her brought downstream as soon as possible if we're to sail to the Isle of Wight in good time."

"I'll bring her to the Hungerford steps in three days' time. She should be ready then; there are just one or two things to make good."

"Excellent."

They reached the bottom of the staircase, and then a sound caught Rowe's sharp ears. It was a young woman's giggle, soft and kittenish, and it came from just behind the door connecting the main house with the kitchens and other offices. Leaving a rather startled Geoffrey standing where he was, Rowe went to fling the door open. A housemaid and her lover leaped apart.

Rowe's gaze was harsh and cold. "What's the meaning of this?" he demanded.

The maid was terrified. "We meant no harm, my lord. Truly we didn't!"

"You know the rules of the house. No servant is to . . ." Rowe broke off, his eyes narrowing as he looked again at her lover. "Aren't you in my wife's employ?"

"Y-yes, my lord." The unfortunate young man was pale with dismay.

"What are you doing here, then? You're supposed to be in Cowes, aren't you?"

"Sir, I . . ."

"Spit it out, man. Have you been dismissed?"

"Oh, no, sir."

"Then explain your presence in London."

"I—I'm on her ladyship's business, my lord."

"What business?"

The young man looked helplessly at him.

Rowe's patience, such as it was, was running out. "If you value your neck, you'll tell me immediately."

"I've a letter to deliver," cried the frightened man quickly.

"That's better." Rowe's voice was silky. "I take it that this missive cannot be for me, or you'd have been more forthcoming, which makes me wonder greatly who it's addressed to."

"My lord, I cannot say." The young man's tongue passed dryly over his lips, and he was trembling. The maid shrank closer to him, her eyes like saucers.

Rowe's good hand suddenly shot out to seize the man's lapel and thrust him bodily against the wall. "You have a letter to deliver, and yet cannot say who it's for? I find that a little hard to believe."

The maid gave a squeal, hiding her face in her hands as Rowe pinned her lover to the wall, his face menacingly close. "Now, then, dolt," he said malevolently, "who is this mysterious recipient?"

"Lord Highclare, my lord," squeaked the man, his already pale face now ashen.

Rowe was motionless, his gaze frozen.

The young man looked as if he would be sick at any moment. "I w-was to deliver it straight to him and then return to the island, b-but I couldn't go w-without seeing Poppy first. We're to be wed, my lord."

The maid burst into tears then and begged Rowe to let her lover go. For a long moment Rowe remained still, but then slowly he released the man's lapel. "Have you already delivered the letter?"

"No, my lord."

"Give it to me."

"But, my lord—"

"Give it to me."

Without another word, the man took the letter from the pouch attached to his belt.

Rowe snatched it, breaking the seal and reading.

Kit, my love,

Since you've gone my life has been desolate. Forgive

me and return to my arms. I love you too much to lose you.

> I yearn for you.
>   T.

Rowe's face was as cold and chiseled as flint as he slowly folded the letter again and then looked at the terrified man. "I want this to be delivered, I'll reseal it using my ring, and when it's been handed to Highclare, you're to go directly back to the island. You're not to say anything about this to Lady Rowe, is that clear? And be warned, if she's told, I'll know, you can count upon it. So, if you value your life, and your sweetheart's position here, you'll do as I tell you. Do you understand?"

"Yes, my lord."

"Very well. Wait here." Rowe turned on his heel and strode back to the staircase.

"I say, Rowe, what the devil's going on?" asked Geoffrey.

"It seems I've yet another score to settle with Highclare," breathed Rowe in a low, taut voice, walking straight past him and up the staircase.

Geoffrey followed him. "What do you mean? What's up?" he asked.

Rowe reached the drawing room and flung the doors open so wildly that the draft set the candle flames gyrating. Thea's portrait seemed almost alive in the moving light.

Geoffrey paused hesitantly at the door, watching as Rowe went to the escritoire and lit a small candle ready to melt the sealing wax. "Rowe? Aren't you going to explain anything?"

"It seems that I've been wearing horns and that Highclare's the man putting them there."

Geoffrey's lips parted in amazement.

The wax was soft and melting, dripping slowly onto the letter and covering what remained of the previous seal. Rowe's voice was so quiet that it was barely audible. "Your precious governess is soon going to be a widow, Lawrence. Highclare isn't going to survive his next race with me, I'm going to settle all scores at one fell swoop, and when I exact revenge, I exact it to the full. When Highclare returns to the island, he'll be returning to certain extinction." He plunged his signet ring into the wax.

21

Southampton quay was extremely busy as Kit's traveling carriage drove smartly over the cobbles. The ancient city's medieval walls rose almost out of the water, the towers and gateways little changed since the day Henry the Fifth's army departed for Agincourt. At the head of its seven-mile-long tidal inlet, where the rivers Test and Itchen flowed together, the port enjoyed an unrivaled situation that protected it from invasion and made it a perfect haven for shipping. Until the rise of Brighton, it had also been a fashionable spa, both for sea bathing and the mineral springs, but now it contented itself with being what it had always been, one of England's most important ports.

The carriage drew up at the *Spindrift*'s mooring, and Kit alighted, turning to hand Louisa down, and then Pattie, who'd traveled with them. He avoided Louisa's eyes and released her hand almost immediately. She hid her unhappiness by shaking out her cream muslin skirt and retying the ribbons of the wine velvet traveling cloak that had originally been intended for Mrs. Siddons. The brisk sea breeze tugged at the wide brim of her straw bonnet and ruffled the long dark-red curl tumbling down her back from the knot Pattie had pinned up at their inn in Winchester earlier that morning.

She glanced around the quay, where the cobbles were littered with sacks, wooden boxes, upturned boats, fishing nets, lobster pots, and every other article always associated with such places. The ring of sea boots was

everywhere, and the rattle of hooves and wheels. Men
talked in many languages, and there was a rather rowdy
meeting in progress before an ancient warehouse that
was evidently now used to keep French prisoners-of-
war. Ships of all kinds were moored alongside the
wharf, and the Isle of Wight packet was just coming in.

Kit was supervising the unloading of their luggage
from the carriage and seeing that it was carried carefully
aboard the *Spindrift*. She watched him. He hadn't
mentioned Geoffrey or the locket again, but both were
ever present. Things hadn't improved at all; in fact, if
anything, they were worse, for now he'd heard from his
mistress and she sensed that something had changed.

The letter had been delivered the night of the opera-
house visit. She'd been lying in her bed trying to sleep
when she'd heard someone ride up outside and knock at
the front door. After a while a grumbling Miller had
answered, and as the caller rode quickly out of the
square again, the butler had come up to Kit's room,
passing her door on the way. She'd been curious about
it all and had peeped discreetly out as he went by. She'd
seen a sealed letter lying on the silver tray he carried.
She'd listened as he knocked at Kit's door. The brief
exchange of words were as clear to her now as if she'd
heard them but a moment before.

"My lord?"

"What is it?"

"There's a letter for you, from the Isle of Wight. You
told me to be sure to disturb you at any time if . . ."

"Yes. Bring it in."

She'd closed the door then.

The following day she'd felt that his manner toward
her had been subtly different, as if she'd assumed a
lesser place; but perhaps she'd imagined it, because she
knew instinctively from whom the letter had come.
What had T written? What had she said to the man she
loved and who loved her?

She looked away from him. What point was there in
torturing herself like this? He'd never promised her

anything more than his name, and she was a fool to want more.

Their journey from London had been taken at a leisurely pace, with an overnight halt in Winchester, where they'd slept in separate rooms. That side of their marriage hadn't changed; there was still no intimacy, and no sign of its approach. In public he was attentive enough, but in private . . .

The thirteen-mile journey to Southampton from Winchester had been accomplished in virtual silence, and now, as they'd alighted, he'd been so quick to release her hand that she'd felt even more strongly that she was of no importance whatsoever when placed beside his beloved T.

Her glance was drawn farther along the quay, where the Isle of Wight packet had now come alongside and was preparing for its passengers to disembark. A stout, gray-haired gentleman on the deck had noticed Kit and was trying to attract his attention.

"Highclare! I say, Highclare!"

Kit turned. "Damn," he muttered under his breath, "it's Glenfarrick." But he smiled and returned the man's salute. "Good morning, Glenfarrick."

The gangplank in place, the man was one of the first to come ashore. He was dressed fashionably, but was a little too rotund to look elegant. His tall beaver hat sported a fine silver buckle, and his silver-handled cane looked very expensive as he strode toward them, using it to flick aside some straw strewn on the cobbles. He was about fifty years old, and rather soft and pink. Louisa immediately disliked him.

His smile was too ready as he doffed his hat. "You sly dog, Highclare! Fancy springing this on us all!"

"Springing what?" inquired Kit with a polite coolness that would have deterred someone less thick-skinned, but not Glenfarrick, whose soft exterior concealed a malicious, scandalmongering nature second to none.

"Why, your match, of course." The man's watery

blue eyes slid toward Louisa, rightly placing her as the astonishing new Lady Highclare. "Word reached the island yesterday, and to say we were all thunderstruck would be putting it mildly. First you dash off into the thundery night without so much as a word about returning in time to take Grantham on tomorrow, then we all learn that you've gone and got yourself tangled up in the bonds of matrimony. What on earth will you think of next?"

"Tell me, Glenfarrick," said Kit dryly, "are you always thunderstruck when you hear of something as commonplace as a wedding?"

"Commonplace? Dear me, Highclare, your match can hardly be termed commonplace! What can you expect when a fellow of your standing takes such an unexpected wife?" asked the man, giving another sly grin. "Er, unexpected, but very lovely, of course," he added quickly, glancing toward Louisa. "Ain't you going to introduce me, dear boy?"

"Certainly. Louisa, allow me to present the Honorable Alistair Glenfarrick. Glenfarrick, my wife."

She suppressed a slight shudder as with a plump, gloved hand he drew her fingers to his full lips. "Sir."

"Enchanted, m'dear. Enchanted. I confess, you're a vision, and you'll set Cowes by the ears."

She smiled, slowly extricating her hand. "You're too kind, sir."

He studied her for a moment and then returned his attention to Kit. "You'll find the island *en emoi* about you both, Highclare. There hasn't been another topic of conversation since the story arrived. I don't know if you've sent word to your grandfather, but—"

"That's my business, surely?" Kit's blue eyes were veiled.

Glenfarrick cleared his throat uncomfortably. "To be sure, to be sure," he muttered. "Well, one thing's certain: you've even got royalty chitter-chattering on the matter. Last night the Duke of Gloucester and Princess Sophia were heard discussing you, and the princess expressed a fervent hope that you'd both be attending the forthcoming ball."

"Ball?"

"In three days' time, to belatedly honor Prinny's birthday. It seems HRH was displeased with his cousins for not showing suitable respect on the appropriate date, and rather than risk incurring his continuing displeasure, they've hastened to arrange a grand ball. Anyone not attending runs the undoubted risk of being dispatched to the Tower, never to be seen again!" He gave a slight chuckle. "I fear Lady Rowe will be among those, for she told me that if she heard one more mention of the Highclare match, she'd exterminate whoever uttered the words! I must say, she was in a decidedly poor humor yesterday; one couldn't glance at her without she snapped one's head off. The sooner Rowe gets here and takes her in hand, the better." His eyes slid quickly toward Louisa, for word of the duel had also reached the island. "Me condolences, Lady Highclare. I didn't mean . . ." His voice trailed away.

She didn't respond, knowing full well that he *had* meant. He didn't say anything by accident; he chose his words very carefully, seeking maximum effect. Kit's gaze hadn't wavered, not even when Thea was mentioned.

Glenfarrick cleared his throat uncomfortably, turning with some relief as a post chaise approached swiftly along the quay. "Ah, there's my rattle wagon. I'm afraid I'll have to tear myself away, my children." He made them both a rather extravagant bow and then climbed into the carriage, which immediately set off at a pace.

Kit exhaled slowly as the vehicle drew out of sight. "Damned gadfly," he breathed. "No doubt the air's fresher at Cowes for his departure."

"I didn't like him at all," said Louisa.

"So I noticed," he replied dryly. "You have quite a way with you when faced with those you find repellent." He glanced along the quay to where a man was selling peppermint cordial. "Have you ever sailed before?" he asked.

"No. Why?"

"The crossing to the island may not be all that long, but it can be quite choppy, even on a good day. I take it that Pattie hasn't sailed either?"

The maid heard him and shook her head. "No, my lord." She'd been looking at the *Spindrift* with some trepidation, for she was terrified at the thought of going out on the sea in such a delicate craft.

"I strongly suggest that you both take some peppermint before we set sail," said Kit, beckoning to the man, "for it's a sovereign remedy for seasickness." He gave the man some coins and took two of the little glasses, giving one to each woman.

When they'd drunk it, he escorted them on board the cutter, ushering them to the hatch at the stern and down into the tiny cabin. The window allowed the sunlight to pour in, and water reflections dappled the walls and ceiling. Outside, Louisa could see the Isle of Wight packet and a small fishing boat slipping in to a narrow berth, accompanied by a flock of excited sea gulls.

Kit left them immediately to go and assist on deck, and Pattie sat down nervously on the bunk, evidently quite convinced that the peppermint cordial wouldn't do her any good at all.

"You'll be quite all right, you know," said Louisa soothingly.

"I prefer my feet to be well and truly on solid ground," replied the maid, staring uneasily out of the stern window at the swaying prow of the packet.

On the deck Louisa heard Kit calling out commands. The *Spindrift* trembled a little as the ropes were loosed. She began to move. Her prow swung away from the quay and her limp sails began to fill. Pattie closed her eyes, still gripping the side of the bunk. It was obvious that she intended to sit there like that until they reached Cowes, and as Louisa didn't want to be cooped up in the bright but stuffy cabin when she could be in the fresh air on deck, she left the maid and went back up the steps.

The quayside was slipping away behind and the vessel was moving smoothly past the fishing boat. Louisa went to stand by the rails, looking back toward the city's medieval walls. The Pilgrim Fathers had looked back like this, and seen those same walls.

There was clear water ahead now, and Louisa turned as she heard one of the crew calling out to Kit. "The wind's ten degrees on the weather quarter, sir."

"Keep her steady," Kit replied. "With luck we'll run before it all the way."

"Aye, aye, sir."

The sails were filling all the time and suddenly seemed to catch the breeze properly. The yacht sprang forward, the water rushing and hissing along her flanks. Southampton began to slip away astern. Sea gulls wheeled excitedly against the blue sky, sometimes swooping low over the water, and their cries echoed all around as the *Spindrift* sped south along the inlet of Southampton Water toward the Solent, some seven miles ahead.

The land rose gently on either side, clad in the soft green of oak woods. To port Louisa glimpsed the ruins of Netley Abbey rising among the trees, while to starboard there was the unbroken splendor of the New Forest. Glancing back, she saw the spires of Southampton standing against the sky, and clustered below them the tangle of masts from the many ships using the port.

Merchantmen plied their way toward the city, moving slowly against the wind, and a swift revenue sloop was coming about a little way to port ahead, close to the mouth of the beautiful Hamble River. The *Spindrift* skimmed toward her, barely altering course as she passed, her wash creaming against the sloop's stern.

Louisa remained at the rail, her bonnet ribbons flapping wildly in the breeze. Her traveling cloak billowed, and she could taste salt in the air and on her lips. It was an exciting taste, filling her with anticipation for the moment when they emerged into the Solent and more open water.

The land continued to slide past, and her attention was drawn to the starboard horizon, where a castle jutted out into the water on a narrow spit of land. It was Calshot Castle, one of the many defensive forts built in the reign of Henry the Eighth. Beyond that spit of land lay the Solent.

Above her head, the sails cracked and strained as the *Spindrift* altered course a little, to take in the gentle eastward curve of the inlet. A flock of wading birds rose as one from the shore, their cries vying with those of the sea gulls that had followed the yacht from the moment she'd set sail.

It seemed that they were quite suddenly in the Solent; one moment the inlet had them in its clasp, the next the shores had splayed away and the *Spindrift* was on wide water, with the Isle of Wight directly ahead. The island stretched magnificently across the horizon, a patchwork of summer color, of fields and woods, hills and bays, with Cowes itself clearly visible at the mouth of the Medina estuary.

There were many ships, some making for Southampton, but others set for Portsmouth or London. A Royal Navy frigate was beating east toward Spithead, where a small flotilla lay at anchor, waiting for her to join them. Tan-sailed ketches plied between the island and the mainland, outpaced by the swifter, more graceful wherries; and a small fleet of fishing boats was moving westward.

Louisa hardly noticed the busy waters, she was too intent upon Cowes. What was she going to find there? Would she know when she encountered T?

Her glance moved to the west of the town, past the beach and onto a distant headland. From the book she'd read in London, she knew that Highclare lay just beyond it.

Her pulse quickened apprehensively. So much was about to happen, and she doubted if any of it was going to be pleasant.

22

They were approaching Cowes Road now, and she saw that there was a yacht race in progress. Two cutters were straining side by side toward a winning buoy by a much larger craft, a particularly elegant corvette, and the spectacle was being observed by a gaggle of other yachts and private barges containing a great number of fashionably dressed people. On the corvette's deck a fine awning had been erected, and beneath it sat a small party that seemed very exclusive indeed.

Kit came to her side at the rail to watch the climax of the race. The sea breeze had stung color into his cheeks, and his windblown hair gave him an almost boyish look. She could see how much he enjoyed being on board the *Spindrift*, for there was a new light in his eyes and an unforced ease in the way he leaned against the rail beside her.

She looked away from him toward the race. "Whose yachts are they?"

"The one in the lead is Lord Grantham's *Eleanor*, the other is Charles Pelham's *Kestrel*. Grantham's bound to win; the *Kestrel* doesn't stand a chance now."

He was right. A moment later, amid cheers and the booming of the corvette's cannon, Lord Grantham's sleek cutter skimmed past the buoy in first place. Kit smiled. "He may have won today, but he won't better me tomorrow."

She watched the two yachts beginning to come about, and then her glance moved to the awning on the corvette. "Who are the people on the large vessel?"

"The royal party. The lady with the bright-yellow pagoda parasol is Princess Sophia, and the plump gentleman at her side is the Duke of Gloucester. The rest are a scattering of earls, a marquess, and several countesses."

She recalled what the odious Alistair Glenfarrick had said on the quay about the hastily arranged ball. "Will we be attending the ball?"

He hesitated. "That rather depends."

"Upon what?"

He straightened. "Upon you, Louisa. I need certain assurances before I'll even begin to think about taking you to such an occasion. The scene you created at the opera house was disgraceful, and I don't intend to risk a repetition, especially not in front of royalty."

It was as if he was lecturing a naughty child! She colored. "There were, as I recall, certain rather extenuating circumstances at the opera house."

"Those circumstances will apply on the island. Rowe is set to arrive soon, and his wife is already present. You're bound to encounter them both, and so naturally I require your word that you'll conduct yourself with dignity and restraint."

"I cannot say how I will respond to Lady Rowe, sir, because I don't know her, but I know her husband, and the way he behaved in London left me in no doubt as to the meanness of his character. I cannot and will not undertake to behave as if I find him agreeable, and I think it ill becomes you, sir, to demand such an impossible thing of me."

"It's hardly impossible for you to conduct yourself civilly, but you expect me to think it is. Very well, since you won't give me the assurance I require, you leave me no choice but to spare society your presence. During our stay on the island, you will remain at Highclare."

She stared at him. "You—you intend to banish me completely?"

"In the absence of your cooperation, I have no alternative. I'm not going to risk an unpleasant scene in front of royalty, and it's quite obvious that you're prepared to do just that. I also have another reason for preferring to keep you away from Cowes society.''

"And that is?'' she asked coldly, still unable to believe he was saying all this.

"I think it preferable to keep you away from all possible contact with Captain Geoffrey Lawrence, whose significance in your life has obviously been rather more than you've been prepared to admit.'' He held her gaze, thinking he saw guilt in the way she drew back from him. He wanted to see innocence, but saw only guilt.

So he'd said it directly at last. She hid her heartbreak behind an outer coldness. "Don't presume to judge all women by your mistress, sirrah, for we don't all betray our marriage vows.''

Anger flashed in his glance, and without another word he left her, to return to his place by the helmsman.

Louisa turned away as well, trembling so much that she had to grip the rail to steady herself. Hurt indignation surged through her. She was being condemned for refusing to dishonor Tom's memory, and she was also being condemned because Geoffrey Lawrence had formed an unwelcome and unwanted passion for her; in the first she was right, and in the second she was innocent. Why couldn't Kit be honest and admit that the real reason he wished to keep his wife safely out at Highclare was so that he could more easily keep assignations with his beloved T?

She stared across at the corvette and its attendant craft. Maybe T was watching the *Spindrift* from one of those yachts, maybe her heart was quickening even now at the thought of being reunited with her lover. Louisa lowered her eyes to the rushing water creaming along the *Spindrift*'s side.

The island was very close now, and she could see the twisting, narrow streets of the older part of Cowes.

Passing the yachts lying at anchor by the entrance of the harbor, the *Spindrift* maneuvered much more slowly now, making her way to her berth by the warehouse. She inched into place, and the ropes were made fast. An ox wagon was rattling along the quayside, and a fishing boat was discharging its catch, surrounded by the usual excited cloud of sea gulls. The Mermaid Inn was doing brisk business, and the sound of a man singing a sea chantey drifted from its open doorway.

The crew was carrying the baggage ashore, and a small boy was dispatched to an inn in the town, where a post chaise could be hired to convey Kit, Louisa, and Pattie out to Highclare.

Pattie emerged from the cabin looking pale and unwell, and it was evident that the peppermint essence hadn't proved beneficial at all. Louisa hurried to assist her ashore, sitting her carefully on a convenient bale of hay until the queasiness passed.

Kit had just stepped ashore as well when a maroon landau with its hoods down approached along the cluttered quay. It contained four very elegantly dressed ladies, their parasols twirling as they laughed and chattered together. He turned the moment he heard it, and his face changed as he realized immediately that it was Thea's carriage. He'd known that sooner or later she and Louisa were bound to come face to face, but now the moment was being thrust upon him and he had no idea how either woman would react—least of all Louisa, who, although she might not realize Thea was the other woman in his life, would certainly identify her as the wife of Tom's murderer. Damn Thea for forcing things like this. It wasn't mere coincidence that brought her carriage along at this precise moment; it was quite deliberate. No doubt she'd seen the *Spindrift* approaching.

Louisa watched the landau as well, having very swiftly detected his reaction to it. Every sense warned her that she and the mysterious T were about to confront each other for the first time.

The landau drew to a halt, its fine team of grays stamping and shaking their heads. The ladies forgot their laughter and conversation, and their parasols ceased twirling as they quite openly surveyed the intriguing new Lady Highclare.

One of them was small and dark-haired, with a well-rounded figure encased in a fussily frilled pink hat and matching pelisse. Opposite her sat two sallow, mousy creatures in pale blue. They were as alike as two peas in a pod and were unmistakably twins. Louisa accorded these three only brief attention, but the fourth, a breathtakingly lovely blonde in cool lemon silk, was a very different matter. Haughty and superior, her magnificent violet eyes hadn't moved from Kit, and there was no mistaking the secret truth written large in them. Suddenly they flickered away from her lover to rest malevolently on his new wife. There was ill will in their steady gaze, the malice of a woman faced with another who'd encroached upon her domain.

Thea studied her unexpected rival, appraising her very carefully. She was displeased to find Louisa prettier than she'd expected, but prettiness was one thing, beauty quite another, and in Thea's opinion Louisa Cherington was hardly a beauty. Nor did she have any right to possess Kit, whose absence had convinced Thea that he was one lover she had no intention of relinquishing. But as Thea gazed spitefully at Louisa, she saw with something of a jolt that there was an awareness and defiance gleaming in the governess's eyes that spoke volumes. In that brief second, the mistress saw the wife pick up the silently tossed-down gauntlet.

The lady in fussy pink wasn't aware of the subtle undercurrents; she was just conscious of a certain awkwardness. She gave a rather too bright smile and spoke to Kit. "La, my lord, how wicked of you to absent yourself from the island without seeking my permission. I'm of a mind to be miffed with you."

Kit returned her smile, deciding to play the situation by ear and hope that nothing untoward occurred. "Lady Grantham, I swear I looked everywhere for you

before I departed, but you weren't to be found. I vow
you must have been with one of your lovers.''

"My *what*?'' She chuckled a little. "Fie on you, sir,
for you're not a gentleman, but I suppose I shall have to
forgive you. It wouldn't do to put you down on the very
eve of your inevitable defeat at my husband's superior
hands.'' She extended her hand to him.

He accepted if, still smiling as he drew it to his lips.
Then he turned his attention to the ladies in blue. "Ah,
the Misses Carpenter, how very agreeable it is to meet
you again.'' He kissed their hands as well. Then, at last,
he was looking at Thea. He had to utter her name—he
had no choice—and then it was up to fate how Louisa
would react. "Lady Rowe,'' he murmured, "you're
looking lovelier than ever.''

Louisa froze. Lady Rowe? His secret mistress was
Lady Rowe? Shaken, she looked away as he slowly drew
Thea's hand to his lips. A sharp hurt passed keenly
through her. It had been bad enough to know that he
loved someone else, but to now discover that that
someone else was Lady Rowe was simply too much.
Shaken, she strove to maintain her composure.

Thea was smiling coolly at Kit. Now that he'd looked
into her eyes again, she knew that he wasn't over her.
He may have taken a wife, but his heart was still drawn
to his former love; she could, and would, win him back.

Lady Grantham was impatient to be introduced to
Louisa. "Sir, you're forgetting your manners. We're all
so eager to be presented to your bride, and you dilly-
dally with idle pleasantries.''

"Forgive me, my lady,'' he replied immediately,
taking Louisa's hand and drawing her forward a little.
"Louisa, may I present you to Annabel, Lady
Grantham, to Miss Ethne and Miss Verity Carpenter,
and . . . to Thea, Lady Rowe.''

Louisa gave no sign of her inner feelings as she smiled
at the first three ladies, murmuring that she was very
honored to meet them. But if Kit fleetingly hoped that
she was going to behave as he wished, that hope was

swiftly dashed as she looked coldly at Thea and said not
a single word.

It was a snub as deliberate as that she'd dealt
Geoffrey in London, and no one could mistake it. Lady
Grantham was a little taken aback, and the Misses
Carpenter exchanged meaningful glances. Thea's eyes
were like ice. How dared this nonentity, this jumped-up
governess, presume to cut her!

At that moment the post chaise approached, drawing
up behind the landau. Thea's cheeks were pink as she
abruptly commanded her coachman to drive on. The
landau pulled smartly away.

As it vanished from sight, Kit rounded furiously on
his wife. "Is there no end to your capacity for misconduct?" he breathed, keeping his tone low so that no
one else on the quay would hear. "What you did just
then was unforgivable, and if I had any lingering doubt
about making you remain out at Highclare, that doubt
is now completely removed."

"I have no doubt that it is, sir," she replied in an
equally low and angry voice, "for you wish to be free to
continue your despicable liaison with your mistress,
don't you? So you meant your marriage vows when you
uttered them, did you? It's patently obvious that dear
Lady Rowe didn't mean hers."

She caught him off guard. He hadn't realized that
she'd perceived the truth; he'd put her conduct down
solely to the fact that Thea was Lord Rowe's wife.

Her eyes were very bright as she looked at him. "Oh,
yes, I know who she is; I'd have to be a fool not to, for
you were both transparent. I marvel that no one else in
society appears to have found you out, for to be sure
you're incapable of concealing your illicit love. I've
misjudged you, sir, for until now I believed you were a
gentleman, but the fact is that you have no honor at all.
Not content with expecting me to behave graciously
toward Lord Rowe, you also expect me to smile sweetly
at his wife, when all the time that wife is your mistress."

A thousand emotions crossed his face, and for a

moment she didn't know how he was going to react, but then he suddenly seized her arm, steering her almost roughly toward the waiting post chaise and bundling her inside.

She sat back against the drab upholstery, fighting back hot tears of anger and hurt. She loved him, but he felt nothing for her at all. He'd promised that he'd show her the respect and consideration due to a wife, but she was being shown neither.

The chaise swayed as the baggage was loaded, and then Pattie climbed hesitantly in, avoiding her mistress's eyes. A moment later Kit climbed in as well, slamming the door behind him and taking the seat opposite Louisa. His blue eyes were still very stormy, and there was a firm set to his jaw.

The chaise drew away, and Louisa kept her glance lowered. The gulf between them had widened still more, perhaps irrevocably. How long could it possibly be before he wished to rid himself of an unwanted, unloved wife he'd so mistakenly married out of duty?

23

The road to Highclare led west out of Cowes, passing through mellow, rolling countryside from which the Solent could always be seen. The roadside was fringed with soft green ferns, and the hedgerows boasted valerian and fuchsia as well as wild roses and honeysuckle, and there were long low farmhouses and cottages built of gray stone. They nestled in leafy hollows, their windows peeping sleepily from beneath thatched roofs, and their gardens were filled with a riot of summer flowers, but especially with geraniums, which seemed to bloom more luxuriantly here than anywhere else Louisa had ever been.

The apricot scent of sun-drenched gorse filled the air from heathland as the chaise pulled up another gentle hill, and then they were descending again, and suddenly the Solent was hidden from view by a high stone wall over which hung the boughs of ancient oaks. There was a shallow river valley ahead, choked green with trees, but before they reached it, some great wrought-iron gates appeared on the right and the chaise swung toward them. The lodgekeeper was alert, swinging them open for the carriage to pass through. Recognizing Kit inside, he quickly doffed his hat. The carriage drove on, moving smartly along a fine avenue of the great oaks that seemed to proliferate all around.

The breeze rustled the leaves, and through the trees Louisa could see a small herd of deer bounding away, startled by the chaise. Suddenly the avenue ended and the drive emerged into an open park set on a southwest slope, and at the head of this park, against a background of trees, was Highclare itself. It was a beautiful red brick house with a Doric colonnade and stone facings, and it presided over a wide terrace reached by a double flight of steps from the end of the drive. The dormer windows of the third floor were housed in a fine hipped roof that boasted a promenade, and in the center of it there was an octagonal cupola containing a gazebo where supper parties could be held on fine summer evenings. The house commanded incomparable views over the island and the sea, and particularly over the park, which stretched westward for about half a mile, terminating at low cliffs above a rocky private beach. Out on the Solent, Louisa could see the little fishing fleet she'd noticed from the deck of the *Spindrift*, and on the mainland opposite lay the ancient town of Lymington, its houses very sharp and bright against the endless green of the New Forest.

The chaise drew to a halt at the foot of the terrace steps, and Kit alighted, pausing for a moment to look up at the house before turning to assist Louisa and then Pattie down. Then he drew Louisa a little aside.

"I know we have differences, Louisa, but before we go into the house, can I beg you to set those differences aside for my grandfather's sake? He's old and frail, and it won't do him any good to see us continually at odds."

"You wrong me considerably if you think I'd conduct myself poorly in front of him," she replied a little stiffly.

"Do I? My short acquaintance with you has left me in no doubt that when the circumstances dictate, you will conduct yourself how you please. My grandfather means a great deal to me, and I want him to be content that ours is a happy marriage."

"How will you do that when you leave me behind while you go to Cowes? And how long will it be before servants' tittle-tattle reaches him about our separate nights? I fail to see how he will be convinced for long."

"You may leave all that to me, Louisa, for all I'm

asking of you is some semblance of warmth in our dealings with each other when he's present.'' He smiled a little cynically. ''Perhaps you'll find it easier if you can put it down to my reverence for double standards.''

''I already had,'' she replied flatly.

''No doubt. Well? Will you do as I ask?''

''Will I be your perfect wife?''

''Yes. To my perfect husband, of course.''

''Of course. Very well, you have my promise.''

''Thank you.'' Something seemed to suddenly catch his eye at an upper window of the house. Louisa had her back toward it and so didn't see the earl watching them. Kit looked quickly at her. ''You've given your word,'' he said softly, ''so let us seal it with a kiss.''

Before she knew what was happening, he'd drawn her close, enfolding her in his arms in an embrace that to any onlooker must have appeared very loving and tender. He kissed her on the lips, taking his time, his mouth moving slowly over hers.

It was a practiced kiss, the art of a man who'd made love to many women and knew how to please and arouse. She knew this, and she didn't want to surrender to her treacherous senses, but they were betraying her with each passing second. The fire was beginning to flare through her veins again, just as it had in the chapel, and she felt as if her body was melting with the heat. An enervating desire burned voluptuously within her, robbing her of the will to resist. She just wanted to surrender to him, to submit her soul and give herself up to the passion that he alone had ever stirred. But he was using her! The cold touch of reality made desire recoil, and with a huge effort she dragged her lips away from his.

He still held her close, his eyes very dark and blue as they looked into hers. It was so good to hold her, false as she was. She was made to be held and kissed, to be made love to. But he wasn't the first to think this; Geoffrey Lawrence had thought it before him. Jealousy and resentment flooded through him once more, and he slowly released her. For the moment, however, all must seem well. He glanced up at the window again, but his grandfather had gone. He met her eyes. "A promise sealed with a kiss, Louisa," he said softly, offering her his arm.

They proceeded up to the terrace. Orange and lemon trees in large terra-cotta pots had been placed along the stone balustrade, and their dark-green, shiny leaves shivered in the breeze sweeping up from the Solent. The cries of sea gulls echoed from the beach, the sound suddenly drowned by the excited baying of two large liver-and-white pointers that bounded out of the main door of the house as the butler opened it. They loped delightedly toward Kit, and the butler tried in vain to call them back.

"Hengist! Horsa!"

They ignored him, leaping up to try to lick Kit's face. He paused to fuss them for a moment and then ordered them sternly to heel as he and Louisa once again proceeded toward the door, with Pattie now keeping a very wary distance because of the dogs.

The butler bowed. "Welcome home again, Master Kit," he said warmly, but then his smile became uncertain as he looked at Louisa. "Welcome to High-clare, my lady," he murmured respectfully.

She wondered how the news of Kit's astonishing match had been received, but she smiled. "Thank you. I'm afraid I don't know your name."

"Newton, my lady."

"Thank you, Newton."

A moment later she'd crossed the threshold of Highclare for the first time. She found herself in a gracious gray-and-white entrance hall where a double white marble staircase rose immediately on either side of the door, leading up to a magnificent gallery landing on the floor above. The pedimented door of what she was to discover was the great parlor was directly opposite the main entrance, and on the floor above, in perfect symmetry, was the door of the dining chamber. Lesser doors opened off the hall and landing, but it was to these two principal portals that her eyes were immediately drawn.

The pointers' paws pattered on the gleaming floor as they danced around Kit, still trying to win his attention. He removed his hat and gloves and handed them to the butler. "I take it from your greeting that news of my marriage has reached here."

"Indeed it has, Master Kit. One of the underfootmen was sent to Cowes yesterday to collect a delivery of the earl's Stilton cheese from the Southampton packet, and the whole town was talking about it. May I be so bold as to offer you my sincere congratulations?"

"Thank you."

She smiled again. "Thank you, Newton." Inside, she wondered what the man was really thinking, for he undoubtedly knew from the gossip that until recently she'd only been a governess, and so he was probably finding it very difficult indeed to be completely respectful.

Kit glanced up the stairs. "When we arrived I noticed my grandfather in the gun-room window. Is he still there?"

"Yes, sir."

She lowered her glance. So that was the reason for the sudden kiss.

Kit turned to the butler once more. "I presume my grandfather has made arrangements for us?"

"Indeed so, Master Kit. He gave orders that the adjoining Venetian suites were to be aired."

"Newton, will you have a cold luncheon prepared for us, it's some time since we breakfasted."

"Certainly, Master Kit." The butler bowed and then hurried away in the direction of the kitchens, which evidently lay beyond a door on the left hand side of the hall.

Kit turned to Louisa. "Shall we go up?"

She drew a long, nervous breath. "Yes."

"It will be all right, I promise you; my grandfather isn't an ogre."

"Maybe not, but I still can't help wondering how he's taken the news about me."

"He'll be happy for us." Suddenly he took her hand, drawing it to his lips and at the last moment turning it palm uppermost.

She was startled at the unexpected intimacy, instinctively going to snatch her hand away, but his fingers tightened and he looked quickly into her eyes. "Remember your promise, Louisa," he said, his voice was low and soft that only she could possibly hear. "Houses like this have ears, there are servants everywhere, and as you said yourself a moment ago, servants whisper."

"I know, it's just that I wasn't expecting you to—"

"Show such apparent tenderness?"

"Yes."

"Then you must expect it from now on, for in this house I am your perfect husband, remember?" Slowly he released her hand.

They began to ascend the staircase, and her heart-beats quickened. In a moment or so she'd be meeting the Earl of Redway. Would he really be glad about his grandson's marriage? Or would he, like the rest of society, really think of it as a misalliance?

The gun room lay on the western side of the house, its windows gazing out over the Solent toward Lymington. It had oak-paneled walls hung with a magnificent display of swords, cutlasses, sabers, rapiers, and fencing foils, as well as pistols, blunderbusses, muskets, carbines, flintlocks, and matchlocks. It reminded her poignantly of another such room, at Cherington Court, and a collection that had had to be dispersed to help settle Tom's debts.

More weapons lay on a large oval table, having been removed from their places on the walls, and Kit's grand-father was standing by the table, lovingly polishing a pistol with a soft cloth. He was a slightly built man of a little less than medium height, with stooping shoulders and thinning gray hair that he wore long and tied back with a black velvet ribbon. He evidently favored clothes that were comfortable rather than fashionable, for his coat was loose and had seen a number of summers, and his breeches were of an easy fit. He put the pistol down the moment they entered, his quick glance moving over Louisa. His eyes were as blue and piercing as Kit's.

After a barely perceptible hesitation, he came toward them, smiling. "Kit, m'boy, I can't tell you how glad I am to see you again, and under such auspicious circumstances. Congratulations, my dear fellow, congratulations." He seized Kit's hand, pumping it up and down with a force surprising for one of such delicate appearance.

Kit turned to draw Louisa forward. "Grandfather, may I present my wife, Louisa."

The earl looked at her. "Welcome to Highclare, my dear. I trust that you will find only happiness here." He came to kiss her on the cheek, and she was relieved to sense the genuine warmth in the gesture.

"Thank you, sir."

"I confess I didn't think this wretch of a boy was ever going to do his family duty, but in marrying you he's more than done that, for he's also managed to please me immensely. You're very beautiful, my dear, and you'll be an adornment to the family and to this house."

She flushed a little, lowering her eyes, for how could he really be so pleased when all society was talking about her past?

He put a hand to her chin, making her look at him. "I mean every word, Louisa, for it doesn't matter to me that recent years have been less than kind to you. I'm only concerned that you and Kit are happy, and from what I witnessed from the window when you arrived, I know that that is indeed so." He patted her hand. "I'm truly sorry about your brother, my dear. That insect Rowe should be hung for his crimes, as I think most honorable men would agree, but for you the past must be the past, because from now on you're going to know only joy.''

His kindness made her feel guilty, and she glanced at Kit.

The earl smiled again. ''It occurs to me that your first day at Highclare should be marked in some way, and so I think I'll have Newton make arrangements for us to dine on the roof this evening. It's a particular treat I like to keep for very special occasions, and what could be more special than this?'' He glanced at Kit then. ''By the way, it's come to my notice that there's to be a grand ball in a few days' time. Did you know?''

''Yes, we encountered Alistair Glenfarrick in Southampton.''

''That mischievous popinjay? Well, there's nothing that passes him by, so he'll have told you all about it. It goes without saying that I won't be attending, but I'm glad to think that Highclare will be represented by both a Lord *and* Lady Highclare.''

''I'm afraid it won't,'' said Kit quickly, ''because Louisa and I have decided not to attend. Haven't we dear?'' He glanced directly at her.

Until that moment she hadn't really believed he would carry out his threat, but now she had to face the fact that he'd meant every word he said about keeping her away from anyone who mightly conceivably cause her to speak her mind.

''Louisa?'' He was still looking at her.

She met his gaze unwillingly. ''Yes, that is what we've decided.''

The earl didn't seem unduly concerned. ''Oh, well, I don't suppose it's all that vital. Besides, newlyweds are expected to spend all their time together on their own, are they not? And where better to do that than here at Highclare?'' He smiled at them both. ''I can't tell you how happy all this has made me, and now I offer no excuse for saying that I look forward to the next happy event, the announcement that I am to become a great-grandfather.''

Louisa felt utterly dreadful, but Kit seemed equal to the moment. He smiled at her, cupping her face in his hands and kissing her on the lips. ''That will indeed be a happy announcement,'' he murmured.

24

As that first day at Highclare drew toward a close, they dined on the roof as the earl had promised. The gazebo beneath the cupola was light and airy, exquisitely decorated with pale-green Chinese silk and comfortable chairs, and had a circular mahogany table of particular elegance. The large French windows stood open onto the roof promenade, and a light evening breeze played over the small dinner party as they lingered in the fading light. Fruit and liqueurs were on the table, and Newton had just withdrawn after lighting the candles. The new flames shivered a little, moving shadows over the delicate silk on the walls, and the wisps of pale smoke were carried away, threading until they became invisible. Beyond the house the summer day had almost closed, and the setting sun was a stain of dull crimson on the skyline. The Solent gleamed like soft gray satin.

Louisa wore the lilac silk and plowman's gauze evening gown she'd had on at the opera house, and there were pearls from the Highclare collection in her hair. There were more pearls at her throat, and over her arms she had a lacy shawl, its ends knotted to hang heavily to the floor.

Next to her the earl was very stylish in a black coat and white waistcoat, a voluminous neckcloth at his throat, and a black velvet ribbon tied in a precise knot to hold back his hair. Kit sat opposite, his fair hair shining in the candlelight, and he was putting himself out to be amusing. He was describing the performance of *Così Fan Tutte*, and he was doing so with such wit and humor that Louisa could again see quite clearly the scene in the opera house that night. She watched him as he lounged easily in his chair. How attractive he was, and how devastatingly charming when he chose to put himself out; surely there wasn't another man in the world to compare with him. How she wished their marriage was founded on more than mere duty.

The conversation drifted on for a little longer, and the sun had almost completely set when the earl put down his glass and looked apologetically at her. "I'm afraid it's time for me to toddle off to my bed. The state of my health has long dictated early retiring and early rising, and I do hope you won't be offended if I leave you on this, your first night here."

She smiled quickly. "No, of course not."

"Bless you. Besides, I've no doubt that you and Kit will prefer to be on your own." He got up, drawing her hand to his lips.

Kit escorted him to the staircase that descended into the house, and then returned. She'd left the table and was standing out on the roof, by the stone balustrade edging the promenade area. The park was shadowy far below, and the Solent was visible only as a faint silvery gleam to the north and west. The breeze toyed with the gauze on her gown, and she drew her shawl a little closer, turning as she heard Kit approaching.

"I wish we weren't deceiving your grandfather."

"Are we deceiving him?"

"You know we are." She searched his face in the darkness. "Why can't you be honest, Kit? You haven't any intention of really making me your wife, because you've realized that I'm not the milksop creature you originally believed I was. I also think that now you've seen Lady Rowe again, you're glad your anger with me has kept us apart, because now you have that most perfect of situations: a marriage that apparently satisfies your grandfather's desire to see you honoring your family duty, but that in fact is conveniently open so that, should Lady Rowe choose to come to you, after all, you'll be able to set me aside. You're using me, Kit, and you're also using my so-called indiscretions with Geoffrey Lawrence as an excuse to justify your own despicable conduct.''

For a long moment he met her accusing gaze. ''Think that if you wish, Louisa; it's your prerogative.''

Her chin rose defiantly. ''Don't let me keep you, sir, for no doubt her ladyship is waiting for you even now. I trust that you'll able to make your peace with her and that she's more trusting than you, for to be sure she'll have a lot to swallow when you promise her faithfully that you haven't consummated your shocking misalliance with Tom Cherington's unlikely sister.''

Anger flashed into his eyes and abruptly he went back into the gazebo, extinguishing the candles. Then he turned to face her again. ''You're right, madam: she *is* waiting for me and I see no reason why I should dally pointlessly here with you when I could be with her.''

Without another word, she walked past him toward the staircase. There were tears in her eyes, but he didn't see them. She'd provoked the argument without really knowing why—she just hadn't been able to help herself—and now her worst fears were being realized: he was going to his beloved Thea.

The villa Rowe had had built some five years before stood in a leafy lane on the hillside overlooking Cowes. Small and elegant, it was set in beautiful gardens and was protected from the lane by a high wall and a screen of evergreen trees. It was approached through wrought-iron gates beside a little lodge, and this lodge was in darkness as Kit rode quietly along the lane. The absence of lights indicated that the lodgekeeper's duties were at an end for the night, which could only mean that Thea had retired to her bed.

He rode past the lodge to where the wall veered away from the lane toward a thicket, then he dismounted and led the horse into the bushes where it wouldn't be seen. He'd left it there many times in the past, gaining access to the villa grounds by climbing the huge oak tree next to the wall. As he tethered the horse, he paused. If he proceeded now, he'd be picking up the threads with Thea again. For a long moment he hesitated, then he went toward the oak tree.

There wasn't a sound from the villa as he dropped down into the gardens. Open lawns stretched toward the house, where there weren't any lights to be seen. Thea's rooms opened on to an elegant balcony on the first floor and could be reached by climbing another tree, this time a mulberry growing against the house. He moved silently, slipping across the lawns and swinging himself up into the mulberry's branches with only the minimum of sound.

The French windows were open, they always were when she was expecting him. He stepped into the dark room beyond. It was an elegant, feminine chamber, furnished in the Oriental style, with pale-blue hand-painted silk on the walls and an immense four-poster bed draped extravagantly with the same costly material. He expected to see Thea lying there, but the bed was empty, the coverlet hadn't even been turned back.

Her absence took him by surprise, for he'd been so certain she'd be there, but then she spoke behind him and he turned sharply to see her sitting in a chair by the fireplace.

"I'm amazed you've come here, sir," she said, "for I imagined your new bride would occupy you on your first night on the island." She rose to her feet, her magnificent figure outlined very clearly, even in the darkness, by the low-cut, flimsy muslin robe she wore. Her hair was very golden, and a slight smile curved her lovely lips, for she was triumphant that he'd so swiftly deserted Louisa. "Why did you marry her, Kit? I'm all curiosity to know. Was it to spite me?"

"Hardly."

"Then why take such a vapid little nonentity as your bride?"

"Louisa isn't vapid and she certainly isn't a nonentity."

It wasn't a reply she cared for, and she turned petulantly away. "You'll be telling me next that the rumors are true and it *is* a love match."

"Does it matter what it is? After all, you refused to leave Rowe and marry me, didn't you? Or was I mistaken that night on board the *Spindrift*?" He leaned back against one of the bedposts, folding his arms as he surveyed her.

"You caught me unawares that night, Kit."

"And if you'd sensed what I was about to ask, would you have given me a different answer?"

She glanced at him. "We'll never know now, will we?" she murmured. "But you're trying to change the subject, aren't you? I asked you why you'd married the governess."

"Shall we agree not to inquire about each other's marriages, Thea?"

It was another displeasing answer. "I'll warrant you'd prefer not to answer my questions, for no doubt you've very swiftly realized how much a fool she's made of you."

"What makes you say that?"

"Oh, the usual malicious chitter-chatter, but from an unexpectedly trustworthy source."

"And what source might that be?"

"Rowe."

He gave a short laugh. "Since when has *he* been trustworthy?"

"Oh, I admit that he has his faults and that the thought of his arrival in Cowes tomorrow doesn't fill me with joy, but one of those faults doesn't happen to be indulgence in idle gossip. That's why I place great trust in what he tells me in the letter I received today." She glanced away, suddenly thoughtful. "It was an odd letter, actually, too loving by far. Rowe never writes loving letters; he sends curt notes."

"You were telling me what he said about Louisa," he prompted.

"You already know that he and Captain Geoffrey Lawrence have become friendly, but I wonder if you know that the handsome captain has been regaling him with salacious tales of the goings-on at Lawrence Park? You've married a strumpet, Kit, a fortune-seeker for whom discretion appears to be an unknown quality. If you wish to be sure your heirs really are your heirs, I strongly suggest you lock her up, because Lawrence is accompanying Rowe to Cowes, and I rather gather that what the good captain enjoyed once before, he fully intends to enjoy again."

"You aren't telling me anything I don't already know, Thea."

She was startled. "You—you know?"

"Yes, and I don't intend to discuss it—not with you or with anyone else. You forfeited any right to that side of my life when you turned me down."

"Then why have you come here tonight? If part of your life is now closed to me, why bother to come and see me like this?"

"Because I thought I owed you at least that."

The triumph she'd felt because he'd deserted Louisa on his first night back began to suddenly fade. She was no longer as sure of him as she had been when he'd entered. Something in him had changed since that night on the *Spindrift*, and now she bitterly regretted turning him down. If only she'd accepted and flown in the face of scandal, for by now the worst of the uproar would be over and she'd be anticipating divorce from Rowe and a future with this man she now wanted so very much. She wanted him now, and intended to do all in her power to win him back.

Quickly she went to him, linking her slender arms around his neck and drawing his mouth down to hers. She pressed against him, exercising all her many wiles, and she felt his arms begin to move to hold her close.

But as he did so, he suddenly saw Louisa, her lips

parted with desire as she reached up to kiss Geoffrey Lawrence. The vision was so sharp and clear that he drew back abruptly.

Thea still clung to him. "Love me, Kit," she whispered urgently, "love me now." She kissed him again. She wouldn't give him up to a creature like Louisa Cherington. She wouldn't.

Before dawn a mist rose over the Solent, and the *Cyclops* was forced to lie at anchor in Cowes Roads, waiting for it to clear. A lookout kept watch on deck, but the rest of the crew was asleep. Down in the cabin, Rowe and Geoffrey had been up all night, and now two empty decanters of cognac stood on the table. Geoffrey was sprawled drunkenly on the only chair, while a much more sober Rowe lay on the narrow bunk, nursing his throbbing arm. Each day the pain seemed to worsen, and now was so bad that his physician had strongly advised against leaving London and had certainly instructed him not to take part in anything as strenuous as sailing; but William, Lord Rowe, wasn't a man to bow to the advice of others, especially not when a burning thirst for revenge had to be slaked. Thea had to be brought to account for her infidelity, and Kit had to pay very dearly indeed for what he'd done. Rowe's eyes glittered coldly as he lay on the bunk, and he was still icily clearheaded in spite of the amount of cognac he'd consumed.

Geoffrey, however, was very much the worse for wear, leaning unsteadily forward to pick up an empty decanter and shake it in a disgruntled way before attempting to put it back. He couldn't balance it and so it fell over, rocking to and fro on the table to the gentle motion of the cutter.

Rowe's attention was drawn to him. "God damn it, man! I thought you could hold your drink better than this."

"Nothing wrong with me." But Geoffrey's voice was thick and slurred.

Rowe drew an irritated breath and said nothing more.

Geoffrey looked accusingly at him. "Why'd you tell your wife my plans for the governess, eh? Why'd you tell her?"

"To gall Highclare, of course. Thea's bound to mention it—she's too much of a cat not to—and she'll have been roused to a fury by his marriage."

"But he knows now," protested Geoffrey.

"He knew already, you fool. He'd warned you off at the opera house, remember? Letting him know through Thea won't make any difference, except that it'll get under his skin." Rowe studied Geoffrey for a moment. "I trust you're still of a mind to possess the lady."

"Yes."

"Good, because I'd hate her to escape. All three of them must suffer for their actions."

"Four."

"Four? What do you mean?"

"My dear stepmama." Geoffrey raised his empty glass in mocking toast.

Rowe sighed irritatedly. Lady Lawrence wasn't of any interest to him, she could go to perdition for all he cared.

Geoffrey despised her, though, and meant to have his full revenge for the business of the locket, which he now firmly believed to have been her work. He'd already put his reprisal into effect. "She'll be rueing it by now, I promise you," he said with a satisfied, lopsided grin.

"Why do you say that?"

"Because I've spiked her guns for her. She can't do as she pleases and get away with it, not when she tries it with me. The atmosphere'll be frosty at the parental home, frosty as hell."

"A contradiction in terms, if ever I heard one."

Geoffrey shrugged.

Rowe got up, wincing as a searing pain lanced through his arm. God damn Cherington! Going to the stern window, he gazed through the mist toward the island. Was Thea lying in Highclare's arms right now?

A nerve twitched at his temple. His glance was drawn toward a shadowy shape that was just visible through the gray haze. It was another yacht, and from her outline he knew her to be Lord Grantham's *Eleanor*, the cutter that would be taking on the *Spindrift* later that very day. Rowe stared at the other vessel, his cold eyes narrowing as a thought suddenly occurred to him. Slowly he smiled.

Geoffrey saw. "What are you smiling about?"

"I believe I've just thought of a way of trapping Highclare into the very corner I seek."

"Corner?"

Rowe gave a low, chilling laugh. "I trust the governess has brought her funeral weeds with her, for she's very shortly going to be a widow. Very shortly indeed."

25

The sun broke through after daybreak, dispersing the mist and giving the promise of yet another beautiful day. Louisa slept late, weary after the previous days' travel, and weary too after crying herself to sleep in the small hours; but before falling asleep, she'd come to a very important decision: she was going to fight for Kit and not surrender to Thea.

The Venetian apartments at Highclare were aptly named, for everything in them had once adorned a *palazzo* on the Grand Canal itself. The doors were inlaid with ebony and ivory, and the columns were made of jasper. There was rich decoration everywhere, not a single surface left plain, and the walls sported subtle rococo designs of long twining stems and flowers in aquamarine and beige. The ceilings were gorgeously painted, and from them hung elaborate chandeliers fashioned from wood and gilded copper, their stems curling into little rosettes, their candleholders fashioned like crowns. The furniture was all of the distinctive Venetian style, lacquered and delicate, but in oddly bulging shapes. The chairs, cupboards and tables were finished in mock-Chinese work in deep-green and gold, and the bed where Louisa lay was particularly rich and ornate, with complicated hangings of the finest damask.

Kit sat on the window seat. The window was slightly open, allowing in the sounds of the sea gulls screeching over the private beach a short way off. He wore a maroon dressing gown over a shirt and beige trousers, and he looked for all the world as if he'd spent the night with his new bride and had risen a short while before without disturbing her. He leaned his head back against the window embrasure, gazing not at the sunlit park outside, but at his wife as she slept. He wished he *had* spent the night with her; he wished so much where she was concerned, but it was not to be. She was so very lovely as she lay there, and in slumber looked so innocent. But she wasn't innocent at all.

The sea gulls screeched again and she began to stir, turning her head so that her dark-red hair caught against the lace on her pillow. Her gray eyes flickered and opened, widening suddenly as she saw him in the window. She sat up quickly, her hair tumbling down over the shoulders of her nightgown.

"Don't look so alarmed," he said dryly. "I'm not about to demand my conjugal rights, I'm merely placing myself where a bridegroom would be expected to be at this hour. When Pattie brings the morning tea shortly, she'll find what she should find: the happy couple enjoying each other's company."

"I admire your attention to detail."

"I said that you could safely leave such matters to me." He rose from the window and went closer to the bed. He couldn't help thinking how attractive she was, her mane of dark-red hair falling unchecked, the flush of sleep warm on her cheeks. "I trust you slept well?"

"Better than you, I'll warrant," she replied.

"Facetiousness isn't very becoming at any time, but least of all at this ungodly hour."

"I was merely drawing a natural conclusion."

"Really?" He studied her for a moment, remembering the manner in which she'd suddenly entered his thoughts the night before. The memory made him even cooler. "Draw what conclusion you wish, it's immaterial to me. I only hope you'll continue to remember your promise concerning my grandfather, for I intend to leave for Cowes within the hour because of the race, and I still have no intention of taking you with me. I trust, too, that you'll be able to amuse yourself during my absence.''

"I'm sure I will, sir, for thankfully I've yet to become reliant on your company.'' She didn't want it to be like this, but somehow there didn't seem to be anything she could do to change things. Each time they came face to face, the sparks flew. Why, oh, why couldn't they go back to the way it was before the locket had spoiled everything? She lowered her eyes. Last night she'd sworn to fight to win him, but how could she when things were always like this? Maybe it was hopeless, but she had to try.

He came to the bedside, leaning a hand on one of the posts to look down at her. "Louisa, I really don't want us to quarrel like this . . .''

Neither of them had heard Pattie's discreet knock at the door, so when she came in, she saw Kit leaning over his wife in what appeared to be a very fond manner.

The moment he realized the maid was there, his reaction was swift. Mindful of the need to give the right impression, especially with Pattie, who'd witnessed so many arguments and so could be relied upon to relate to the rest of the servants the glad tidings of the newly-weds' reunion, he bent quickly to kiss a startled Louisa full on the lips, putting his hand to the nape of her neck, his fingers curling in her warm hair. It felt so right to kiss her, and yet everything about her had been wrong from the very beginning.

Following so swiftly on her resolution to fight for him if she could, she was for once equal to the moment, startling him in turn by slipping her arms around his neck and returning the kiss. She gave herself to the embrace, her lips moving warmly and luxuriously beneath his as she took full advantage of the situation. It was sweet to hold him, and in spite of her actions being calculated, she was still aware of her responding senses. As she eventually drew back, she didn't have to try to make her voice sound husky, for it was anyway.

"I—I shall miss being with you today, my darling,''

she said softly, tracing the outline of his lips with her fingertip, "but I do understand that a yacht race isn't suitable for a lady and that my presence would only distract."

He'd been caught so off guard that for a moment he was rendered speechless. Surprise lingered in his blue eyes at first as he straightened, but then it was replaced by suspicion. Where had she learned such amatory skills if not in Lawrence's knowing arms?

She sensed his reaction and was filled with hurt dismay, but still she smiled. "Good luck in the race. I'm sure you'll win."

"I'm sure I will too, especially with your blessing behind me," he murmured.

"You have more than my blessing; you have my love." Oh, how true, if only he knew.

He glanced at Pattie, who'd put the tray down and was preparing to pour the tea. "Not for me, if you please. I'm about to get ready to go to Cowes."

"Very well, my lord." The maid bobbed a curtsy.

He turned toward Louisa again, lowering his voice so that the maid couldn't possibly hear. "I'm sorry to leave you like this, but you really give me no choice."

She met his gaze. "And you give me none, Kit."

For a moment he continued to look into her eyes, then suddenly he took her hand and raised it to his lips. "I will see you tonight," he said.

Her fingers tightened momentarily over his. "I meant it about the race. I wish you all the luck in the world."

He smiled. "Thank you." Then he was gone, closing the door softly behind him.

She lowered her eyes. Her lips were still tingling from the pleasure of kissing him. Had she played her cards wisely? It was said that a wife held all the trumps when it came to fighting off a challenge from another woman. Well, if that was so, then Lady Highclare was going to have to become a very canny cardplayer, for Thea, Lady Rowe, wasn't just any other woman, she was *the* other woman, the great love of Kit's life.

Pattie brought her a cup of tea. "What clothes would you like me to set out for you, my lady?"

"The yellow-and-white-checkered lawn, I think."

"Yes, my lady." The maid hesitated, smiling shyly. "My lady . . . ?"

"Yes?"

"I hope you don't mind me saying, but I'm so very glad that you and his lordship have made it up. I'm so happy for you."

Louisa managed a weak smile.

Kit had left for Cowes when she went down to take breakfast with the earl in the small east-facing breakfast room on the ground floor. There was gray-and-white floral paper on the walls, an oval table covered with a crisp white cloth, elegant chairs with gray velvet seats, and a sideboard laden with the earl's surprisingly robust choice of breakfast dishes, from beefsteak pie and York ham, to deviled kidneys, scrambled eggs, and one of the Stilton cheeses brought by the Southampton packet. The smell of fresh-baked bread hung in the air from the dish of warm rolls in the center of the table.

Sunlight streamed in through the window, and Hengist and Horsa were sprawled sleepily in a patch of brightness on the carpet. They stirred and got up, tails wagging, as she entered, her primrose-and-white-checkered morning gown bright in the sun.

The earl had been reading his newspaper, but he immediately set it aside, getting to his feet and coming toward her. He wore a floor-length powder-blue dressing gown, and there as a tasseled cap on his head. He kissed her on the cheek and then drew out a chair for her. "Good morning, my dear. I'm so glad you've decided to stay here today, for I'll have you to myself."

"Good morning, sir."

"Louisa, you're part of the family now, so I wish you would call me grandfather. Shall we begin again? Good morning, my dear."

She smiled, liking him more each time she was with him. "Good morning, Grandfather."

"That's better. Now, then, what would you like to eat? Some beefsteak pie? It's very good."

"I'm afraid I couldn't possibly manage pie for breakfast, but a little scrambled egg would be very nice." She felt uncomfortable as he went to the sideboard to serve her. "I'm sure it's not right that you should be waiting on me."

"Nonsense. I've dreamed for so long about having Kit's wife to dance attendance upon that I'm positively wallowing." He spooned a very large helping of the eggs onto a plate and put it before her. Then he poured her some coffee from the extremely elegant silver pot before resuming his seat. "Kit was very sorry to leave you behind this morning."

"I—I'm sure he'll feel free to concentrate more on the race if I'm not there."

"No doubt you're right. I wish he wasn't quite so keen on racing the *Spindrift*, for it can be a very dangerous activity, as the loss of the *Mercury* bears full testimony." He was silent for a moment, glancing at her. "My dear, are you really sure you wish to forgo the grand ball?"

She couldn't help the slightly guilty color that entered her cheeks. "Yes, quite sure." The reply lacked all conviction, and she knew it.

"I know how possessive new bridegrooms can be, especially if their brides are as pretty as you, and I doubt if Kit is any different. He wants to keep you all to himself and thus deny others the opportunity of dancing with you, but understandable as his attitude may be, it's still no reason for making you stay away if you really wish to go."

She felt very awkward and gave him a weak smile. "I—I really don't want to go."

"Well, if you change your mind and feel you'd really like to go, after all, just let me know. I'll tell Kit that *I* insist on you both going, and then he can grumble at me but will not blame you." He smiled. "Now, then, what would you like to do this morning?"

"I thought I might take a ride, if that's all right."

"All right? My dear, this house is your house, you're at liberty to do as you please. Of course you may ride. I'd come with you were it not that my riding days are long since over. But you shall not go entirely alone, I'll send Hengist and Horsa with you, they'll protect you."

Hearing their names, the dogs padded over to him, resting their heads on his lap while he stroked them.

An hour later, accompanied by the hounds and with the sun high in the sky, she rode down through the park, her mustard-yellow riding habit—once destined for the Countess of Effingham—a bright splash of color against the fresh green all around her.

She rode toward the cliffs above the private beach, reining in for a moment to look down at the waves breaking on the rocks and shingle. The taste of salt was on her lips, and the breeze fluttered the little plumes springing from her beaver hat. Hengist and Horsa waited beside her.

Something, she didn't know what, made her look toward the wooded river valley to the south of the park. For the briefest of seconds she thought she saw a man on a large chestnut horse but then he'd gone, melting so quickly back into the trees that she thought she must have imagined him.

She didn't give him any more thought, remaining on the cliffs for a little longer before turning her horse southward and cantering toward the woods, Hengist and Horsa loping beside her. She little realized the danger that lay ahead as she rode innocently into the cool shade of the trees.

26

As Louisa rode slowly through the woods at Highclare, the Rowe landau was driving smartly out of the villa gates and down the lane toward Cowes, conveying Lord and Lady Rowe to watch the race.

Thea wore a matching pelisse and gown of salmon-pink sprigged muslin, but although the color was cheerful, her face was pale and anxious behind the veil attached to her little hat. A gaily fringed pagoda parasol was held stiffly above her head, and her whole figure was tense. On his return, Rowe had immediately made it plain that he knew all about her infidelity with Kit and was going to punish her severely. Without warning, her position was as precarious as Louisa's had so recently been, and the specter of ruin was staring her in the face.

Rowe had threatened her with divorce, but for the moment it was a suspended sentence, held over her like the sword of Damocles. Immediately after the regatta she was to be banished to his remote estate in Scotland, a place far removed from any social life, and she was to remain there for an unspecified time to dwell upon the awfulness of her fate should he finally decide to publicly cast her off. It was a dreadful prospect for one who'd always reveled in the luxury and excitement of high society, and for Thea it was a particularly ironic sentence, for too late she was conscious of what she'd willfully thrown away when she turned Kit down. Now the scandal and downfall she'd dreaded so much then were looming ominously before her anyway, and without the prospect of riding out the storm with Kit at her side, for Louisa Cherington was his wife now, a fact upon which Rowe did not hesitate to cruelly play. It gave him savage satisfaction to see how afraid she was of his vengeance, and how bitter at her lover's unexpected marriage. It also gave him pleasure to see how desperate she'd been when first he'd faced her with her unfaithfulness. She'd wept and begged him to forgive her, promising him eternal fidelity from now on, but he'd laughed coldly in her face, telling her that her fate would remain in the balance until he saw fit to decide.

The first houses of the town appeared ahead, and Thea gazed blindly at them, the parasol now twisting with a bravado she didn't feel. Fleetingly her thoughts turned from herself to Kit. She knew that Rowe had something dreadful planned for the man who'd dared to make love to her, and that whatever it was was timed to take place very soon, but that was all she knew. She trembled inside, but already Kit had faded from her mind as she thought anew of her new future.

Rowe sat beside her, his face cold and set. His dark-green coat had been placed carefully around his shoulders, because his arm now hurt too much to put it on properly. His legs, encased in cream cord trousers, were stretched out on the seat opposite, and the tassels on his Hessian boots swung to and fro to the motion of the carriage. He'd pulled his top hat forward on his head, so that his face was in shadow, but the thin line of his mouth and the grim set of his jaw were only too plain to see. A pale light shone in his eyes as he contemplated the imminent extinction of Christopher, Lord Highclare; if all went as planned, within twenty-four hours his hated rival would be no more. It had to be twenty-four hours, his own weak physical condition dictated the timing. He needed a day to recover his strength after the rigors of sailing from London. A plague on Tom Cherington's soul, for it was his fault that Highclare's consignment to perdition must be put off for another day. The *Spindrift* and her accursed master had to be allowed a stay of execution before they met the same end as the *Mercury* and the *Eleanor*. He smiled as he thought of the *Eleanor*, for Grantham's prized yacht was now at the bottom of Cowes Roads, having met with a strange accident in the misty dawn, and so the long-anticipated race would have to be abandoned. But the racing fraternity wouldn't be denied a race, for the *Spindrift* was about to acquire a new challenger, one much more lethal than the *Eleanor*—the *Cyclops*.

The landau rattled down through the streets of Cowes, emerging at last onto the quay. The cobbled area was crowded, for every fashionable soul on the island had gathered for the race preparations. The Duke of Gloucester and Princess Sophia had deigned to put in an appearance before being taken out to their corvette, and were seated in an open carriage outside the Mermaid Inn, sipping the hostelry's very finest coffee, brought deferentially out to them by the landlord himself.

Thea looked at the crowd and then glanced to where the two yachts should have been moored. The *Spindrift* was in her accustomed place, but of the *Eleanor* there wasn't a sign. Thea's brows drew together in puzzlement.

Rowe's coachman had instructions to drive as close to the *Spindrift* as possible, and as he slowly maneuvered the restive team through the crowd, snatches of very strange conversation carried to Thea.

"Damned peculiar show, eh?" one gentleman was saying. "The whole damned Solent to choose from, and the damned wherryman has to barge into the *Eleanor*!"

"She went down without a murmur, just her buoy left to show where she'd been."

"Grantham's in a fine old stew; she cost him a small fortune."

"Sank like a stone, dear boy, but then those in the Highclare camp claim she sailed like one."

"The wherry's master looks sick, as well he might;

he's just managed to dispatch one of England's best yachts to Davy Jones' locker! The fellow swears he doesn't know how it happened; he says his vessel was made fast and couldn't have slipped her moorings like that. But it happened, we've the *Eleanor*'s empty place to prove it.''

Thea listened with growing unease, for one glance at her husband's face had been enough to tell her that he knew rather more about the mysterious loss of the *Eleanor* than anyone else on the quay. Her disquiet increased as the landau halted by the *Spindrift* and Rowe's icy gaze was directed at Kit, who was on deck talking to Charles Pelham and a very agitated Lord Grantham.

The landau had come to a halt beside the Grantham barouche and Lady Grantham leaned across immediately to speak to Thea above the general buzz of excited conversation. ''My dear, isn't it all a terrible tragedy?''

''What's happened? Is the *Eleanor* . . . ?''

''Sunk, my dear. Apparently she went down in less than a minute. A wretched wherry came adrift and collided with her.''

''Oh, dear,'' said Thea lamely, ''how dreadful.''

Lady Grantham nodded, glancing at her husband. ''Poor Thomas is quite cut up about it. He treasured that yacht, and he was so looking forward to taking Kit Highclare on. *Mais, c'est la vie, n'est-ce pas?*''

Thea gave a weak smile, glad of her veil. Her glance slid again to study her husband. He was lounging back on his seat, his good hand resting protectively over the wrist of his wounded arm, and in that split second she knew beyond a doubt that he was directly responsible for the loss of the *Eleanor*. But why had he done it? What possible purpose could such an act serve?

At that moment Charles Pelham became aware of the Rowe landau. He removed his hat and sketched a bow. Kit turned quickly, his shrewd glance taking in Thea's veil before coming to rest on Rowe's cold visage. He inclined his head briefly before returning his attention to the disconsolate Lord Grantham, who stood with his hands thrust deep into his pockets.

Rowe sat slowly forward, raising his voice so that he could be heard above the crowd. "Grantham, I gather the race is off."

"It is."

"An idiot with a wherry, I believe."

"Damn his eyes."

Rowe tilted his hat back so that the glitter in his eyes was suddenly clearly visible as he looked at Kit. "Highclare, I don't think these good people should be denied their race, so I've an interesting proposition to put to you."

The words caused an immediate hush, and Kit turned, his glance suddenly much more guarded.

Rowe gave a chill smile. "I challenge you, Highclare. I'll take you on tomorrow, when my arm has had a chance to recover a little. A race around the island, just as we did before."

"Correction, Rowe, just as *you* did before. I wasn't racing you when you managed to put the *Mercury* on those rocks, you did it all by yourself."

Rowe's eyes flickered with intense dislike. "That's your version. I prefer the truth. However, we digress. I've issued a challenge, Hichclare. Do you accept or not? I don't think you can refuse, can you? We have so much to settle."

Everyone assumed he was still referring to the *Mercury*, and perhaps to Tom Cherington's untimely death, but Kit knew better. Suddenly he understood why Thea was wearing a veil; Rowe knew about their affair.

Rowe was looking inquiringly at him. "What do you say, Highclare? Do we have a race? Or are you too craven to take me on?"

Some gasps and a quiver of anticipation rippled through the crowd, and even the duke and princess sat forward eagerly.

Faced with such a challenge, there was little Kit could

do but accept. His honor was at stake. He nodded. "We have a race, sir."

A great cheer went up, for suddenly there was the certain prospect of a race much more exciting and hazardous than the one lost forever with the *Eleanor*.

Amid the noise, Kit stepped ashore and came over to the landau. "What are you up to, Rowe?" he asked, his voice carrying to those in the carriage, but inaudible to everyone else because of the general hubbub.

Rowe was smoothly sure of himself. "Up to? I don't know what you're talking about, Highclare. I've merely done the spirited thing and challenged you to a race. Don't tell me that after accepting so very publicly, you've had second thoughts and have turned coward."

"I haven't had second thoughts, but I suggest that you do if you've any notion of trying anything underhand tomorrow."

Rowe sat back, a taut smile curving his thin lips. "Tell me, where is your charming bride?"

"I'm sure you don't really want to know."

"On the contrary, I'm very interested. You see, if she's out at Highclare, she'll be receiving a visitor. Lawrence has ridden there just to see her, and I'm sure she'll be delighted. But, then, you know all about that, don't you?" Rowe rapped his cane on the floor of the landau. "Drive on."

The landau pulled away, and Thea didn't dare look back at Kit, although she longed to. She wanted him, but she wanted her high-society life of luxury and plenty still more, and she'd do all that was necessary to keep her place at Rowe's side.

Kit remained where he was on the quay. His eyes were dark and angry. If he returned to Highclare now, would he find Louisa in Lawrence's arms?

27

As talk of the new race took over on the quay at Cowes, Louisa was still enjoying her ride at Highclare. With Hengist and Horsa still beside her, she rode slowly along the bank of the river in the wooded valley to the south of the park. Through the trees on the other side of the water, marking the boundary of Highclare, there was a high perimeter wall beyond which she couldn't see.

The river was clear, with fish darting in the sun-dappled water, and the banks were fringed with ferns that dipped so low they almost trailed in the current. There were ferns everywhere, cool and feathery beneath a canopy of oak trees, and she knew that in the spring it would be a place of bluebells. A blackbird was singing its heart out, and a kingfisher darted over the surface of the water, a vivid speck of bright blue that was gone in a moment.

Louisa gave only a little thought to the horseman she'd glimpsed earlier—if glimpse him she had—although from time to time she glanced around, wondering if maybe he'd been an estate worker, a gamekeeper perhaps.

A rustic bridge spanned the river ahead where the valley ended and the wooded land flattened, and the two pointers suddenly ran toward it, crossing over and vanishing among the oak trees on the far side. She saw them again as she reached the bridge. They were moving along a broad ride that had been cut through the trees, and at the far end of this unexpectedly open area she

saw that there were some wrought-iron gates set into the
perimeter wall. Through them she could just see a flat
expanse of marshy creek, with the Solent itself in the
distance.

Kicking her heel, she urged her mount across the
bridge toward the gates. She only meant to peep
through, thinking that such gates were bound to be kept
locked, but as she reached them, Hengist and Horsa
began to dance around excitedly, as if waiting to be let
through, and she realized that simply by sliding a bolt
across, she could open the gates and go out onto the
marsh.

As the gates swung open, the two dogs dashed out
into the wide openness beyond, immediately picking up
a scent and setting off along a narrow spit of land
between two withy-edged fingers of water creeping in
from the sea. The flocks of seabirds on the marsh were
startled by the hounds' sudden appearance, and rose as
one into the sky, filling the air with their noise.

For a moment Louisa hesitated by the gates, something again making her glance back into the woods, but
there wasn't anything to be seen, only the gentle motion
of the oak leaves as they stirred in the light breeze. She
rode out then, watching the dogs until they vanished
from sight among the withies. If she'd glanced down at
the ground, she'd have seen fresh hoofprints that
showed she hadn't been the first that morning to open
and close the gates; she'd also have seen that the other
horse had entered Highclare, not left it.

She followed a barely perceptible path that told of
firm, safe land. It led down toward a wider expanse of
creek, where an isthmus of land reached out into the
water, ending at an ancient medieval chapel by a landing
stage. The tide was in, so there weren't any disfiguring
mud banks, just the inlets of water and the reeds and
flowers of the marsh.

The seabirds continued to wheel and twist noisily in
the air. Hengist and Horsa were giving voice somewhere
in the distance, but she couldn't see them. She reached

the chapel and dismounted, tethering the horse to the tamarisks that had been planted there in times gone by as a windbreak, then she went to sit on the landing stage, to rest for a while before riding back to the house.

The marsh was colorful. Bright-yellow purslane was washed by the high tide, and blue-purple sea asters nodded in the breeze. The startled birds were beginning to settle again now, their noise dying away so that she could just hear the dogs, invisible on the marsh as they still followed the scent. She gazed at the glittering water where it lapped among the reeds, each gentle surge of the tide making a bed of pink sea lavender sway in unison.

How long she'd been sitting there she didn't know. It was all so peaceful and beautiful that she felt quite relaxed, able to think about all that had happened to her. But even as she reflected on her feelings for Kit and how she could possibly emerge victorious against a rival like Thea, the birds suddenly rose in another alarmed cloud, their wings flapping and their cries splitting the quiet. Something had frightened them again. But what? She hadn't heard Hengist or Horsa returning; indeed, they'd been silent for several minutes.

Slowly she got up. Something was wrong. Suddenly she sensed that there was someone behind her, and she turned with a sharp gasp. The horseman she'd seen earlier was by the chapel, an unpleasant smile on his lips as he savored the fact that he had her alone and trapped. It was Geoffrey Lawrence.

He dismounted, tethering his horse next to hers and then coming toward her, the braiding on his uniform gleaming in the sunlight. Halting at the beginning of the landing stage and thus blocking her escape, he sketched a mocking bow. "We meet again, Miss Cherington. Ah, forgive me, I keep forgetting that it's Lady Highclare now."

"Please leave me alone." Her heart was racing with fear.

"I'm merely passing the time of day, my lady," he replied.

"Wh-why have you come here?"

"To see you."

"I don't want to see you, sir. I don't want to have anything more to do with you. Please allow me to pass." Her riding crop clutched tightly in her hand, she went slowly toward him, her glance moving nervously toward her tethered horse. It seemed so very far away. He stood squarely in her path, and she had no hope of passing him. "Please stand aside, sir," she demanded.

"Ah, the voice of authority. My, my, so recently a mere governess, but now a lady of quality. How the pendulum doth swing."

"Please stand aside," she said again. Her fingers clenched over the riding crop, although she knew it was a very feeble weapon against a man like him. But it was all she had . . .

He toyed with her. "By all means," he murmured, pretending to stand to one side.

It was a chance she had to take. Gathering her cumbersome skirt, she made to dash by, but he seized her wrist, throwing her roughly on the springy grass just beyond the landing stage and then pinning her down bodily by flinging himself on top of her.

A cry was torn from her lips as she desperately tried to wrench herself free, but her struggles seemed to make him all the more determined—and all the more strong. With a low laugh he twisted her wrist back, forcing her to look up into his face, only inches from her own. "So, my *lady*," he breathed, "you think you'll escape from me yet again, do you?"

"Let me go!"

He shook his head, his eyes moving hotly to her bodice, where the riding habit's cloth strained tightly over her breasts as she tried to struggle. His tongue passed over his lips and he looked into her terrified eyes again. "We're at liberty to talk now, aren't we, my dear? At last there aren't any disagreeable social barriers to disturb your sense of propriety, for we're equal now, aren't we? Well, maybe one of us is more equal than the other, for to be sure you'll one day be the Countess of Redway, while I'll never amount to more than mere Sir Geoffrey, but what does that matter, mm? I've been looking forward to this, governess—I've dreamed about it night and day—and I intend to savor you to the full."

"You wouldn't dare," she cried, casting desperately around for some sign of help, but there wasn't anything, just the marsh and the disturbed birds.

"Wouldn't dare?" He laughed derisively. "My poor little fool, how little you know me."

"My husband . . ."

"Already doubts your virtue, and if you're unwise enough to say anything to him about this, he'll think his suspicions more justified. No, my dear, if you want to keep your fancy marriage, which I can see you do, you won't be saying anything about this little, er, interlude."

She could feel his breath on her face as she stared up at him. He meant to rape her! He meant to force his vile attentions on her and believed he could use her desperation to keep Kit as a means of keeping his actions secret! Tears stung her eyes, and Kit's quiet voice seemed to echo in her head: "Madam, if Lawrence had any reason to send you that locket, as far as I'm concerned you already *are* a Mrs. Siddons. I vow your act of sweet innocence was breathtakingly convincing . . ." He'd never believe she hadn't arranged to meet Geoffrey, never!

With another low laugh, he pressed down on her, grinning into her terror-stricken face. "Oh, Louisa," he breathed, "you should never have refused me, for I'm not a man to take refusal lightly. You're about to discover that, just as my dear stepmother will by now have discovered that she cannot flout my wishes and get away with it. I punish those who displease me, my dear, and sometimes—just sometimes—I punish those who please me as well. Your beauty pleases me, Louisa, you've ravished my senses since the first moment I saw you, but now I intend to gratify those senses. I'm going to take you, governess, and there's nothing you can do about it.''

He forced his mouth down on hers, ignoring the feeble flaying of her arm as she tried to beat him off with the riding crop. The blows rained uselessly upon him; he was oblivious to them all as he forced her lips apart, bruising her. She could feel his hands moving over her, sliding over her breasts. She writhed beneath him, and her struggles aroused him more and more. He ripped at the buttons of her bodice, and then his hard fingers were pressing her warm skin, seeking her breast, forcing, prying, and hurting.

She struggled all the more, and then she felt his other hand beneath her skirt, sliding up to clasp her thigh. She cried out then, suddenly finding the voice to scream. The piercing sound lanced over the marsh, echoing above the racket of the birds.

She felt his lips on her throat as his hands moved hotly all over her, and every fiber of her being recoiled in revulsion; but she was powerless and completely at his mercy. Please, don't. Please.

Suddenly Hengist and Horsa erupted from the withies, splashing through some shallow water and bounding past the frightened horses to where Louisa was struggling helplessly. Their every instinct was to protect her, and with loud bays of warning, they leapt against Geoffrey, knocking him violently aside.

She needed no second chance but scrambled away, sobbing as she ran to her horse. She fumbled desperately with the reins, for it was as if her fingers didn't belong to her. As she mounted, she heard Geoffrey's frightened cries as the dogs attacked him. He cowered back from them and then tried to get away, but he lost his footing, stumbled, and fell into the deep water of the creek by the landing stage. He flailed about, trying to tread the water in his heavy uniform as Hengist and

Horsa gave loud voice from the shore, delighting in his vanquishment.

Louisa managed to mount and urged her horse away. Immediately the dogs left their prey and followed.

Geoffrey thankfully managed to wade ashore, dragging himself up onto the grass and lying there for a moment to regain his breath. His heart was pounding and his mouth felt dry with lingering fear. He'd thought he was going to drown, or that the dogs were going to tear him to shreds, and so he lay thankfully on the grass, taking great gulps of air.

The nearby woods echoed as once again Hengist and Horsa gave defiant voice, and with a sharp gasp of renewed fear, he got up and ran to his horse, mounting and spurring it swiftly away from Highclare. The governess had managed to escape him yet again.

28

Louisa managed to reach the house and the sanctuary of her suite without anyone seeing her. Once inside she quickly took off the torn, mud-stained riding habit and then hid it at the back of the wardrobe. Still fighting back tears, she washed her face and hands, and then recombed her hair, pinning it up into a creditable-enough knot. Putting on the primrose-and-white gown she'd worn to breakfast, she surveyed herself in the cheval glass. Did she look as distressed and upset as she felt? Her eyes gazed anxiously back at her, and her lips trembled a little. She felt defiled, as if Geoffrey Lawrence's hands still moved over her skin. She drew a long, steadying breath. No one must know what had happened on the marsh, because if Kit found out he'd never believe she was innocent. Taking up her shawl, she left her rooms.

She found the earl in the gun room, and he smiled as she entered. "Louisa, my dear, you're back as well!"

"As well?"

"I saw Kit riding back a moment or so ago. The race must be over already."

"Oh." Her heart sank. She didn't want to face Kit just yet; she needed a little time to pull herself together.

The earl was polishing a rather ancient flintlock. "Did you enjoy your ride?"

"Very much."

"Were Hengist and Horsa a nuisance?"

"Oh, no!" She glanced gratefully at the two pointers, who were stretched on the floor asleep.

222

"From the mud all over them, I rather guess you went onto the marsh."

"Yes."

"You must take care out there, my dear, there's water everywhere and sometimes you simply cannot see it. Next time I wish you to take someone with you, someone who knows the creek well."

"I will."

"Good. Ah, is this Kit now? It sounds like him." The earl slowly put the flintlock down as he detected the anger in the brisk approaching steps.

Kit came in, his piercing, suspicious gaze swinging directly toward his wife. Had she come fresh from her lover's embrace? Did she think she'd gotten away with her assignation?

The earl was looking at his grandson. "You're back very early. How did the race go, if go it did in so short a time?"

Kit hesitated, wanting to say so much to Louisa, but knowing that he couldn't in front of his grandfather. "The race was canceled; Grantham's tub went to the bottom at dawn."

The earl's jaw dropped in amazement. "The bottom? In weather like this?"

"A wherry broke from her moorings in the fog last night and rammed it."

"Heaven forbid. I'll warrant there was great disappointment at being deprived of the big match."

"They'll have their race. I've been challenged by Rowe instead. We meet tomorrow."

The earl pursed his lips disapprovingly. "You'd have been wiser to refuse him."

"He left me no choice."

"He's never forgiven you for the loss of the *Mercury*."

"There's nothing I can do about that." Kit's glance moved fleetingly toward Louisa again. She looked so lovely, but he could see something in her eyes that told him his suspicions were well-grounded.

She met his gaze, conscious of a chill foreboding that somehow he'd found out about her encounter with Geoffrey. She toyed anxiously with the folds of her skirt.

The earl suddenly glanced at his fob watch. "I believe I may have an appointment with one of my tenants. I'll just go and check." Inclining his head, he left them.

Kit faced her immediately. "I understand from Newton that you went for a ride earlier."

The awful foreboding intensified. "Yes."

"Did you meet anyone?"

He knew, somehow he knew! She forced herself to meet his eyes. "No."

"So, there isn't anything you feel I should know?"

"No." Guilt swept miserably through her and she had to tear her glance away.

He came to her, roughly seizing her wrist. "Are you quite sure about that?" he breathed, his jealous fury on the point of finally bubbling over.

She could only stare at him, her tongue suddenly tied.

To him her silence signified a guilty conscience, and his fingers tightened savagely around her wrist. "Well? Have you nothing to say?"

"You're hurting me!"

If he was, it was as nothing to the pain she was causing him. He loved her, in spite of everything he loved her, but she'd done him only wrong. "I don't like being lied to, madam. You had an assignation with Lawrence, didn't you?"

"No! I won't deny I saw him, but I certainly didn't deliberately meet him."

"You lie, madam, just as you've always lied!"

"I'm telling you the truth."

"I'm not a fool, Louisa. You were up to something this morning. Why else were you so accommodating about being left here while I went to Cowes? Do you imagine I'll stand idly by while you put horns on me?"

With a gasp she struck him with her other hand, the bitter sting of her fingers marking his skin. Tears were wet on her cheeks, and her lips shook. "You—you hypocrite! How dare you insult me by crediting me with your own despicable standards! You lack all honor, Kit, and I can't believe I ever thought of you as a gentleman, for that is the last thing you are."

For a moment she thought she'd goaded him into striking her in return, but then the door opened and unexpectedly the earl came back in.

Kit released her immediately, stepping away and avoiding his grandfather's eyes. "I have things to attend to, so if you'll excuse me . . ." His voice trailed away and he went to the door, leaving it open as he strode along the corridor.

The earl turned inquiringly to Louisa, but she was still too overcome to say anything. She wanted to hide her distress from the old man, but somehow she just couldn't. Tears shone in her eyes and she was trembling.

He went to her in great concern. "My dear, what ever has happened?"

The tears rolled miserably down her cheeks as he took her hands and drew her to the sofa, making her sit down and then joining her. He took a handkerchief from his pocket and dabbed at the tears. "Please don't cry, my dear, I'm sure nothing is as bad as that. Even the most adoring of lovers have quarrels. Do you want to tell me about it?"

"I c-can't."

"Nonsense, of course you can," he said soothingly, patting her shaking hands. "Besides, I doubt very much if you'll be telling me anything I haven't already perceived for myself. To begin with, your marriage isn't quite what it appears to be, is it?"

She stared at him through her tears. "Why—why do you say that?"

"Come, now, you can't pull the wool over this old bird's eyes. Your marriage isn't the love match you'd have me believe, is it?"

Miserably she shook her head.

"Do you want to tell me about it?"

She hesitated, but then drew a long breath and nodded. "Yes."

"I'm listening, my dear," he said, still holding her hands.

She told him everything, except Kit's affair with Thea, for that wasn't her secret to tell. She told him she'd fallen in love with Kit, and she even described what had happened to her on the marsh.

At that he leapt to his feet, his face pale with outrage. "The blackguard!"

"Hengist and Horsa came when I screamed. They saved me."

"I'll have him flogged off the island!"

"Please, I'd rather nothing was said."

"But the felon attacked you!"

"I know, but it would just be his word against mine, and who will believe a former governess? It will be said that when I was at Lawrence Park I was more liberal with my favors than I should have been."

"But why should they think that?"

"It's what Kit already believes. That was what he'd said a moment ago when you came back. Somehow or other he'd found out that I'd seen Captain Lawrence, and he didn't believe that the meeting was an accident."

"And he believes such ill of you simply because of that locket?"

"Yes, and because he heard me mentioned in a conversation between Captain Lawrence and Lady Lawrence. Captain Lawrence admitted wanting to seduce me, and I think Kit wonders how much I may have encouraged such thoughts in his head."

"And Lady Lawrence was jealous of you?"

"Yes."

The earl's lips pursed thoughtfully and he sat down again. "Somehow that business with the locket smacks of a woman's hand, a jealous woman." He smiled gently at her, patting her hand again. "My poor Louisa, you've suffered a great deal, haven't you?"

She lowered her eyes. "Have I? How can that be when I've made one of the most advantageous matches imaginable?"

"Wealth isn't everything, especially when one loves in vain." He studied her face for a moment. "You haven't told me everything, have you?"

"What do you mean?"

"I mean that you haven't told me about Kit's less-than-creditable affair with Lady Rowe."

She stared at him. "You know about that?"

"My dear, I have eyes in my head. The wretched creature came here one day with a group of other ladies and gentlemen, and I perceived certain glances passing between her and Kit. I came to the correct conclusion about their relationship and was therefore extremely relieved to discover that she was already very much married. She wasn't at all the sort of woman I wished to see ensconced here at Highclare, for she didn't appear to have an honest or sympathetic bone in her admittedly beautiful body. You are the perfect woman for Highclare and for Kit, Louisa, and I intend to do all in my power to help you keep him."

"You—you do? Even though I've been deceitful?"

"Deceitful? In what way? Are you telling me you aren't in love with him, after all?"

"No, of course not."

"Then as far as I'm concerned, you haven't been deceitful." He looked earnestly into her eyes. "Will you place your marriage in my capable hands, my dear?"

"What do you mean?"

"Exactly what I say. Will you place your marriage in my hands?"

She hesitated. "Yes."

"Good. To begin with you must go to Cowes with Kit tomorrow, whether he wants you to or not. He's not to be allowed to go anywhere where that creature will be free to exert her influence over him. Promise me that in the morning you'll be ready to go with him. I'll go as well, and I want you to come down to the breakfast room the room the moment you see the carriage come to the front. Will you promise to do this for me?"

She searched his face and then nodded. "Yes, I promise."

29

It was evening and she was dressing for dinner. She hadn't seen Kit since their argument, for he'd gone out for a ride that had kept him away from the house for hours, and when he'd returned, he'd been closeted alone in the gun room with his grandfather. He was still there.

She knew the earl was worried about the race with Rowe and wanted it stopped. She was very anxious indeed for Kit's safety too, for what with Rowe's singularly unpleasant reputation and the fact that he considered he had a number of grievances against Kit, it was impossible to believe the race would be conducted by the rules. According to the earl there were many places along the course—including the rocks where the *Mercury* had foundered—where any number of deliberately dangerous maneuvers could bring about another fatal shipwreck. It didn't seem likely that Rowe was spurred by the prospect of the *Cyclops* coming in first; it was the prospect of extinguishing his hated rival forever that was driving him, and the earl intended to do all he could to dissuade Kit from taking part. She doubted very much if Kit would agree to such a thing, for to do so would be to lose face and would call his honor into question.

She looked at her reflection in the dressing-table mirror. Pattie was pinning up her hair, and the dark-red tresses glinted in the fading sunlight as the day drew to a close. The maid deftly twisted the hair up into a complicated knot, teasing one long curl out so that it fell to the nape of her mistress's neck. A jeweled comb from the Highclare collection was placed in the knot, and it sparkled brightly at the slightest movement. She wore the Marchioness of Holworthy's beautiful blue silk evening gown, which had a low-cut square neckline and tiny puffed sleeves, and a hem that was heavily embroidered with silver threads and spangles. Her thoughts drifted back to Geoffrey's assault upon her on the marsh. She'd had a long bath, but still she felt soiled and tarnished by his touch.

The door openly suddenly behind her, and without ceremony Kit came in. He looked immediately at Pattie. "Will you bring me Lady Highclare's riding habit?"

Louisa's lips parted. She'd hidden it at the back of the wardrobe because it was so torn and dirty. Why was he asking for it? There was only one answer: the earl had told him what really happened on the marsh, and now he'd come to check for himself whether there might be a grain of truth in it.

The maid searched as instructed, but then turned in puzzlement. "I—I can't find it, my lord."

Louisa lowered her eyes. "You'll find it on the floor at the very back."

The maid stared at her and then searched again, slowly drawing the squashed, ruined garment out. Seeing the state it was in, she looked askance at Louisa.

Kit took the riding habit and then dismissed the maid. As the door closed behind her, he turned to face his wife. He'd wronged her. In this he'd wronged her very much indeed. "Will you tell me what happened?"

"What point is there? You won't believe me because you've already decided I'm guilty."

"My grandfather told me Lawrence attacked you, but that's *all* he told me. He said I must learn the rest from your own lips."

"And if I tell you, will you then declare that there's no smoke without fire and I must have encouraged everything?"

He looked away guiltily, for at first that was exactly how he had reacted. Dear God, if only things were different between them, if only jealousy and pride didn't fill him, and if only she hadn't given him so much cause to feel both destructive emotions . . . But she had, except that in this particular instance he'd mis-judged her. "Just tell me what happened, that's all I ask."

"Very well." She told him everything, but couldn't look at him while she did so. Dull color stained her cheeks and she toyed nervously with the hairbrush Pattie had replaced on the dressing table. Her voice shook, for with each word the assault returned to her; she could feel Geoffrey pressing down on her, taste his lips, and hear the ugly sounds of his lust.

Kit remained very still throughout. His face was very pale, and his eyes bright with anger. There was no doubting she was telling the truth, it was written so clearly on her face. He despised himself for having said what he had earlier. She'd been subjected to a dreadful attack, and he'd accused her of going gladly to meet her attacker. She hadn't gone to meet Lawrence, he'd way-laid her. But had she met him before, at Lawrence Park? Had she gone gladly enough then? Doubts milled in his head, and with a curse he flung the riding habit across the room. "I'll have his vile heart out for this," he breathed, his voice tightly controlled.

She turned toward him. "Aren't you going to accuse me of inviting his attentions?" she asked coldly.

"I was wrong to say what I did earlier, and I ask you to forgive me."

"Do you ask my forgiveness for ever having doubted me?"

His eyes met hers. "For that I'd have to forget the existence of the locket."

"Then I don't forgive you for anything, sir. Things remain as they are between us."

He nodded slowly. "I fear they must," he said softly. "I also fear that Lawrence must be made to pay for what he did today."

"He isn't worth bothering about, Kit," she said quickly, suddenly sensing the level of his anger.

"I cannot and will not let it pass. I'll have his sickening life for this."

"Please don't do anything rash, you'll only regret it."

"I won't regret anything."

"You're not above the law, Kit."

"Nor is he. You're my wife, Louisa, and today he would have raped you, so do you really expect me to stand idly by and do nothing about it? I'm going to make him suffer, both for what he did and for what he would have done."

"You've made your opinion of me quite clear over the past week or so, Kit, and now I can only believe your reason for wanting to punish Captain Lawrence is that your insufferable male pride has been bruised because he laid hands on me."

"Is that what you really think?"

"Yes," she replied without hesitation. "What else should I think after all you've said and done since the arrival of that cursed locket? You're not concerned about me right now, you're concerned about yourself."

"It's your prerogative to think what you like, just as it's my grandfather's to request me to cravenly stand down from the race against Rowe, which is what he did this evening. You're both wrong in your judgment of me, Louisa, as I trust you'll both know in the end. Good night to you." With a curt nod of his head, he turned and walked out.

As his footsteps died away, tears shone on her lashes.

It was dark as Kit rode along the lane toward the Rowe villa. The gates were closed and the lodge was in darkness, but he could see the French windows of the drawing room standing open, the light of the candles within shining palely over the shadowy lawn.

He left his horse in the usual place, climbing the tree and dropping down the other side of the wall. He could hear piano music, and Thea's sweet voice singing. He made his way across the lawn, pressing back against the wall at the side of the terrace before the drawing room. Moths fluttered in the pool of light from the bright chandeliers within, and Thea's singing was clearer now.

By turning his head a little, he could see the room reflected in the great gilt-framed mirror on the wall close to the windows. Thea was wearing her damson silk gown, with plumes in her golden hair. Rowe was leaning on the piano, his face cold as he watched her. His black coat was resting around his shoulders, and Kit could see how gingerly he held his arm, wincing now and then as it pained him. His face was sallow, lacking even its usual pale color, and it was quite obvious that he'd suffer the legacy of Tom Cherington's lucky shot for some time to come.

Geoffrey was standing by a console table. He wasn't wearing his uniform, it needed drastic cleaning after the dowsing he'd received on the marsh, and he looked a lot less impressive in a plain dark-blue coat and beige trousers. There was a large glass of cognac in his hand, and as Kit watched, he drained it, turning immediately to replenish the glass with another generous measure. He didn't look at all relaxed; in fact, he looked very ill at ease, suddenly putting the glass down and taking a letter from his pocket. It wasn't a long letter, and its contents evidently upset him a great deal, for he closed his eyes for a moment before folding it and putting it away again. Then he drained the second glass.

Thea's singing came to an end and she smiled sweetly at her husband. "It's so pleasant to be here with you like this," she said untruthfully.

He wasn't at all impressed. "Indeed? You do surprise me," he murmured acidly, straightening and turning to Geoffrey. "What in God's name *is* that damned letter you've been looking at all this evening?"

"It's from my father."

"Do all his communications have this effect on you? You've been as sick as a dog ever since it arrived, sicker than you already were after the latest fiasco with the governess."

"You read it and see if you still think it's amusing," snapped Geoffrey, thrusting it into his hand and then pouring himself yet another liberal glass of cognac.

Rowe glanced at him. "You're very generous with my brandy," he observed coolly, managing with some difficulty to unfold the letter because of his wounded arm. He began to read aloud. " 'Sir, This is . . .' " He broke off in surprise. "Sir? A little formal for a father to his son, don't you think?"

"Just read it."

"Very well.

Sir,

This is to acquaint you with the fact that your heinous disloyalty is now known to me in full, as is the infidelity of the woman who has been my wife but who is soon to be divorced from me forever. If you thought by spite only to strike at her, you were mistaken, for your actions have redounded upon yourself as well. You're no longer my son, sir, you are disowned, and should you attempt to set foot on my land again, you will be thrown off. Emma is my sole heir now and will inherit my entire fortune. You will have nothing.

Ashley Lawrence, Baronet.

Rowe handed the letter back. "Dear me, you have made a mess of things, haven't you? Tell me, are you capable of doing anything properly?"

Geoffrey colored. "Damn you," he breathed, reaching for the decanter again.

Rowe stopped him. "I think you've had enough. Why don't you toddle outside for a little fresh air?"

For a moment Kit thought Geoffrey would balk at being denied the cognac, but then with a muttered curse he put his glass down and came toward the open windows. Kit pressed farther back out of sight as he came out onto the lawn. Thea began to play again, her trilling voice drifting out into the darkness.

Geoffrey stood on the edge of the light from the house, reaching into his coat for a cigar and his lucifers.

He didn't see Kit, he didn't know anything until a hand suddenly came from behind, clamping roughly over his mouth and almost ramming his unlit cigar down his throat. With a muffled cry, he struggled violently as he was dragged toward a shrubbery and pushed out of sight of the house. He whirled about immediately, swinging his fist at Kit's chin and almost connecting. Kit jerked back just in time and kicked the other's feet from under him, so that he fell heavily to the ground. Instinct made Geoffrey dangerous; he grabbed a handful of earth and tossed it fully into Kit's face, blinding him for a moment. With an oath, Kit struck out, catching him squarely on the chin.

Geoffrey's eyes became glazed and he went limp. Seeing him lying there, Kit almost forgot himself, reaching out to seize him by the throat and shake him furiously for all he'd done to Louisa.

Geoffrey moaned, recovering sufficiently to try to pull the choking hands away, but Kit was remorseless, his rage and contempt so great that his only thought was to continue until the other was no more. But then Louisa's words returned to him. "He isn't worth bothering about, Kit . . . Please don't do anything rash, you'll only regret it . . ." She was right. Slowly he relaxed his hold and for the second time that day Geoffrey gulped great breaths of air he'd thought never to breathe again.

Kit stood over him. "I want you off this island on tomorrow morning's packet, and if I hear a single whisper connecting your name with my wife's, I swear I'll finish off what I started today. Do you understand me?"

Geoffrey stared mutely at him.

Bending, Kit seized his lapel and shook him like a rat. "Do you understand me?" he repeated.

"Yes," rasped Geoffrey, terrified. "Yes, I understand!"

"You'd better mean it, my friend," said Kit with soft menace, "because if you don't, you'll be very, very sorry.'' He flung him disdainfully away, looking toward the house where Thea sang on, not knowing that her lover was so close. Then he slowly melted away into the shadows, leaving Geoffrey lying there.

It was a minute or so before Geoffrey crept out of the shrubbery and stumbled back to the house. He stood swaying weakly in the candlelight and Thea's singing halted on a scream.

By the time a furious Rowe had gathered some servants to search for the intruder, Kit had long since gone.

30

The following morning, carefully following the earl's instructions, Louisa breakfasted alone in her room and then dressed to go to Cowes. Kit still knew nothing of the intrigue going on behind his back. His grandfather hadn't said anything to him, and he certainly didn't know anything from Louisa, for he'd ignored her existence completely since returning to Highclare after his confrontation with Geoffrey.

She waited by the bedroom window, toying nervously with the drawstring of her little pink reticule. Her white muslin gown was scattered with pale-pink spots, and over it she wore a rose velvet spencer that was left unbuttoned to show off the intricate ruching decorating the gown's high-waisted bodice. Her gypsy hat was tied on with wide white ribbons, and Pattie had once again dressed her hair so that a long curl tumbled down over her left shoulder.

Outside the sun was shining from a clear sky, and there was a light breeze stirring through the trees in the park. On the Solent there were a number of private yachts, their sails billowing as they sped over the blue water. It was perfect weather for sailing. She stared unhappily out. Fate hadn't answered her silent prayers; there was no gale to force a postponement of the race, and soon Kit and the *Spindrift* would be sailing out to whatever vile revenge Rowe had planned. Her heart tightened. Please let him come safely through it. Please.

A carriage drove from the stables, its gray-lacquered panels gleaming in the bright morning light. The team

of perfectly groomed strawberry roans tossed their fine
heads, their harness jingling as they came to a standstill
below the terrace. She drew a long breath. It was time
for her to go down to the breakfast room, where Kit
would be faced for the first time with his wife's
intention to accompany him.

He was seated at the breakfast table with his back
toward the door as she entered. The earl rose immediately, coming around the table toward her. He
wore a pea-green coat and beige breeches, with shining
top boots, and his hair was tied back with a dark-green
velvet ribbon. He smiled, giving her a secret wink to
signify that Kit wouldn't be able to do anything about
her presence. "Ah, there you are at last, my dear."

Kit got up the moment he realized she was there, and
his expression was far from pleased. A chasm yawned
between them this morning after all that had been
said so coldly the night before. She'd said she
couldn't forgive him, and he knew he couldn't forgive
her.

The earl kissed her. "I understand you've already
breakfasted, my dear, so we can leave immediately, but
first I must have a brief word with Newton. I'll see you
both in the carriage." He squeezed her hand
encouragingly and then hurried out.

Kit faced her. "I imagine that you and my grandfather think yourselves very clever for manipulating the
situation like this. Well, I'm sorry to disappoint you,
but I really do not care if you come to Cowes now or
not; it's of no consequence to me where you are or what
you do. Well, that's not quite so, for it matters to me
that you conduct yourself with dignity in society. Do I
have your word?" He put his hand up immediately to
stop her from replying. "Perhaps you'd find it easier to
comply if I reminded you that any misconduct today
will take place in front of my grandfather, and I doubt
if you'll wish to embarrass him."

"You're quite right, sir, I have no wish at all to cause
the earl any disquiet." Oh, how she hated being like

this. She hesitated, suddenly looking earnestly at him. "Kit . . ."

"Spare your breath, you said enough yesterday."

"And so did you." She held his gaze. "No matter what we may think of each other, it makes no difference to the fact that this race today is the height of madness. Rowe isn't worth it, so don't give him the ultimate satisfaction of putting an end to you. Please, Kit." Without warning she found herself on the verge of confessing her love, and with a huge effort she bit the words back. What point was there in telling him, he didn't love her and never would.

"I have no intention whatsoever of standing down from the race, Louisa. Now, then, shall we go?" He offered her his arm.

Slowly she slipped her hand over his sleeve, and they left to cross the entrance hall and emerge into the morning sun. The breeze played with the brim of her gypsy hat, and her muslin gown fluttered prettily around her ankles as they reached the carriage and he assisted her inside, where the earl was already waiting. When Kit had taken his seat and closed the door, the vehicle drew away.

Very little was said as they drove through the park and then emerged through the gates into the road. She sat with her hands clasped in her lap, very aware of Kit as he sat opposite, his leg brushing the folds of her skirt. He wore a navy-blue coat and buckskin breeches, and his boots were the tall ones he used for sailing. His top hat was tilted back on his fair hair, and he rested one elbow on the windowsill, a gloved hand before his mouth as if to conceal the expression on his lips. As she looked at him, he glanced down for a moment, just as if he were lowering his guard; it made him seem suddenly very vulnerable. She wanted to reach out to him, but knew he didn't want her comfort. He didn't want anything from her.

He felt her eyes upon him and met her gaze. She was so near, and yet so very far.

It seemed they reached Cowes all too quickly, the carriage rattling down through the narrow cobbled streets toward the quay, where everyone had gathered in readiness.

Not having been present the day before, Louisa and the earl were taken aback by the excited crush, and they looked out in astonishment as the carriage made its slow way along the cobbled quay to where the *Spindrift* was moored forward of the *Cyclops*. The breeze had begun to stiffen, rocking the yachts and flapping their rigging audibly against their masts. Farther along the quay the Mermaid Inn was doing brisk trade, and the usual sound of music was drowned by the clamor of a flock of sea gulls around a fishing boat that had just come in. The birds' cries echoed along the crowded quay as the Highclare carriage came to a standstill alongside the *Spindrift*.

The earl alighted first, and his appearance caused an immediate stir, for he hadn't been seen outside Highclare for years.

Kit was about to alight as well when Louisa put her hand on his arm. "Kit . . ."

"Yes?" His blue eyes swung toward her, veiled and offering no encouragement.

"Please don't go through with this race."

"I've already said all I'm going to say on the matter."

"Is your pride worth your life?"

He shook his arm free and stepped down, more disturbed than he liked by her last words, for hadn't he said virtually the same thing to her brother before the duel? Taking a deep breath, he turned to look at her again, holding out his hand.

Her fingers trembled as she alighted, and she was conscious of the surge of interest as everyone craned their necks to see the noteworthy new Lady Highclare.

The earl was very aware that there would have been a great deal of speculation about his reaction to such an unexpected bride, and so he seized the opportunity to convey his attitude to them all. He drew her away from

Kit, smiling at her and dancing very deliberate
attendance as he introduced her to person after person.

She moved automatically among them, murmuring
empty politenesses and giving smiles that meant nothing
at all. She wasn't interested in any of them; her thoughts
were entirely with Kit, but he made no move to follow
her. From time to time she glanced around for a glimpse
of Rowe or Thea, but as yet there seemed no sign of
them, they certainly weren't on board the *Cyclops*, nor
was there any sign of their landau. She also glanced
around for Geoffrey, but she couldn't see him either,
for which she was immensely thankful; he was one
person she never wanted to see again.

Along the quay the sea gulls were becoming more and
more quarrelsome, swooping and diving around the
fishing boat, their cries filling the air. The two yachts
swayed at their moorings, and on the *Spindrift* the crew
were beginning to get ready to sail, but on the *Cyclops*
there was still no sign of activity as they waited for
Rowe to put in an appearance.

At last another carriage was heard approaching, its
clatter only just audible above the noise of the sea gulls.
Thinking that it must be the Rowe landau, Louisa
turned to look in the direction of the sound, but by the
respectful stir of the crowd she swiftly realized that the
new arrivals weren't the Rowes, but the Duke of
Gloucester and his sister, Princess Sophia. Her pulse
quickened. Was she about to be presented to royalty?
Her eyes fled nervously toward Kit, who was coming
quickly over to her.

The royal carriage, a splendid black-and-silver vehicle
drawn by cream horses and sporting liveried footmen,
came slowly along the quay, the duke and his sister
acknowledging the cheers of the crowd. It drew to a halt
alongside the Highclare vehicle, and the duke opened
his door to lean out and look at Kit. "Ah, there you are,
Highclare. Going to give us a run for our money, eh?
What?" He raised a quizzing glass to his rather bulbous
eyes, surveying Louisa with considerable interest.

Kit drew her forward. "Your highness, may I present my wife."

The duke continued to survey her. "Charmed," he murmured. "Absolutely charmed."

The princess leaned out then, graciously inclining her head and smiling.

Louisa had already sunk into a low curtsy, which she hoped was as graceful as it was respectful. "Your highnesses."

The princess looked chidingly at Kit. "Fie, sir, you should not be staying out at Highclare; you should be here in Cowes so that we may enjoy your bride's delightful company more often. I trust you'll be attending the ball?"

It was tantamount to a royal command, and Kit had no option but to consent. "We will, your highness."

"Good. I trust too that you'll keep a dance for me, for I've a mind to be seen treading a measure with the most handsome man in town."

"Your highness." Kit bowed.

The royal pair sat back again and the duke closed the carriage door, rapping his cane on the roof so that the coachman urged the cream horses on again.

The earl slid over to stand next to Kit and Louisa. "Well, my boy, I think you can be proud of your bride, for she acquitted herself very well just then."

"Yes." The single word was clipped.

"Is that all you have to say? Don't tell me you're in a pet because you've got to attend the ball, after all? I don't know what's got into you, but I do know that your recent conduct is most out of character. What's the matter? I can't believe that you're still hankering after that Rowe hussy, not when you have a divinity like Louisa."

Kit was caught completely off guard by his grandfather's revelation that he knew about Thea. His glance went accusingly toward Louisa.

The earl shook his head sternly. "Don't blame her, boy, I've known for some time. I also know all about

your sham of a marriage, I wormed it out of Louisa
when you made her cry yesterday. You don't come out
of this very well in my eyes, Kit, but I'm prepared to
concede that you must have a very good reason for
behaving as you do.''

With this, the earl took Louisa's hand and once again
drew her away from Kit, leading her through the crowd
to continue meeting the bewildering succession of titled
people who all seemed eager to make her acquaintance.
Quite suddenly, her attention was snatched away by the
utterance of a single word: Lawrence.

It was one of the Misses Carpenter who said it. She
was seated in the Grantham landau with her sister and
Lady Grantham. ''Lawrence Park must have been in
turmoil,'' she was saying, her voice barely audible
above the continuing noise of the sea gulls. ''Poor Sir
Ashley received the news very badly indeed.''

''What news?'' inquired Lady Grantham.

''That Captain Lawrence and Lady Lawrence were
lovers.''

Lady Grantham was startled. ''How terrible! How
did he find out?''

''Quite by accident. Do you know Lady Dales?''

''Your aunt? Yes.''

''Well, she was driving through Brentford recently
when her carriage drew up next to Sir Ashley's. He
asked her if her health was now fully recovered. She
replied that she hadn't been ill, to which Sir Ashley
responded that he thought she'd been most unwell and
had been visited overnight by Lady Lawrence. My aunt
knew nothing of this and said so. Sir Ashley drove
home, evidently in a great stew, and when he got there,
he found a most peculiar communication waiting for
him. It was anonymous and informed him that his wife
had a lover.''

Miss Carpenter sat back, pausing for dramatic effect.
''Well, the note may have been anonymous, but the
sender could be identified easily enough because the
paper reeked of the special Spanish cigars Captain

Lawrence had made specially for him. Thinking that his son was trying to break news of Lady Lawrence's infidelity with someone else, Sir Ashley faced her with the note's charges, at the same time mentioning from whom the communication had come. She broke down immediately and shocked poor Sir Ashley to the core by confessing all, including the fact that her lover was none other than Captain Lawrence. It seems there'd been some bad feeling; she'd done something the captain resented very much, and he'd thought only to punish her by sending the note, instead of which it all came back on his head as well.

"Sir Ashley wouldn't believe her at first, accusing her of vindictiveness, but she told him that she and the captain had stayed overnight at the Green Dragon in Brentford. Sir Ashley checked and found that this was indeed so. He acted swiftly after that, throwing her out of the house and disinheriting his son. Now his little daughter is his sole heir. Captain Lawrence is leaving the island on this morning's packet, I saw him embarking a few minutes ago. No doubt he hopes to win his father's affection back, but I don't think he will succeed."

Lady Grantham sat back, amazed by it all. "But how on earth do you know all this?"

"Well, after encountering Sir Ashley, my aunt Lady Dales was concerned that she might have said something out of turn, and so she went to Lawrence Park. She had it from Sir Ashley himself, so you may believe that every word is true."

In spite of her own problems, Louisa smiled to herself. Lady Lawrence and Geoffrey had got what they deserved, and now Emma would be happy again, enjoying the love of her father just as she had done before the advent of his malicious wife.

The sea gulls were still squabbling by the fishing boat, fighting over the scraps thrown out from the morning catch. Beyond their clamor she heard another carriage approaching along the quay, and as the crowd parted to let it through, she saw that it was the Rowe landau. Its hoods were down and Thea and Rowe could be plainly seen. Thea was exquisitely lovely in lime green, the soft plumes of her little hat fluttering prettily in the breeze.

Louisa's glance was drawn unwillingly toward Kit. He was gazing at his bewitchingly beautiful mistress.

31

The Rowe landau drew up behind the Highclare carriage. The horses were sweating and stamping, as if they'd been driven at speed all the way from the villa on the hillside, and they were nervous, capering a little at the crush of people. The coachman endeavored to keep them steady, but the nearside leader was particularly uneasy, tossing its head, its eyes rolling. It reared up a little as the sea gulls farther along the quay set up a renewed clamor when more fish were discarded from the catch. There were gasps from the ladies in the crowd as the horse lurched momentarily toward the very edge of the quay, its hooves striking sparks from the cobbles.

In the open carriage, the two occupants could be clearly seen by one and all. Thea had seldom looked lovelier than she did today, for lime green suited her particularly well. There was a hint of rouge on her lips and cheeks, and her violet eyes seemed a little uneasy, but that was the only sign she gave that all was not well in her life.

Beside her, Rowe looked even more drawn than the day before, and it was obvious to everyone that he was in greater pain from his wounded arm. A fawn coat was resting gingerly around his shoulders, and he held his arm awkwardly, as if the slightest movement caused him utter agony. His hat was tilted uncharacteristically back on his head, allowing the sunlight to fall fully on his strained face, revealing its ghastly pallor.

The horses were still very restive as he alighted, stepping down on the side away from the edge of the quay. He moved carefully, protecting his arm at all times, and the crowd began to murmur, for it was obvious to everyone that he wasn't in any condition at all to take part in the race.

Kit thought so too and went quickly over to him to offer to postpone the race.

Rowe turned immediately, a cruel twist to his pale lips. "Well, Highclare, I trust you're ready to be humiliated, for that's what's about to befall you today."

"I'll never be ready for humiliation, Rowe, but I am ready to put the race off until you're fully recovered." Kit glanced at Thea, whose lovely eyes hadn't left him.

Rowe's laugh was cold. "Postpone it? Never." He spoke in a loud-enough tone for everyone to hear.

"Be sensible, man, said Kit, "everyone can see you're not up to it."

"Can they, indeed? Well, I'm up to it, all right, make no mistake. Be a coward if you wish, Highclare, but don't expect me to aid and abet you. The race goes on."

Kit's eyes had flashed with anger at being publicly called a coward, and now he gave a stiff inclination of his head. "Very well, if you wish the race to proceed, proceed it will."

Seeing that he was about to turn away, Thea suddenly stretched out her hand to him, needing to touch him again, even though Rowe was watching. "May—may the best man win, Lord Highclare," she said.

Kit hesitated, but then took the hand and drew it to his lips.

Louisa felt a deep pain as she watched. Next to her, the earl watched as well. "My dear, he's your husband, not hers. You told me you'd resolved to fight for him, so do it. Don't allow her even an inch. Just follow your heart, do what it tells you and you won't go wrong."

Kit had left Thea now and was coming back toward her. Louisa stared at him. Do what her heart told her? It was telling her to run to him, to hold him close and tell him how much she loved and needed him.

The earl urged her again. "Claim him, Louisa. He's yours."

Suddenly the shackles seemed to fall from her and everything was crystal-clear. Of course she had to go to him and confess her love, she'd been blind not to do it before. Gathering her skirt, she hurried across the few yards separating them, startling both him and the onlookers by flinging her arms around him and kissing him passionately on the lips. There were gasps at such an uninhibited display from Lady Highclare, and she caught Kit completely unaware, but she was oblivious to everything except the need to at last show him how she really felt.

Thea stood motionless by the landau, her violet eyes flashing as she recognized Louisa's actions for what they were. The creature loved him and actually had the presumption to try to win him.

Rowe was paying little attention to what was going on on the quay, for one of his crew had called him over to the water side of the landau to examine one of the hasty repairs carried out to the cutter before she'd left London. He stood on the very edge of the quay, the inky, shining strip of water between the harbor and the yacht lying directly below; it was an ever-changing strip of water because the *Cyclops* was moving at her moorings.

Kit didn't want to respond to Louisa, but he couldn't help it. He needed to hold and kiss her. His hands moved slowly to her waist, pulling her close, and there were cheers from the watching crowd as he returned her ardor. Dear God, how he loved her . . .

Her face was flushed as she drew back to look into his eyes. "I love you, Kit, I love you so much that I can't go on any longer without telling you. I haven't meant any of the dreadful things I've said, I only said them because you hurt me so much. I'm innocent of doing anything wrong, please believe me."

A gladness sang through him. He didn't care about anything except that she loved him. He cupped her face in his hands. "Louisa, I . . ." He broke off because suddenly the sea gulls' noise rose to a deafening crescendo. Pandemonium broke out by the fishing boat as one bird managed to fly off with the last fish and was pursued by the others up the quay. They swooped low, their wings startling and very white, and their furious cries resounded from every corner of the harbor.

It all happened in a moment. The landau's nervous team shifted uneasily, the nearside leader once again tossing its head and rearing a little. The coachman shouted a warning to Rowe, who still stood with his back toward the horses. He whirled about, realizing too late the danger he was in. The rearing animal struck him full force on his wounded arm and he gave an agonized scream as a searing pain engulfed him. He lost consciousness, his knees sagging, and Louisa's breath caught on a horrified gasp as he slowly fell over the edge of the quay into the dangerously deep and narrow water below.

For a moment everyone was stunned. The sea gulls continued their noise and the unhappy coachman strove to control the horses, afraid that at any moment they'd panic completely and drag the landau after Rowe into the water.

Kit, who'd been as thunderstruck as anyone, recovered from the initial shock and reacted quickly, dashing to the edge of the quay and tearing off his coat and boots before climbing over the lip of the wharf and dropping down into the constantly changing water below. The *Cyclops* was closing in a little, the breeze edging her toward the quay, and a woman screamed as it seemed that the yacht would crush anyone caught between her and the quay, but then the breeze dropped and the yacht became still.

Thea remained where she was as everyone else pressed forward to see what was happening. Her thoughts were suddenly far from Louisa's fight for Kit. Let Rowe be dead, let him be dead! She wanted to be free of him.

Lord Grantham had hurried down some stone steps

leading to the water, and he called to Kit. "Get him over
here if you can. Is he still alive?"

Rowe's body was floating in the narrow water, the
Cyclops looming menacing over him, but he was faceup
and so at least couldn't drown. A deep gash marked his
white forehead, and blood was oozing swiftly from it as
Kit managed to reach him. "He's alive, but he's losing a
lot of blood!"

A murmur spread through the crowd, and Thea
breathed in sharply, her eyes bitter. Alive. She wasn't to
be free of him! The joyous prospect was being snatched
away as swiftly as it had been set before her. She
collected herself then, for if Rowe had survived, she
must ape the distraught wife. With a belated but
admirably convincing sob, she hurried to the top of the
steps just as Lord Grantham, assisted now by several
other gentlemen, pulled Rowe out of the water.

Lady Grantham and the Misses Carpenter hurried
dutifully to comfort her, endeavoring to pull her away
from such a distressing scene, but she gave a remarkably
consummate performance, refusing to budge until she'd
seen that her husband was all right. She bent tearfully
over his unconscious body as he was carried to the top
of the steps, and had to be restrained from flinging
herself on him as they set him down for a moment.

No one watching could have guessed that her anguish
was all an act—except Louisa and the earl, of course,
who both looked on in disgust as she wept her crocodile
tears.

Kit hauled himself from the water, accepting his coat
and boots from a small boy who'd brought them down
to him in the hope of a penny or two. Kit obliged him
and then pulled on the boots, glancing up to the top of
the steps to where Lady Grantham and the other ladies
were still trying to calm Thea's hysteria.

Through her effusive sobs, Thea was watching him all
the time. Her glance lingered on the way his fair hair
curled tightly with the wet, and how his shirt and
breeches clung revealingly to his body. She wasn't going

to surrender him to a mere governess—he was hers, and he'd always be hers! As she saw him begin to come up the steps, her sobs increased, and the moment he reached the top, she ran to him, flinging her arms about his neck just as Louisa had done only minutes before. She cried out her gratitude to him for saving her husband's life, and she pressed against him, seeming for all the world like a distraught woman thanking her husband's savior, but all the time she was exulting in embracing him in front of his wife.

As the men carried Rowe away to the nearby Mermaid Inn and a boy was sent to bring the surgeon, who resided in a street not far away, Louisa watched stricken as Kit put his arms around his sobbing mistress to comfort her. What a fool she'd made of herself, confessing her love and baring her innermost soul, only to see him reaffirming his love for another woman in front of the whole world. He was still Thea's, and he always would be.

32

Kit was aware that Thea was in danger of drawing too much attention, and so he quickly moved away from her, appealing to Lady Grantham, who still stood nearby with the Misses Carpenter. "Would you look after her while I go and see what's happening with Rowe?"

"Yes, of course." Lady Grantham hurried willingly forward.

Thea had no intention of being separated from Kit. "No," she cried tearfully. "No, I must see my husband as well, I won't stay out here."

Lady Grantham was appalled. "But, my dear, it will not be a place for a lady."

"I must be with my husband." Thea looked imploringly at Kit. "Take me with you. Please, I beg of you."

Such a heartbroken appeal was impossible to refuse, and although he still felt uncomfortable, he offered her his arm and they proceeded through the crowds toward the inn. Thea couldn't resist tossing a victorious glance back at Louisa, who remained with the earl.

The earl was much concerned. "Louisa, you must go too, don't allow her any chances at all."

"He doesn't want me, he's made that perfectly clear." Her voice shook a little.

"Nevertheless . . ."

"Please, my mind is made up, I'll stay out here."

He fell silent, seeing that for the moment she was too upset to be reasoned with. But in a while he had every intention of putting pressure on her again. She'd agreed to put her marriage in his hands, and he wasn't going to allow Thea such an easy victory.

The surgeon had arrived only a moment before Kit and Thea entered, and was leaning over Rowe's still-unconscious body, applying a dressing to the bloody wound on his forehead.

The low, beamed room was crowded with gentlemen, including Lord Grantham and Charles Pelham, who stood at the foot of the narrow bed. The windows had been closed to shut out the noise from the quay below.

Thea waited with convincing anxiety, twisting a handkerchief in trembling, anguished hands. The surgeon straightened, drawing a heavy breath. Lord Grantham looked anxiously at him. "Well? How is he?"

"Not good, not good at all, sir. I'm afraid there's nothing I can do for him, he's lost far too much blood already and is still losing it. Perhaps it's as well, because from what I've seen of his arm . . ." The man shook his head. "It should have been amputated days ago. For his sake I think what happened today was a kindness, for now he'll go quickly."

Thea was staring at him. Rowe was going to die, after all? Ever mindful of her very public anguish, she gave a heartrending cry and began to rush to the bedside, but Lord Grantham restrained her.

"My lady, my lady, he's in no condition!"

"But I must see him! He's my husband and I love him dearly!"

Kit shifted his position uncomfortably, averting his eyes.

Lord Grantham saw nothing amiss in her conduct, but still held her back from the bedside. "Please don't stay here, my dear, it will only cause you pain. Allow me to take you down to my wife, let her look after you . . ."

"No!" Thea was still determined not to be separated

from Kit, but now saw he was siding with Lord
Grantham.

"He's right," he said, "you shouldn't be here."

Her mind was racing. "Very well," she said at last,
her glance falling on the landlord, who was hovering
anxiously in the doorway. "Landlord, do you have a
room where I can be private? I wish to be on my own for
a while."

The man nodded quickly. "Oh, yes, my lady, there's
a parlor off the taproom where you can be quite alone."

She looked at Kit. "You'll come and tell me the
moment . . . ?" She broke off wretchedly, believable
tears shining in lovely eyes.

He had to consent. "Yes, of course."

"You promise?"

"I promise."

Satisfied that he would do as she asked, she went out
of the room with the landlord, and as the door closed
behind her, the surgeon spoke again. "I didn't like to
say anything in front of her ladyship, but Lord Rowe
will not see many more minutes out, he's slipping away
quite quickly."

As if to prove him wrong, Rowe stirred slightly, his
dull eyes flickering and opening. Their fading glance
moved straight toward Kit, as if he sensed he was there.
"Highclare." The single word was said so feebly that it
was barely audible.

Kit moved unwillingly to the bedside.

Dislike poured out of the dying man's eyes. "You
escape me, after all," he whispered. "I'd have put an
end to you, on the same rocks as the *Mercury*. I'd have
sent you to the bottom as surely as I sent the *Eleanor*. I
had it all planned, it could not fail."

Lord Grantham and Charles Pelham exchanged
shocked glances, and a stir passed through the other
gentlemen.

Rowe's bloodless lips were curved in a parody of a
smile. "Tom Cherington has had to wait, but he's got
me, after all. Your governess will . . . will dance

on . . . my grave . . .'' His eyes were closing and he slipped back into unconsciousness.

Out on the quay, Louisa was seated in the Highclare carriage with the earl. He'd been holding his tongue, but now he decided it was time to press her again.

"My dear, I must remind you that you're leaving that woman precious minutes with Kit. Do you want him or not?"

"It doesn't matter what I want anymore, he's made it clear what *he* wants."

"Has he? Are you telling me that he didn't respond to you when you kissed him in front of everyone? Was it my imagination that he held you close and returned your kiss?"

She raised her sad eyes to his face.

He took her hands. "He's your husband, Louisa, *your* husband, the man you vowed to love and cherish and who made those same vows to you. I don't think he uttered them any more lightly than you did, so you must go to him now, you *must*."

"I can't," she whispered, her eyes filling with tears.

"You're twice the woman she'll ever be, and I don't think she really stands a chance against you. Go to him now, my dear, it's your duty."

Her duty? Did everything always come down to duty?

"It's *your* place to be with him, Louisa, not hers. Go in there now and deny her what she seeks to steal from you."

She hesitated then, wanting to find strength in what he said.

He smiled, releasing her hands. "Go to him, my dear, for if you don't, you'll never forgive yourself."

She was suddenly swayed. He was right, she had to go. Gathering her skirt, she alighted from the carriage and hurried toward the inn.

The earl sat back, smiling. There was more than a mere kitten in the new Lady Highclare, there was a little of the tiger as well.

Lady Grantham and the Misses Carpenter were by the inn door as Louisa approached, and they seemed to be trying to see into a window immediately next to it. A maid was just drawing the curtains, and before she did so, Louisa caught a glimpse of Thea languishing tearfully inside on her own, a handkerchief held pathetically to her eyes. Louisa hesitated and then made up her mind; it was time to face this other woman.

She managed to slip unseen past the ladies, who were too busy discussing the awful events of the morning to notice her. The taproom was crowded as gentlemen jostled for service with the sailors and fishermen who always frequented the inn. The landlord saw her immediately and came hurrying over, recognizing her from having watched her arrive earlier.

"Lady Highclare, I'm afraid his lordship is upstairs with—"

'It's Lady Rowe I wish to see.''

He looked a little uncomfortable. "Her ladyship wishes to be alone, she's very distressed."

"I'm sure she'll see me," she replied, looking toward the door of the room where she'd seen Thea.

He was in a quandary, but then decided that he'd do as Louisa wished. "Very well, my lady, if you'll come this way."

He conducted her through the taproom toward the door, and immediately he knocked, Thea began to sob loudly within, her voice catching as she answered. "Yes? Who is it?"

"Lady Highclare wishes to see you, my lady."

There was sudden silence, the sobs stopping as quickly as they'd begun. "Very well, show her in."

He opened the door and Louisa went inside. The door closed behind her, shutting off the noise of the taproom, and she was alone with Thea.

The darkened room was small and sparsely furnished, with two high-backed settles on either side of an inglenook fireplace. The walls had been recently whitewashed, the floor was red-raddled, and a table stood in the center of it. Thea still occupied the only other chair, and because the curtains were drawn, it was at first difficult to see her face, but then she rose to her feet, her lime-green skirt rustling as she came closer.

"So, governess, we meet at last. Have you come to concede defeat?"

"No. Why should I? I have his ring, you don't." Louisa held up her left hand. The band of gold gleamed softly in the subdued light.

"You may wear it for the moment, my dear, but you won't for very much longer. Kit made a great many decisions that first night he was back on the island. He told me that when I was free he intended to set you aside. He regards you as a millstone of monumental embarrassment, did you know?"

"I don't believe you, you'd say anything to try to destroy me."

"Don't flatter yourself, governess, for I really don't need to try, you were destroyed the moment your name was linked to Geoffrey Lawrence's. Kit will never forgive you."

Louisa held her ground. "Maybe you were looking the other way when he kissed me on the quay just before the accident."

Thea turned sharply away. "You begin to bore me, governess. Kit is a red-blooded man, he was bound to respond to such a wanton display as yours. You threw yourself on him, and really, it was very embarrassing. I could tell he found it discomforting, and so could everyone else I heard passing comments. You made a fool of yourself, my dear. Why don't you just remove yourself from his vicinity, for you're not going to win." She turned spitefully back. "I'm waiting here for him now, he's coming to me the moment Rowe's breathed his last."

Louisa stared at her. "Lord Rowe is dying?"

"Yes. What price your precious wedding ring then, mm?" Thea smiled unpleasantly.

Louisa was shaken, for somehow it hadn't occurred

to her that Rowe's injuries were fatal, after all. How could she possibly compete if this woman was free? What hope did she have?

The door suddenly opened and to her dismay Kit came in. "Thea, Rowe died a few moments ago, and . . ." He broke off, seeing Louisa.

Thea smiled triumphantly, going to him. "I've been waiting for you, darling," she murmured.

He spoke to Louisa. "Please wait outside."

"But, Kit . . ."

"Do as I say. I'll be out directly."

She stared miserably at him. Everything Thea had said was true. With a choked sob, she hurried past, pausing just outside to glance unhappily back. The door was swinging to, and she caught a glimpse of Thea slipping her arms around him, her lips upturned yearningly to meet his.

It was too much to bear, Louisa pushed tearfully through the taproom, causing no small comment in her haste. She dashed out into the sunlight past Lady Grantham and the Misses Carpenter, and she heard their amazed gasps as she ran along the quay toward the carriage."

The earl saw her coming and opened the carriage door in great concern. "My dear, whatever is it?"

He helped her inside and closed the door again, drawing the blinds down so that no one could see, for everyone had noticed her distress. He took her trembling hands. "Please tell me, Louisa. What's happened?"

She bit her lip, trying to blink back the tears. "It's her he wants, I know it beyond any shadow of a doubt. He's going to set me aside so that he can marry her."

"But Rowe . . ."

"Lord Rowe is dead. She's free now, and that's all Kit has ever wanted. He thinks of me as a millstone and I embarrass him."

The earl was taken aback. "Kit said *that* to you?"

"No. He told her and she told me."

His eyes cleared. "Then I think we can regard it as a fairy tale. You've fallen into her trap, my dear; there isn't a shred of truth in what she says."

"Isn't there? When I left they were in each other's arms."

"Oh, surely not . . ."

"I saw them. There was no mistake." She swallowed, her voice breaking. "I've played and lost, and now it's time for me to leave while I still have any pride."

"Leave? No, I won't hear of it!"

"Please. Let me go, I can't bear it anymore. I want to leave as quickly as possible—on the afternoon packet if possible."

"But what will become of you, my dear?"

"I'll manage." She gave a wry smile, her lips trembling. "I'm sure I'll find a position, for what a talking point it will be to be able to say that you've employed the notorious Lady Highclare as governess?"

"Please don't talk like that . . ."

"I'm sorry, I can't help it. Too much has happened to me and this is the end. Can I return to Highclare now?"

"Please reconsider."

"I can't. It's all over, and I know it."

He nodded sadly. "Very well, my dear. I'll come with you."

"No, there's no need. Besides, I think I'll be better on my own."

"If you wish. Send the carriage back."

"Yes."

He climbed out, slamming the door behind him and telling the coachman to drive to Highclare. As it drew away, he turned to look darkly at the Mermaid Inn, then tugging his hat on firmly, he walked toward it.

He arrived just as the harassed landlord emerged from the doorway to beg Lady Grantham to come and help as Lady Rowe was having hysterics. Lady Grantham didn't wish to be seen entering a low establishment, but felt that circumstances were somewhat extenuating and so she followed the man inside.

The earl moved in their wake, for where Lady Rowe was, there was Kit to be found as well.

The taproom was hushed because of the noise coming from the little parlor. Thea's loud sobs echoed through the building and became louder as the landlord opened the door and ushered Lady Grantham inside. Kit was standing before the fireplace, his hands clasped behind his back, his eyes downcast. Thea was in the chair, her face hidden in her hands as she wept, and at first she was so distraught that Lady Grantham couldn't do anything with her.

The earl stood by the doorway, looking on with reluctant admiration. By God, the creature was a superb actress. She missed her vocation by not going on the stage. Her tears seemed so real that no one could know they were false.

At last Lady Grantham coaxed Thea from the chair and, putting a soothing arm around her shoulder, led her from the room. The men in the taproom parted to allow the two women through, and a moment later the Grantham barouche had been brought to the door and was conveying Thea away.

The earl went slowly into the parlor, closing the door behind him as a buzz of conversation broke out in the taproom. Kit looked up. "Grandfather?"

"Do you really intend to foist that—that strumpet on Highclare?"

Kit seemed puzzled. "I beg your pardon?"

"I don't recollect your hearing to be in any way impaired, Christopher. I asked you if you meant to bring that crocodile-teared creature to Highclare."

Kit's eyes cleared then. "There was nothing crocodile about her tears, Grandfather; they were real enough, I promise you."

"Am I supposed to believe she's grieving for that maggot Rowe?"

"No."

"Then what exactly are you saying?"

Kit smiled at him. "Let me put it this way, what is it

that you'd like to hear me say more than anything else? What is it that you've been conniving at for the past few days?''

The earl stared at him, and then a slow smile broke out on his delighted face.

33

Louisa's carriage was almost at Highclare. It had passed through the gates and was driving up toward the house. Since leaving Cowes, she'd striven to hold her tears at bay, because she'd now have to face Newton and possibly some of the other servants. She'd left the carriage blinds down, for it was somehow easier when she knew no one could see her. She sat with her eyes downcast. How could she ever have hoped to win? She'd foolishly dreamed of playing invisible trumps and emerging the victor, but everything had been stacked against her all the time. Governesses didn't win the hearts of lords like Kit, and she'd been the ultimate fool, reaching out toward the flame only to burn herself very badly indeed.

The carriage drew to a halt below the terrace and she alighted, instructing the coachman to return to Cowes and then hurrying up the steps. Newton, having perceived the carriage's approach, opened the door quickly. Hengist and Horsa bounded out to greet her, and she paused for a moment to fuss them before going into the entrance hall. She hoped she appeared collected as she faced the butler. "Would you tell Pattie to go to my suite and pack my things. I shall be leaving Highclare today and I won't be returning."

He was totally taken aback. "L-leaving, my lady?"

"Yes." She'd already decided what she was going to do in the meantime in order to avoid curious eyes. "If I'm needed at all, you'll find me on the roof." She didn't wait for him to say anything else, but gathered her skirt to go up the stairs.

The astonished butler remained where he was for a moment, watching as Hengist and Horsa trotted up behind her, then he returned to the kitchens to break the news to Pattie.

The gazebo's French windows were closed, and the sunlight streaming unchecked in through the glass made the little building as hot as a greenhouse. She stepped out onto the roof promenade, taking a deep breath of the cool, fresh air. Hengist and Horsa padded beside her, seeming determined to keep her company. She stood by the stone balustrade, looking across the park and the Solent toward the mainland. From up here it was possible to see for miles.

Impulsively she untied her gypsy hat and took it off. The breeze felt good on her face, and after a moment's hesitation, she reached up to unpin her hair, shaking the dark-red curls so that they fell heavily about her shoulders. She was still very close to tears, but could hold them back, as if she'd found some inner strength to carry her through this last part of her ordeal.

Hengist and Horsa sprawled beside her in companionable silence, almost as if they understood how she was feeling. She stared at the magnificent view without really seeing it. It seemed a lifetime now since she'd been a governess at Lawrence Park, with no prospect of ever being anything else. The highlights of that existence had been her occasional meetings with Tom, but those meetings had been very few and far between. She'd seen so little of him over the past year that sometimes she still couldn't believe that he'd gone forever; it was as if she'd suddenly receive one of his hastily scribbled notes asking when they could next meet in Brentford. She'd never receive such a note again, but her existence was soon to return to what it had been before, provided she could find a position. She'd spoken bravely enough to the earl, but would anyone really wish to employ a woman who'd be talked of as a discarded adventuress? What hope did she really have of finding respectable employment?

Suddenly her thoughts were interrupted by the sound of drumming hooves. A horseman was riding swiftly toward the house. It was Kit, she recognized him straightaway. But why was he coming here now? Why wasn't he with the woman he'd chosen? As she watched, he reined in. His face was upturned directly toward her as she stood so clearly silhouetted on the roof, then he urged his mount on, leaving it by the terrace steps and hurrying into the house.

A few moments later she heard him coming up into the gazebo. Hengist and Horsa heard him too and went to meet him, their tails wagging. He paused by the open French window, patting the dogs for a moment and looking toward her. "Louisa, I must talk to you."

She braced herself, determined to cling to what was left of her pride. "We have nothing to say to each other, Kit."

"My grandfather tells me you intend to leave."

"Yes."

"Please don't, for I'd much rather you stayed."

She gave a small, rather wry smile. "I'm sure you would, for if I go people are bound to talk about you and Lady Rowe. Well, I'm afraid you'll have to endure their wagging tongues, because I will not stay here and be humiliated anymore."

"The last thing I've ever wanted to do is humiliate you. You're my wife, Louisa, and you mean a great deal to me."

"Oh, please don't keep up this pretense," she said, her voice shaking a little. "We both know the truth: it's Lady Rowe you've chosen, not me."

"On the quay this morning you said . . ."

"A lot of very foolish things," she interrupted quickly, conscious of the telltale color flooding into her cheeks. She turned away. "I'd be grateful if you'd forget all about it, for it wasn't of any consequence."

"Wasn't it? Are you telling me you didn't mean any of it?"

"Does it matter? Lady Rowe is now free and you've made your wishes very clear. You don't want an embarrassing ex-governess encumbering you any longer—not even for duty's sake."

"My grandfather told me what she'd said to you, but it wasn't true. Please look at me, Louisa, for I'm telling you the truth."

Unwillingly she faced him again.

Leaving the dogs where they were, he came toward her. "I've never spoken ill of you to her, as she knows only too well, and now she also knows why I've never done so. Do you want to know why, Louisa?"

She hesitated.

"Please, Louisa, I want you to know, and if you refuse me now, then the misunderstandings and mistrust will triumph, and you and I will both be the losers."

"I don't want to misunderstand, Kit, and the last thing I wish to do is mistrust you, but . . ."

"There aren't any buts. Nothing I'm about to say to you will hurt you, I promise you upon my honor. I want you to know my side of all this, it's important to me . . . to us both, I hope."

She searched his face for a moment and then nodded. "Very well."

He came to stand next to her, leaning his hands on the balustrade and staring across toward the mainland. "I'll begin at the very beginning. The day I went to Lawrence Park to see you, I was acting solely out of duty and conscience. I'd given my word to Tom and I felt guilty about letting my grandfather down, but I was also suffering from what I believed was my unrequited love for Thea. You were my way out of it all, enabling me to both do my duty and clear my conscience, while at the same time standing between me and a wrongful love for another man's wife. I'd always despised myself for my liaison with her, because I was betraying my principles by indulging in an adulterous affair, but I honestly loved her and I wanted her to become my wife.'' He paused. ''I'm not trying to excuse my actions where she was concerned, I'm trying to explain them. Do you understand?''

She met his earnest gaze. ''Yes, I understand.''

He took a deep breath. ''As you know, my journey to Lawrence Park was interrupted at the Green Dragon, where I overheard certain things. Rightly or wrongly, I found myself wondering about your character, but when I met you, I very quickly realized that you'd been Lawrence's innocent victim and that you'd never have encouraged his advances. Louisa, what I didn't realize then was that in those early minutes with you, my reasons for asking you to be my wife had undergone a very subtle but very important change. I wasn't asking you because I felt duty-bound, I was asking you because I wanted you. If there's such a thing as love at first sight, then it happened to me that day.''

Her heart seemed to stop within her. She stared at him. ''Kit . . .''

He put a finger to her lips to stop her words. ''Let me finish, for I must say it all.''

His touch burned against her skin. She wanted to clasp his hand, but didn't dare. If she reached out now, the dream would slip away before her outstretched fingers. Her heart still seemed numb, as if it had halted in this breathless moment, never to beat again.

His hand moved to rest against her cheek. ''Louisa, I meant every word of my marriage vows, I wanted to worship you with my body, I wanted to love and cherish you, and take care of you forever. My thoughts were all of you, there was no room left for Thea, she'd ceased to exist for me.''

''I thought . . .''

''You thought I loved her and that you weren't worthy anyway, but if you could have seen into my heart, you'd have known how wrong you were. Couldn't you sense the truth when I comforted you after the funeral? Didn't you feel it when I kissed you in the chapel? I wanted to give my passion free rein, but at the same time I didn't want to seem insensitive. You'd lost Tom and your life had changed beyond all recognition; you were lost, vulnerable, and totally in my hands. A false move on my part might have driven you from me forever, and I couldn't bear the thought of losing you before I'd really come close to you in the way I needed to be close.'' He smiled a little. ''I'd never felt that way about Thea, and I know now that what I felt for her fell far short of my feelings for you. No, don't say anything yet, for I must tell you absolutely everything so that you'll understand and maybe forgive me for what I've said and done to you.'' His thumb moved gently against her cheek.

''As I said, I nearly told you the truth in the chapel, but somehow the moment didn't seem quite right, and I decided instead to wait until we were alone together for the first time as man and wife. I meant to make love to you that night, Louisa; my body and my heart ached with the need to hold you close and share that precious intimacy I craved so much from you. Dear God, if only you knew how much I regretted that fateful decision, for between the chapel and our first night together there came the locket, and as quickly as I'd been consumed with love for you, so I was equally consumed with jealousy. I thought that Lawrence possessed what I loved so very much, and my bitterness made me behave the way I did toward you. I wanted to hurt you as much as I believed you'd hurt me, but at the same time I still loved you to distraction, and so I said hurtful things.

''Louisa, I didn't intend to see Thea again after our marriage, but when we quarreled yet again that first night here, I petulantly decided to do exactly what you'd accused me of—I went to her. But when I was with her, I knew how wrong I was, for there wasn't anything left in my heart for her, all I could think of was you. I should have finished it with her once and for all that night, leaving her in no doubt that there was no going back, but in spite of the fact that I'd seen her for what she really was, I couldn't bring myself to be too cruel. I was a fool, because I left her with hope, and that led to her conduct today."

He paused again, his hand falling away from her cheek as he turned to gaze over the park again. "Louisa, I really did think that you'd deliberately met Lawrence that day on the marsh; in my blind jealousy it was all I could think, especially when Rowe taunted me with as much, but you were wrong when you accused me that night of acting out of injured male pride when I found out the truth from my grandfather. I was bitterly ashamed of what I'd said to you, because you meant everything to me and the thought of him hurting you like that was more than I could bear. I didn't want to face you coldly like that. I wanted to hold you in my arms and make you believe how much I loved you, but instead . . ." He drew a long breath. "I was very close to killing him for what he'd done to you, and for the way he'd come between us all the time, but I came to my senses and let him go. I've come to my senses in every way now, Louisa, for I've told Thea that I love you and that it's over once and for all. I know what you think you saw at the Mermaid Inn, but if that door had closed a little more slowly, you'd have seen me very deliberately and definitely disengaging myself from her. I told her that Rowe's death and her freedom made no difference to me, because it was you that I loved. If her tears were false before, they certainly weren't after that.

"Louisa, I know my actions on the quay must have appeared very damning and hurtful to you, but they weren't what they seemed. I didn't go to her because I at last saw a chance of winning her; I went to her because I thought she was genuinely distressed by the accident." He gave a wry laugh. "Don't misunderstand me, I didn't believe she was weeping for Rowe, but I did believe she was shocked by what had happened to him, and there's a world of difference between comforting someone you believe to be upset and comforting that same person because you love her. There is also a world of difference between condemning and confining you because I disliked your show of spirit when faced with those you despised, and doing the same because I in fact admired that show of spirit, but was jealous to the very quick and wished to keep you well away from Lawrence. It's the latter that is the truth, Louisa, for I was proud of the way you stood up for your principles and beliefs, but I was so eaten up with jealousy that I behaved despicably.

He put his hand to her cheek again. "I think I've told you everything now, I've bared my soul and confessed my love. Please tell me that what you said to me on the quay was the truth and that you love me too."

"Oh, Kit," she whispered, tears of joy shimmering in her eyes, "if only you knew how I've longed to hear you tell me you love me. I adore you, and I have done almost from the outset. I want you, I want every part of you, I don't want to be shut out from anything. You mean the world to me, and leaving you would have been the hardest thing I've ever had to do."

His hand slid back to coil in her hair and his eyes were dark. "You'll stay with me now, won't you?" he murmured softly.

The air had been singing around her, and now she felt as if she lacked all substance. She'd become ethereal. He loved her and wanted her, and it wasn't a dream, it was really happening. Against all the odds, the governess had won the heart of her lord. She suddenly found herself remembering Tom's last letter, and she smiled a little.

"Why are you smiling?"

"Because Tom told me to be happy with you."

"And are you?"

"Yes. Oh, yes."

"There's so much happiness yet to come," he said softly, drawing her toward him. His fingers twined richly in her hair as he kissed her, and she could feel emotion sweeping her away as he pressed her close. She was conscious of his body against hers, and the slow, luxurious movement of his lips over hers. It was a kiss to entice her wanton senses, stirring them into that shameless passion that he alone had ever aroused. She felt no modesty at all; she wanted him to possess her.

He drew back a little, cupping her face in his hands, desire to match her own reflecting in his blue eyes. "This is no matter of duty, Louisa," he whispered, "this is a matter of love, a love that should have been acknowledged long before now. It's time you were my wife in every way, for my need cannot be denied any longer. I'm already your husband, but now I must be your lover too." He took her hand and led her to the steps in the gazebo.

Hengist and Horsa rose expectantly to their feet, tails wagging, but he looked sternly at them. "The marriage bed is one place where you're not welcome, my friends, you must stay here."

They recognized the word "stay" only too well, and their tails stopped wagging. They watched as Louisa and Kit descended the steps, and then they lay down again, their heads on their paws. Their ears twitched a little as a door closed somewhere, and then there was silence.

A little later Louisa lay in Kit's arms in the great Venetian four poster bed. She felt warm and loved, and happier than she'd ever imagined it was possible to be. "I love you so, Kit," she whispered.

His arms tightened around her. "As I love you."

"Our marriage won't ever be a matter of duty again, will it?"

"No. Never again."

Her lips were soft and pliable as he kissed her.

COMING IN APRIL 1988

Secrets of the Heart

Mary Balogh

Past mistakes and misunderstandings tore them apart —but present passion promises to melt the barriers between them . . .

The marriage between Sarah Owen and the Duke of Cranwell should have been a perfect one. But in the bliss of their wedding night, Sara's shameful secret is revealed, ending their world of love almost before it has begun . . . When their paths cross again, Sara knows it is folly to hope that the Duke will forgive her. But even as she resolves that they must part forever, she finds that her level head is no match for her hungering heart. . . .